Are those her ribs through which the Sun
Did peer, as through a grate?
And is that Woman all her crew?
Is that a DEATH? and are there two?
Is DEATH that woman's mate?

—THE RIME OF THE ANCIENT MARINER

A WHISPER CAME

A WHISPER CAME

A CAPE COD MYSTERY

KEITH YOCUM

For Denise, my partner in crime

CHAPTER 1

A light northerly breeze coated the crisp salt air with a pleasant fragrance. Jack could taste the end of spring. He pushed the pole deeper into the sand and nudged the small flats boat closer to the shore.

His customer stood near the bow, his fly rod poised to start the whipping motions to cast his tiny lure. Jack liked Phil, a Fidelity fund manager. Phil was obsessed with saltwater fly-fishing, as were most of Jack's customers. In the hierarchy of charter boat captains, the fly rod specialist was the prima donna of the trade. Their boats were small and shallow-hulled, perfect for nuzzling into the sandy flats of Chatham's Monomoy Island.

A fly rod charter captain stalked his fish slowly and methodically, like a blue heron tiptoeing through the marsh.

Their patrons, like Phil, were affluent, obsessed, and intense. Spending hours on the water was a release from their hectic lives, and they relied on Jack's nuanced knowledge of the waterways around this part of Cape Cod.

Phil paid well and always left a solid tip, whether he landed fish or not. Phil loved fly-fishing this time of year and never failed to schedule an outing. Rampant tourism was still weeks away, so they didn't have to outwit the yahoos on overpowered boats that threw off wakes like aircraft carriers.

No, this was the perfect time to stalk *Morone saxatilis*. Fresh from spawning in the upper reaches of the Chesapeake Bay and Hudson

River, the early striped bass habitually skimmed along Cape Cod from Buzzards Bay, through Nantucket Sound and around the tip of Monomoy Island and north to Provincetown.

Early in the season, the fish came in small schools, brown sea lice clinging to their purple dorsal scales.

Jack had launched his eighteen-foot flats boat out of Harwich's Saquatucket Harbor that morning and arrived twenty-two minutes later at the western side of teardrop-shaped Monomoy Island, a mile north of the tip.

Phil's first cast tested the breeze. His nine-foot rod whipped five times, each forward flick adding yardage to the cast. Phil stripped the line back into a basket on his waist, gently teasing his handmade fly to look like a skittering, three-inch, silver-and-green tinker mackerel.

Jack poled in a little closer to shore and Phil readied for his next cast.

"Hey," Phil yelled. "What's that?" He pointed the bone-thin black rod to his right.

Jack strained to see into the sun's glare bouncing off the shimmering Nantucket Sound water.

"I don't see anything," Jack said.

"Right there." Phil pointed again.

Jack scrunched his eyes and tried to focus through his polarized lenses. Now he could see something.

"Is that what I think it is?" Phil said, turning back to look at Jack.

"Let me get a little closer," Jack said, pushing the pole into the sand and pivoting the stern. He shoved the boat slowly in the direction of the floating object.

"Shit," Phil said. "I can't believe it."

"Shit," Jack said.

The two men looked at each other. Two chattering common terns passed overhead and abruptly circled back over the object.

"What should we do?" Phil said.

Jack laid the pole in its holder along the boat. "I'll call it in. Sorry, Phil. Didn't expect to run into something like this today."

"Shit," Phil said again, shaking his head.

Jack reached down and pulled the microphone off its holder and turned the marine VHF radio to sixteen. He typically left it at nine to listen to the harbormaster's channel.

"This is *Sunrise* calling the Chatham Coast Guard. Come in Coast Guard, over."

Jack adjusted the radio's squelch to reduce the static and waited. The boat drifted gently in Nantucket Sound.

"*Sunrise*, this is Chatham Coast Guard, over."

"This is *Sunrise*. We're about one mile north of Monomoy Point, on the Nantucket Sound side. I'm on a charter with a customer. We're about fifty yards from shore. There appears to be a body in the water, over."

"*Sunrise*, this is Coast Guard Chatham. Can you repeat? Over."

"We have found a body in the water and want to report it, over."

"*Sunrise*, what kind of body? A seal or whale? Over."

"A human body, over."

"*Sunrise*, are you certain it is a human body? Over."

"One hundred percent positive it is a human body, over."

"*Sunrise*, is the body intact? Over."

"The body appears to be intact, over."

"*Sunrise*, are you certain the individual is deceased? Have you attempted to revive them? Over."

"Negative, we have not attempted to resuscitate. The individual is obviously deceased. There is no movement, and the body is facedown, over."

"Standby, *Sunrise*. Please remain with the body for now. We're dispatching a boat immediately. It will take approximately thirty minutes to reach your destination. Remain on this channel. You will be contacted by the boat in transit. Please repeat your precise location, over."

"Shit," Phil said again, staring at the facedown body of a woman, her arms spread out as if she were flying. Her long, dark hair floated like seaweed around her head. She appeared to be dressed in a white cotton blouse and thick, dark skirt. The backs of her hands shone unnaturally white and her fingers appeared to be curled into her palms.

"I'm sorry, Phil. I had no idea," Jack mumbled.

◉

The aluminum Coast Guard boat with its orange float collar slowed as it approached. Its blue flashing lights were nearly lost in the sun's glare.

Three guardsmen in their dark blue uniforms stood at the bow, scanning the water.

Jack and Phil pointed in unison to the body drifting near them. One of the guardsmen yelled and pointed. The boat nudged closer. Jack could hear the radio exchange taking place between the boat and the station, as the boat's captain confirmed that there appeared to be a woman's body in the water.

"Can we leave now?" Jack yelled to the Coast Guard boat. "I'm just a charter guy and this is my customer. It's been kind of upsetting and I'd like to get out of here."

"No, sir, you cannot leave yet," one of the guardsmen yelled back. "We need to ask you a few questions. Please remain here while we retrieve the body. Can we see your boat registration please, and a driver's license for you and your customer?"

Jack turned to Phil. "Crap, I was afraid of that. I'm sorry, Phil."

"Yeah, I figured they'd want to talk to us. I need to call my wife," Phil said. "This really sucks."

Jack sat down in the small captain's chair and sighed. He had never seen a human body in the water before. A dead gray seal, yes; a dead pilot whale, yes; an illegally caught dead sailfish dumped by a commercial fishing boat, yes. A dead woman, no.

He idly scanned the shoreline as the boat rocked gently. He could see the muddy red top of the deactivated Monomoy Point Lighthouse jutting above a dune like an oversized carrot. The wind had stiffened, and he was glad to be in the lee of the island. It would be a bouncy ride back in.

◎

Twenty-five miles west in Nantucket Sound off Hyannis, Carl Lane bounced in the wind with two charter customers. They had hit the black sea bass hard last year around the same time, and Carl was glad to have repeat customers this early in the season on his charter boat—a 26-foot center console with twin, 200-hp outboards.

The fish finder showed a school of bottom-feeders directly below them, but the artificial reef of concrete and boulders was a trap for snags. The faster the drift, the heavier the sinker that was required. But the heavier sinker also meant that a snag was more likely, especially with weekend fishermen. The size limit on black sea bass was fifteen inches, but these customers didn't mind catching and releasing undersized fish; they simply wanted to *catch*.

One of the poles bent suddenly and Carl prayed it wasn't a snag. If it was, they'd have to cut the line, re-rig, and start over again. Meanwhile, the other fisherman might hook a fish, complicating things.

The good news was that two customers had started drinking beer on the ride out, so they were less particular about what they caught, as long as they caught something.

The bearded customer turned to Carl. "I'm on!" he yelled.

"You sure? Not a snag?"

"Nope, it's a fish all right."

"Well, bring her in then," Carl yelled back, grinning.

As he throttled up to counteract the boat's drift, Carl's phone rang. It was Noog, a fellow charter fisherman. They often chatted by phone to share tips on locations to find fish.

"Whazzup?" Carl said.

"You heard yet?" Noog said.

"Heard what?"

"The body," Noog said.

"What body?"

"They found a body off Monomoy. A woman."

"No shit."

"No shit, man."

Carl watched as the bearded customer pulled a scup the size of a dinner plate out of the water.

"Gotta go," Carl said, hanging up.

"Nice fish!" Carl said, moving to the bow. "You guys want it?"

"Is it big enough to keep?" the bearded guy asked.

"Sure is. But it's a thin fillet. Your call."

"Yeah, let's keep it," the customer said.

Carl kept his rubber boot on the fish as he removed the hook with his pliers. He tossed the fish in the cooler and rebaited the line.

"Let's keep catching, guys!"

CHAPTER 2

Stacie saw the email pop from Frank Stanford, the assistant Metro editor.

"Need someone to follow up on a body washed up on Cape Cod. You finished the Green Line piece?"

Crap, she thought. Cape friggin' Cod. No way she was driving down there today.

"Almost done," she wrote back. "Don't we have a stringer down there?"

"On vacation," Stanford shot back.

"How about a Northeastern intern? Good experience for them."

"Here's a link to a tweet from the *Cape Cod Times*. Call the Coast Guard and see what you can get out of them. See if it needs follow-up."

"OK," she answered.

"Smitty loves Cape Cod stories, Stacie," he wrote back.

Smitty was the *Boston Globe* editor Charles Smith, and indeed Stacie knew he liked stories about classic New England towns and locations. He liked it better yet if there was a story about a body found in a classic New England town.

She looked up the *Globe*'s internal list of media contacts for the Coast Guard. It showed a number from Coast Guard headquarters in Boston.

What a crappy end to a crappy week, she thought.

Calling federal agencies was always a fraught process, and Stacie knew the moment she mentioned she was from the *Boston Globe*, there would be a change in behavior. No media contact from a federal agency wanted to make a dumb mistake, so they tended to delay getting back to the reporter until they could get their story straight.

Stacie left her phone number and returned to the story on an MBTA accident involving a pedestrian on the Boston College line.

She hit send, and simultaneously her cell phone showed a text message from Marie, her best friend.

u ok today?

yup. onward and upward, she texted back.

he's a conceited jerk. hope you know that now

yup

hang in there, Marie answered.

i'm strong like bull

ha girl

Her office phone rang.

"Hello, this is Stacie Davis."

"Stacie, this is Ensign Steve Cortland of the US Coast Guard Boston returning your call."

"Ah, yes, thanks. I'm calling about a report of a body found off Cape Cod. Can you tell me anything about that?"

"We have very little information at this time, but I can confirm that our station in Chatham reported they retrieved a body in the waters off Chatham today. We don't have much more information than that, to be honest."

"Was it a fisherman?"

"No, it was a woman."

"Did she fall off a boat? Or drown swimming?"

"We have nothing else to report at this time. When I have more information, I'll be glad to call you back."

Stacie knew to keep pressing the media person before they jumped off the line; invariably they had more information but weren't authorized to release it. And the last thing she needed was to see one of those obsequious Boston TV reporters broadcast more detailed information than she had. Handsome or beautiful broadcast reporters were masters at sucking up to media spokespeople.

"Was the body found on a swimming beach? Was a shark involved?"

"Wait a minute, Ms. Davis. I didn't say anything about a shark. There's no evidence a shark was involved in the woman's death. Please don't report that."

"Where in Chatham was the body found? Chatham has water all around it."

"The body was recovered off of Monomoy Island, which is part of the National Wildlife Refuge System."

"Who found the body?"

"It appears a charter boat captain found the body. Listen, Ms. Davis, I really can't comment any further on this matter until we have more solid information. I promise I'll call you back when I have more."

She gave him her cell phone number and hung up.

◉

"Sir, Seaman Apprentice Jones is kinda upset. He didn't, uh, feel good about pulling the body out of the water."

Petty Officer Krojec was upset with the body retrieval but had no intention of showing it. The 25-foot Defender was at full throttle, its dual 225-hp outboards roaring as the boat flew over the light chop. He and Seaman Sims were inside the enclosed cabin, while Seaman Jones and two other crew members were outside on the starboard walkway, staying away from the tarp-covered body in the stern. They were nearing the Stage Harbor entrance and would need to throttle down for the last leg to the dock.

Krojec knew they would be asked a thousand questions back at the station, and he was sure he followed protocol for collecting information from the charter captain and his customer. They had taken photographs of the body in the water before retrieving it.

Krojec was taking the body to the commercial dock in the harbor, where he would be met by the harbormaster, the local police, and an ambulance. He was proud of how composed he appeared to the crew.

Still, Krojec didn't like pulling the lifeless body of the woman onto the boat. He couldn't resist looking at her paper-white porcelain face as she lay on the deck. Her dark hair was plastered around her forehead like a pile of eel grass. He expected to be repulsed by her decomposing face but instead was surprised at how serene and normal she looked.

◎

Stacie both loved and hated the fact that the *Globe* had moved from the old, out-of-the-way Morrissey Boulevard newsroom to the new building in the downtown Financial District. She loved the bustle of people and the purr of the service industry downtown but hated the crushing traffic.

She took a brisk walk down Congress Street toward Post Office Square, one of the few areas of greenery in the dense Financial District. It was a pleasant, late-spring day and she needed to feel the sun on her face. Summer was coming. A new page was being turned in her twenty-seven-year-old life story. She listened to a new Spotify playlist, her earbuds nearly popping out with the thumping bass line.

Stacie made every attempt to look like a woman in command. Her stride on the busy sidewalk was strong and decisive. At five feet six inches tall and 118 pounds, she was a fit, attractive woman. She kept her auburn hair medium length and stylishly swept to one side. She knew men found her attractive, but she also learned at an early age to ignore them. For a hard-nosed reporter obsessed with facts, her motto had been substance over style.

And she thought she'd found a substantial man in Neil.

A single text had shattered that promise.

After an evening when they had argued over a Netflix show she found insipid, he sent a text message:

this just isn't working. sorry Stacie. it's me, not u

u bet its u, she texted back. *have a good life. and that show still sucks*

But it wasn't just the Netflix show, of course. Their relationship had been off-kilter for a while and it had nagged at Stacie. Neil was consumed by the software industry, and all his friends were equally consumed by it. He was the marketing director of a hip, Boston-based start-up that created and sold a category of business software called Software as a service, or SaaS. Stacie vaguely knew what these products were, and she had feigned deep interest in the SaaS ecosystem so that Neil could talk to her incessantly about the industry.

Over time, though, Stacie came to realize that Neil was not actually interested in her work or hearing how challenging it was to chase down an accident victim or state official who was dodging her call. He simply liked having her around for the novelty and status it inferred upon him. She was a reporter for the *Boston Globe,* and he touted it when they were out socially. His friends would ask her about a controversial story in the news as if she had something to do with it, and then would just as quickly move on to gossip about the SaaS industry, job promotions, and managers they hated.

Their argument about the Netflix show was simply an endless replay of their core problem as a couple: Neil was right most of the time, and Stacie wasn't.

◉

The Spotify song abruptly stopped, interrupted by an incoming phone call. She looked at the number; it looked vaguely familiar.

"This is Stacie Davis."

"Ms. Davis, this is Ensign Cortland from the Coast Guard, Boston."

"Oh, yes. Thanks for calling me back. I just need to grab my notepad." She stopped at a crowded bench in Post Office Square and sat down, to the displeasure of two guys chatting about a venture capital investment gone sour.

"OK," she said. "I have my pad."

"We can confirm that a female was pulled from waters off Chatham this morning. She was deceased. Because the body was found in federally protected waters, the Wildlife Service is working with town and county authorities to investigate the death. We'd like you and the other members of the media to follow up with the Cape & Islands District Attorney since the investigation is being coordinated by them."

"Ensign Cortland, can you tell me whether the woman's body showed signs of a shark attack? Or any visual damage? Do you know the name of the deceased? Her age?"

"As I said, please contact the DA's office. The Coast Guard will not comment further since we have nothing to add. Please, Ms. Davis, contact the DA."

"All right. Thanks."

It was colder than she expected, given the brisk breeze forced between the tall buildings in the Financial District. Stacie looked at her notepad. There were several words with a circle around them—DA Cape/Islands.

While she wanted nothing to do with this story and was anxious to hand it off, the fact that the body *may have been* the result of a shark attack piqued her attention. Like all good reporters, she had a well-developed competitive streak, and anything to do with sharks on Cape Cod was bound to get the attention of senior editors. For a lowly general assignment reporter looking to be noticed, sharks were certainly one way to do so.

◉

Dr. Harold Gupta had seen many bodies in his years as a medical examiner. The monotony of cutting open chest cavities, checking internal organs, and sawing open skulls was rote work by now. He did it methodically, rarely stopping to muse over a body.

Yet he was intrigued by this one.

It wasn't the woman's face, or the black hair, or her strong arms, now wrinkled from salt water immersion.

Rather, it was her clothing that caught his attention. The woman—he estimated she was in her twenties—lay on the stainless-steel table, face up to the harsh clinical lighting. He pinched the thick, black skirt that ran from her thin waist, around her hips, and down to her booted feet. The cloth was unusually thick, almost like muslin. He had never seen a body clothed in this kind of fabric before, and he kept pressing it between his gloved fingers.

"What is it?" Sal Manteo, his assistant asked.

"Oh." Gupta looked up, almost embarrassed. "The material. Odd stuff."

Manteo grabbed a piece of the skirt fabric and rubbed it between his fingers.

"Thick," the assistant said.

"Yes. A broad weave. Heavy cotton. Unusual."

Manteo had worked for Gupta for many years and had grown used to his short, grunted sentences. Nothing seemed to bother the man who cut open several hundred bodies a year in a well-ordered autopsy. So, Manteo perked up a bit with the doctor's sudden curiosity.

"Where is it from?" Manteo asked.

"What?" Gupta said, his thick eyeglass lenses flickering in the high-wattage lights.

"The cloth. Where is it from?"

"I don't know," he said absently, looking down again. "Odd."

Manteo released the skirt material, then reached up to grab a piece of the white blouse material. He rubbed it back and forth in his fingers.

"Also seems thick," he said.

"Yes," Gupta said, grabbing a piece of the blouse. "Unusual design. No bra."

They had not cut off her clothing yet, but Manteo saw there were no telltale bra straps showing through the damp cloth on her shoulder. Her breasts were spread out under the cloth, unsupported. The more he looked at her, the more intrigued he became. There *was* something odd about her clothing

Gupta suddenly moved to the bottom of the table and raised one of her shoes several inches off the table. He bent to look closely at the black, thin-soled boot that rose above her ankle. He let her boot fall back on the table and pulled her skirt up; Manteo helped pull the fabric up to her waist.

A small live crab the size of a thumbnail fell to the floor, and Manteo squashed it with his foot.

Both men stared at the woman's undergarments. They were made of strong, white cotton, with a drawstring around her waist. They extended down to above her knees, ending in a decorative lace flare.

"Mmm," Gupta said.

"What are those?" Manteo asked.

"Underwear."

"Really? Not especially practical."

"Practical?" Gupta said.

"Well, every time you peed, you'd have to undo your underwear and slide them down. They look more like pajamas."

"No," Gupta said. "These are fine." He reached up to the body's groin and tugged at the undergarment. It had no crotch and the woman's dark pubic hair poked through.

"What the hell is that?" Manteo.

"It's female underwear."

Manteo looked at his watch. If Gupta kept this up the autopsy would take twice as long to complete.

"We better get going," Manteo said.

"Yes, I suppose," Gupta said, fingering the skirt material again.

◉

The harbormaster's desk was cluttered with office flotsam: a Secret Santa gift coffee mug doing duty as a pencil holder, a glass paperweight encasing a plastic miniature lighthouse, a large clamshell holding a tangle of paper clips and rubber bands, an ancient, rusting stapler left by the prior harbormaster, and a modern, underused desk telephone.

Dan Stilton, the Chatham Harbormaster, motioned for Coast Guard Station Chief Captain Hansen to sit.

Stilton pushed the phone toward his guest and knocked a ballpoint pen and a metal ruler onto the ground.

"Shit," Stilton said.

"No problem, Dan," Hansen said, picking up the items.

"OK, let's get this over with," Stilton said. "This is a crazy time of year, with all the summer residents showing up launching their boats. Half of them forget to turn in their mooring permits. It's a shit show, let me tell you."

"Well, I've got two new guardsmen and each one looks like they're fifteen years old. And they act like it too."

Both men laughed.

Stilton looked at a pink message slip and carefully dialed a number with the phone on speakerphone.

"First Assistant District Attorney Mary Martin, please," Stilton said. The two men stared at each other, waiting.

"Martin here," the phone blared.

"Mary, this Chatham Harbormaster Dan Stilton, and with me is Captain Hansen from the Coast Guard station here. We had a note that you wanted to speak to us, preferably at the same time."

"Yes, thanks, Dan, and Captain Hansen. I'm following up on the body that was found off Monomoy today. The medical examiner has the body now, but can you help me fill in the blanks a little?"

"Sure," Stilton said, hunched awkwardly over the phone. "A body was discovered by a charter boat captain early this morning, about seven fifteen, on the Nantucket Sound side of Monomoy Island. They were on a fishing trip. They saw the body floating and called the Coast Guard on channel sixteen, right, Captain?"

Captain Hansen leaned forward toward the phone. "Yes, that's correct. We got a call from the charter boat at seven fifteen—I can get the exact time from the log later, but that's about right for the timing."

"Was it a phone call from a mobile phone?" Martin asked.

"No, it was a marine band call. We monitor channel sixteen and started a conversation with the caller. We dispatched one of our boats immediately and asked the charter boat guy to stay on station with the body until we arrived."

"How did the charter captain sound?"

"Um, well, I've only spoken briefly with the crewmen who responded to the call, but I gather he was kind of upset."

"OK. What happened when they got to the body?"

"Well, there was the body of a woman floating facedown in the water, about fifty or sixty yards from shore. It was a relatively calm morning on the west side of Monomoy, so they got the body on board quickly, and questioned the charter captain and his customer. They also took some pictures of the body in the water before retrieving it."

"You have the contact information of the boat's occupants? Including phone numbers, driver's licenses, and so on?"

"Yes, we do."

"Did the charter guy follow the Coast Guard boat in to shore?"

"Um, good question. I don't know for certain. I believe he followed it in partway, but he's out of Saquatucket Harbor, so he peeled off at some point."

"I'll give you my email address in a minute, but could you send me the two boat occupants' contact information?"

"Sure."

"OK, back to the body," Martin said. "I gather there was no identification on the body?"

"Correct," Hansen said. "But I want to make it clear that our guys are only required to make a cursory examination of the body, checking pockets, and stuff like that. There may be items the medical examiner found, but she had no obvious identification on her."

"Jewelry? Watch? Cell phone?"

"Negative. Nothing, I'm afraid."

"A real Jane Doe," Martin said.

"I suppose so," Hansen said, looking at Stilton.

"Any sign of obvious trauma? Neck bruises? Head injury? Shark bite?"

"Nothing that we could see," Hansen said. "Definitely no shark bites that the crew noticed."

"Dan, you there?" she said.

"Yes," he said, leaning forward again.

"I talked briefly with the police chief there, and he said there were no reports of missing people in Chatham. You've got a commercial fishing fleet there, correct?"

"Yes, we do."

"Any information from those guys on a missing crew member?"

"It's the beginning of the season here, so things are a little quiet. But no, the boats that are out have not mentioned anything. Captain Hansen, anything on your end?"

"Nothing we've heard. No one has notified us of a missing crew member."

"I don't suppose your crew could estimate how long the body had been in the water?"

"No, ma'am, we aren't qualified to make that kind of call. Sorry."

"Not a problem, just thought I'd ask."

"Dan, do you have a list of Chatham-based commercial boats that are out to sea and might be in the area?"

"No, we don't keep an official list of boats that are out. Boats come in and out all summer and into the fall. But I can ask around. Like I said, it's early so there wouldn't be many boats out. Scallopers mainly."

"Captain Hansen, how about pleasure boats? You receive any notice of a man or woman overboard? Any distress calls?"

"None, I'm afraid."

"Well, we're handling the investigation in the DA's office," Martin said. "You'll be hearing more from us I'm sure. Please contact me immediately if you hear anything that would help identify the body and where she came from. At this time, it's being treated as a suspicious death until we get additional information, like suicide or someone going skinny-dipping after drinking a gallon of vodka."

"She was fully clothed," Hansen said.

"Yes, of course. But you get my drift."

CHAPTER 3

Carl started the long trip back with his two slightly inebriated customers who seemed to revel in the salt spray and roaring outboard motors behind them in the stern. The day had gone well, and he had a couple of legal black sea bass and scup to fillet.

The boat had planed and was skimming the light chop as he raced east in Nantucket Sound back toward his mooring in Stage Harbor. Carl checked emails and texts. He scrolled through the furious Twitter threads about the body found off Monomoy.

There were occasional deaths in the waters off the cape, mostly due to cardiac problems involving older fishermen, or accidents in heavy weather. Sometimes a reckless, alcohol-infused vacationer would flip their boat on the rips off Monomoy or get tossed in the water trying to enter the north break at low tide.

But Carl could not remember the last time a body was found that far from the mainland. There was instant theorizing about the woman who died, including everything from suicide to a domestic fight gone awry on a private yacht.

she got natalie wooded, Noog texted.

lighten up; bad juju to diss the dead, Carl jumped in.

just another cross-dressing gray seal, someone else tossed in.

Carl frowned and put the phone back in his pocket. God, I hope the whole summer isn't going to be like this, he thought.

◉

"Drowned?" Martin said.

"As I said, that is my preliminary judgment on the cause of death," Gupta said. "We're waiting on toxicology, of course. But even if the woman was intoxicated or OD'd on heroin, she still drowned. Saltwater in the lungs."

"And no evidence of sexual assault?"

"None."

"No ligature marks, bruising on the body?"

"None."

"How long was she dead?"

"About six hours or so."

"You estimated she was mid-twenties, yes?"

"Yes."

"No evidence of shark attack?"

Gupta sighed heavily into the phone.

"Mary, you asked that earlier, and my response is still the same—no sharks. You all should get sharks off the brain."

"I'm just anticipating what I'm going to get asked, that's all," she said.

"I understand."

"Tattoos, identifying marks?"

"Just some scars on her left hand and a large mole on her inside left thigh."

"Scars? What kind of scars?" Martin said.

"Small scars, in the palm mostly. Old scars, not new."

"What caused them?"

"No idea, but her hands were calloused. Probably from some repetitive manual work."

"Interesting," Martin said.

"If you say so."

"When do you expect the final report?"

"After toxicology, maybe two days."

"Anything else you want to add? You always have something to add, Harold," she said.

"Not at this time."

"What does *that* mean?"

"It means nothing," he said.

"Oh, come on. Now you've got me interested. That's not like you. What's up? Don't worry. I'm not writing this down. What do you have?"

"You always write things down. You never forget anything I tell you, whether you write it down or not. You'll get my report in two days."

"Shit, Harold. Come on. A woman is dead, found floating south of Stage Harbor. I'm not an oceanographer, but if she *were* floating for six hours, I don't think the tides would have dragged her that far from land. South Monomoy is uninhabited except for the Wildlife Service folks at the lighthouse. And they had no one at the research building that night. I need some help here."

Gupta shifted in his office chair, and it squeaked mightily, betraying its vintage.

"Her clothes," he said.

"Her what?"

"Clothes."

"What about them? No underwear? Tears in the cloth?"

"No, nothing like that. They were odd."

"Jesus, Harold. What the hell does that mean?"

"I don't know. That's your job. I'm just a medical examiner."

◉

Stacie looked at her monitor and groaned out loud.

"Give me a friggin' break, would ya?"

An editor on the night desk was asking for clarification on the age of the pedestrian that was hit by the Green Line car at Cleveland Circle.

"The *Herald* reported that the injured man was fifty-two years old; your story says he's fifty-three. Can you confirm age, please?" the email stated.

Well, for one, the *Boston Herald* sucks, Stacie thought of writing back. She looked at her notepad and flipped through the pages until she found the remarks from the MBTA spokesperson. She had written down "male, age 53," along with a jumble of other quotes.

A good reporter gets these things right, she knew, and the spokesperson could have gotten it wrong, or she may have gotten it wrong, or

19

the *Herald* writer could have gotten it wrong.

"Crap," she said, dialing the MBTA's Norman Lemoine.

"Lemoine here."

"Stacie Davis from the *Globe*. Need to check the age of the guy hit yesterday in Cleveland Circle: fifty-three or fifty-two? *Herald* said fifty-two; I got you down as saying fifty-three."

"Hang on, Stacie," he said.

She heard papers rustling in the background.

"OK, let me see, um … he's fifty-three. *Herald*'s got it wrong."

"They suck," she said.

He laughed. "Anything else?"

"Nope. Thanks."

She shot back a note to the copyeditor confirming the age.

Her cell phone lit up with a text.

can we talk? It was from Neil.

Stacie held the phone in her hand, staring at the message as if it were a confusing missive from another planet. She was not surprised that he was having second thoughts about dumping her. Heck, she was just as conflicted. But she was also hurt and sad. Deep down inside she knew that there was something fundamentally uneven and unhealthy about the relationship. Neil liked the *idea* of their relationship, but he didn't seem to like *Stacie.*

bout what? she wrote back.

about us, he answered.

neil please leave me alone. Someone out there will take u on, but it won't be me

come on, he persisted. *let's talk*

u were right. it's not working. best we stop now

Stacie, stop it. let's talk

please. i mean it. blocking u now

Stacie didn't actually block him, but she put down the phone and leaned back in her chair and scanned the half-empty newsroom. She felt jubilant, but sad and lonely at the same time; she was mostly sad, though.

◎

Carl nursed his beer while he scanned the marine weather forecast on his phone. A family of four was scheduled for the morning, and it was the perfect charter for this time of year. The family had booked a charter the previous year. The parents, a well-heeled couple from Wellesley, Massachusetts, wanted their ten-year-old son and eight-year-old daughter to enjoy the outdoors and have the thrill of catching fish.

He could deliver scup and black sea bass; maybe an errant sea robin and a flounder thrown in as well. The kids loved catching anything, and the parents loved watching the kids catching anything. These were easy trips with lots of smiles and peals of delight.

That is, as long as the weather cooperated. This time of year, fog was a problem. And wind off the water, even from the warm southwest, was not fun for most passengers in Nantucket Sound.

Carl was praying the high-pressure system that was moving east would stall to allow a mild westerly wind to flow off the land and keep temperatures moderate. He needed the business now that his winter indoor painting gigs were ending.

"Whazzup?" Noog said, sitting down next to Carl at the bar.

"Not much. Good charter today. You?"

"Had three guys from Connecticut," Noog said. "They insisted on going to the rips, even though I told them a million times that it was early for the rips."

"Did you go?"

"Yep. All the friggin' way down there and ran them up and down Pollock rip until one of them nearly barfed. Then we hit the reef off Harwich, and we landed some sea bass. Burned a lot of friggin' gas on that one. And the tip sucked as well."

"So, a great day all around then," Carl laughed, raising his glass.

"Fuckin' A," Noog said, clinking the two glasses together. "Better than my bartending gig. Mostly."

Both men returned to their phones and silently scrolled through email, texts, Facebook, Instagram, and a slew of news links.

"Hey, what about the chick that they pulled from Nantucket Sound?" Noog said.

"Yeah. What the hell is that all about?" Carl said.

"Some rich snob was on his way to Nantucket on his fifty-foot schooner and didn't like the way his omelet was prepared. So, he tossed the cook overboard. Problem solved."

Carl laughed. "Makes perfect sense. I hate undercooked omelets."

They returned to their phones. Noog answered a text, and Carl read the weather report for the fifth time.

"So, what do you really think happened to that woman?" Noog said.

"Hell if I know. Suicide probably. I mean, there's no boats out there for her to fall from. Weird stuff."

"It was a bad omelet, I'm telling you," Noog said, returning to his phone.

"Probably," Carl said.

◎

"I can't believe he called you!" Stacie said, taking a sip of wine. "What a total jerk."

"Yeah, it was a little awkward," Marie said, repositioning herself on the couch to look directly at Stacie. "He sounded so desperate. I think he really misses you, and he knows he screwed up."

"Ya reckon?" Stacie said.

"Maybe you should just talk to him again. See what he has to say."

"You're kidding."

"No, I'm not. Just talk to him. Have a cup of coffee. What could be wrong with that?"

"Marie, please," Stacie said, taking another sip. In truth, Stacie was tempted to talk to Neil, but those temptations were growing milder by the day. They were simply not meant for each other.

"Well, if you don't want to see him, don't see him. Let's leave it at that. You're a big girl; trust your instincts."

Stacie stood up and looked out the huge window in Marie's Boston condo on Clarendon Street.

"I wish I made as much money as you and could afford a place like this," she said.

"Yeah, but you have an exciting job. You're a freakin' reporter for the *Boston Globe*, doing interesting stuff. I'm a director of HR at a bank. I'd give it up in a second to have your kind of life."

"No, you wouldn't," Stacie laughed.

"Well," Marie said, "I would if it came with stock options. And a health club membership. And free parking. And a 401k match."

"You bitch," Stacie laughed.

"Smarty-pants reporter," Marie said, finishing off the last of her wine. "Let's get out of here. You need to meet some men and you need my help. I know a good bar that collects professional men with high net worth."

"I need to meet a man with high net intellect."

"They don't make them anymore."

"Well, then high net worth will work."

◉

Jack Wentzel sat next to his wife Louise on the couch in the family room, his right hand on her knee.

"Go ahead," State Police Detective John Clancy said.

"Well, like I said, we'd only been out there for about thirty-five minutes. I don't think Phil had made more than a couple of casts when he spotted the body."

"And that was around seven ten in the morning?" Clancy said.

"Yeah, about that. I called it in as soon as I got close enough to see what it was."

"What did it look like?" Clancy said.

"The sun was in front of us and I just couldn't see what was in the water. You see all kinds of crap floating out there. At first, I thought it was a dead seal. But Phil was in the bow and he saw it. Then I saw it."

"Can you describe what the body looked like?"

"Looked like? What do you mean? I don't understand."

"Describe what you saw."

"Um, well, the body had its arms out, like this," he said, raising his arms like airplane wings.

"The body was facedown?"

"Yeah. But I couldn't tell whether it was a man or woman because of the glare from the sun, so I poled the boat a little closer. Then you could see that it was a woman because she had a dark skirt and a white blouse. She had long black hair that kind of floated around her head."

"Did you check to see if she was alive?"

"No, she was dead. I wasn't about to the mess with a dead body."

"How do you know she was dead?"

"Well, she was facedown, and in the time we watched, she never moved or tried to breathe. After a minute or two, it was obvious she was dead."

"Were there any other boats in the area?"

"Nope. Just us."

"Did you see boats anywhere else that morning?"

"Yeah, saw a couple of bigger charter guys going out. That's about it."

"Do you remember the names of those other boats?"

"No, but if you checked with the harbormaster, they might know."

"Did you notice anything floating near the body? A purse, a piece of paper, a driver's license? Anything?"

"No. We didn't see anything."

"What did your customer Phil do during this time?"

"He was pretty upset. And so was I. We just kind of looked at each other, and then I called it in to the Coast Guard."

"And you didn't try to turn the body over, or see if she was alive?"

"Why the heck would I do that? She was dead. I don't want to see a dead woman's face. Hell, what if the face was a mess and crabs were eating it? No way I was going to look at that."

Jack's wife covered his hand on her knee with hers and stroked it gently.

"And you'd never seen this woman before?" Clancy asked.

"No. I mean, I don't even know what she looks like. I never saw her face. The Coast Guard pulled her out."

"Well, I just need to ask you these questions. You and your client Phil were the first people to discover her body, and people who stumble on bodies are important. They often observe important facts."

"Listen, I'm a charter boat captain out of Harwich, and I have a small business that lasts for about four to five months a year if the weather co-operates. I don't need any bad publicity about this thing. I'm just trying to make a living."

"We understand that, Jack, but we're trying to figure out who this woman is and how she got there."

"You don't know who she is?" Louise spoke for the first time.

"No, ma'am. She's still a Jane Doe at this time."

"Do you know how she died?" Louise asked.

"We're working on that," Clancy said.

"Do you think she was murdered, or something like that?" she asked.

"We're working on that."

CHAPTER 4

Her cell phone woke her. The clock radio showed it was ten past six in the morning.

"Hey," she said. "What's up, Nancy?"

Nancy Nunes was the overnight assistant Metro editor.

"You have the Cape Cod body story, right?"

"Yeah. Not much there yet. I wrote something yesterday."

"*Cape Cod Times* reports this morning that the woman is a Jane Doe and drowned. No one knows who she is or how she got there. Not calling it a murder or a suicide yet. Got a call from Smitty ten minutes ago and he wants someone on it. Tag, you're it."

"Really?"

"Really. I'm outta here in twenty minutes, but you need to get down there. I don't know who's on the desk next, but they'll be chasing you down. I'm sending a photog too."

"Nancy, it's a friggin' body. On the cape. I can do this remotely."

"Negative. Smitty wants boots on the ground. Get your ass moving, girl."

"I'm having my period. And I'm depressed. And I broke up with my boyfriend."

"Poor thing."

"Shit, Nancy. And I have a hangover."

"All the better. Move it. Smitty is all over this."

"If I cross the Sagamore Bridge, Nancy, I may never come back. You know that, right?"

"That would be fine by me. They need better waitresses down there."

◉

"Have you checked with the harbormaster?" Cape & Islands District Attorney Felix Barone said. In his third consecutive elected term as DA, Barone was a quiet man by nature. He spoke in short sentences that, oddly, were almost always questions. At five feet ten inches tall, with thick black hair and a pronounced nose, he was a fitness fanatic renowned for his workout routine.

"They don't keep track of commercial boats or charter fishermen, or anyone for that matter," Martin said. "Not unless they're applying for a mooring permit or a temporary permit. It's not the FAA, Felix. And it's the cape, if you know what I mean."

Barone had a habit of frowning when he concentrated, so Martin often could not judge his mood.

"And the guys who found the body?"

"They look pretty clean. We're still looking at their backgrounds, but their story checks out. And there's the issue with the time of death."

"Remind me again about that. Gupta says she was in the water for six hours?"

"Yeah, which means she started floating at one a.m. or so. The guys who found her—who barely know each other—found her at seven a.m. or thereabouts. Hard to see them as suspects since both had alibis for one o'clock that morning. I'm not focusing on them."

"Mmm," Barone said, rocking gently in his large office chair.

"No missing persons that match?"

"Not on the state and federal list. Still checking."

"Gupta's sure she drowned?"

"He said there's saltwater in her lungs. No bruising, ligature marks. Nothing. No syringe tracks on her arms. Nothing on her body to show she was injured or assaulted."

"Toxicology?"

"Girl was clean. Like completely clean. Not a trace of any drug or alcohol."

"When's the artist's rendition going to be ready? You using that crazy guy from Northampton? Why not the new software they have to build a face?"

"Her body was in good shape, so we could release a photo of her, which as you know is ghastly and generates tons of complaints from the public. Or we can get someone to draw her face. We've done it before, and it works fine. We'll have it later today. Yeah, I know you don't like the artist, but he's the best we have. We could show him a face that's been crushed like a Halloween pumpkin, and he'd give us a drawing. He's good. But nutty."

"Mmm." Barone rocked. "Anything else?"

"We're still checking to see what commercial and recreational boats were in the area, though, like I said, that won't be comprehensive. We're also looking at recent dockings on Nantucket and the rest of the cape. Going to check with New Bedford, Boston, and even Gloucester."

"I got two calls asking if a shark was involved," Barone said.

"Jesus, Mary, and Joseph," Martin said. "What the hell is wrong with people! Sharks?"

"I'm just mentioning it."

"I understand. It just gets frustrating at times."

"You'll be asking for help from the public?"

"Yes, released to the media this morning."

"Nothing else?"

Martin bit the inside of her cheek as she contemplated.

"What?" Barone said. "What's on your mind? Tell me."

"I'm sure it's nothing."

"For chrissakes, Mary, spill it."

"Gupta's acting a little strange on this one."

"And that means what, exactly?" Barone said about Gupta.

"I don't know what it means. He's a little odd, as we all know. But he was very measured when I spoke to him. As if he was weighing each word precisely. I pressed him but he didn't expand his description of the body or cause of death."

They stared at each other.

"Maybe Gupta was in a bad mood. I'd be in a bad mood if I had to cut open skulls every day with an electric saw."

"Yeah, maybe," she said.

Martin, six years after joining the DA, and just two as first assistant district attorney, was still not sure how to handle Barone. He never lost his temper, though he showed frustration with cases that garnered media coverage. At thirty-six years of age, Martin was starting that painful process that all assistant district attorneys go through: how long to stay in the job.

Though she had risen to first assistant DA, the pay was still exceptionally low compared to the private sector. Assistant DA turnover rates were high as young lawyers gathered experience and moved on. She was tired of mentoring the painfully earnest youngsters pouring out of law school. And her husband was pressing her to cash in on her experience.

But she had a weakness—she liked the rough and tumble side of the business. Civil law was chess, but criminal law was an outright contact sport. Martin reveled in it. Maybe one day she'd run for Barone's job when he retired. If he retired.

She could see herself sitting behind his desk one day and would accessorize it in precisely the same way as Barone. Floor-to-ceiling shelves of law books that were never opened, grip-and-grin framed photos covering the walls. Puff piece profiles from newspapers in gilded frames. And of course, she'd keep the requisite near-religious photos of John F. Kennedy and Ted Kennedy.

◉

By the time Stacie got to Plymouth on Route 3, her phone had rung three times: once from Neil that she let go to voicemail, once from Mike Forrest, the photographer she talked to briefly, and the last one from Stephen Hanes, the Metro editor.

"Yeah, I'm heading there now," she told Hanes. "I'll be sure to file something from Chatham later today."

"Color," Hanes said. "Smitty loves local color. Gnarly fishermen, *lobstah* boat captains, seagulls crying out for more French fries."

"I got it," she said. "Isn't there anyone down there to help out?"

"Vacation."

"Yeah, forgot."

Stacie drove a 2017 canary yellow, convertible Mini Cooper S. She bought it on a lark one day when her old Toyota Camry needed new brakes and tires. She loved driving with the top down, even when it was chilly. She kept a Red Sox baseball cap in the car to keep her hair under control. Today it was just too cold to drop the top, but she had been tempted. New Englanders exhibit strange behaviors in the spring.

Crossing the ancient Sagamore Bridge, its iron girders repainted a hundred times in a grim gray color, she glimpsed the canal flowing underneath. Stacie loved the ocean and the cape and was only half kidding when she told Nunes she might not return if she crossed the bridge. She had long fantasized about chucking her complicated dating life and hectic job to save stranded dolphins and turtles.

Of course, it was an impossibly romantic and impractical fantasy, but isn't that what fantasy is—a moment of pretending to ease the stress?

By the time she got to the first exit on Route 6, her phone rang again.

"This is Stacie Davis," she said into the car's hands-free microphone.

"Stacie, this is First Assistant DA Mary Martin returning your call."

"Yes, thanks for returning the call. I was wondering if you had time to meet in person today. I'm following up on the body found off Chatham."

"Well, there's not much more to give you besides what's already been released. I don't think a face-to-face is called for. The body is still not identified. We're checking all the databases and can't find a match so far. The *Globe* has everything that was released. The DA's office has nothing more to offer."

"The cause of death was drowning; do you suspect foul play?"

"We're considering everything at this point, Ms. Davis. Later today we'll be releasing an artist's rendition of the woman's face, and I'm sure we'll get some response from the public. I assume the *Globe* will publish that image."

"Of course. We'll help in any way."

"That's good to hear. Listen, I've got to run, but feel free to call me any time if you have any questions."

"Great, thanks for your help."

Stacie hung up and chuckled. That last bit of largesse on the part of the assistant DA was pure bullshit. The last thing that woman wanted was a call from Stacie. Call her anytime? Um, how about *never*.

◉

They sat in the hectic seating area inside the Route 6 rest area. The open tables were flanked by a Dunkin' Donuts, a Burger King, and a sandwich shop. Besides the milling crowd of travelers, there was a constant flow of drivers rushing to the bathrooms.

Stacie kept scanning her phone for texts and emails, while Mike, the *Globe* photographer, did the same.

"They got file photos of the DA but nothing on Mary Martin," he said. "They want her shot. And the boat captain. You have his phone number?"

"Nope. But I have his website. I was going to try to interview him, so let me hit him first and see if we can get him to see us at the same time."

"Go for it," Mike said, sipping a large Dunkin' coffee. "I want to get back before rush hour, if that's possible. Got tickets for *Jersey Boys* tonight."

"Cool. We'll be out of here before you know it," she said, as she dialed the number on charter boat captain Jack Wetzel's website. Predictably, it went to voicemail.

"Hey, ah, Jack, this is Stacie Davis from the *Boston Globe*. I was wondering if you have a few minutes to chat with me today in person. I'm on the cape right now and would like to stop by. It wouldn't take long. Just following up on the body that was found recently." She left her number and hung up.

"Bet he doesn't call," Mike said.

"That's a possibility. Guy's probably crushed with calls. But I talked to the harbormaster and he's good for a visit. If nothing else, you can get a shot of him and some fishing boats behind him."

"And *shahks*. We need pictures of *shahks*."

They both laughed.

"Friggin' *shahks*," Stacie muttered while she thumbed through her messages.

◉

"Is this what you want?" Harbormaster Stilton said, standing in the parking lot next to the commercial trap dock on Stage Harbor Road in Chatham.

31

"Can you just move a little to your left? Yeah, that's perfect." Mike fired off a bunch of frames on his Nikon and asked Stilton to move again.

Stacie looked at her watch. It was already four twenty in the afternoon, and she had almost nothing of value from anyone in town. Stilton offered no new information, and the police chief deferred all questions to the DA's office.

She thanked Stilton for his help, then chatted with Mike outside her car.

"Look, I've got to find a place to file a story, probably a Dunkin' somewhere. You got everything you need?"

"Yeah; got some lighthouse stuff, and of course, the harbormaster. I'll send them in right now. You all set?"

"For now. I won't get home until late. Kind of sucks."

"Sorry. Wish I could help. I just take pictures."

"You could help by having a beer on me when you get home."

◉

For all the cloying nostalgia about Cape Cod as a fun-filled, family summer playground, Stacie knew there was an unpleasant side as well. The drug scourge had penetrated lives there and left families devastated and kept law enforcement busy. But there was yet a darker side.

Sitting in front of her laptop in a Dunkin' on Route 28, she searched the *Globe* archives and the internet to discover that unidentified bodies had been showing up there for years. The most famous case was the Lady of the Dunes.

In July 1974, a teenage girl stumbled upon a woman's body found in the dunes near Provincetown's Race Point Beach. The victim's skull had been crushed on the left side, and her hands and even some of her teeth had been removed. The body rested on a beach towel.

The identity of the woman was never determined, even after her DNA was used to approximate a facial image that was widely disseminated. No one reported her missing. She is buried in St. Peter's Cemetery in Provincetown. Her grave marker reads: "Unidentified Female Body Found Race Point Dunes; July 26, 1974."

More recently, in June 2014, the body of a man was found on Town Neck Beach in Sandwich. The man's head and limbs were removed. Even with new DNA technology, improved databases, and software that can create facial images, the man had never been identified.

She had filed a summary article earlier that afternoon but was told to file a more complete version later for the morning print edition.

Stacie took a deep breath to clear her mind, then started typing on her laptop, periodically looking at her notes or scanning a *Globe* archive article. It took her forty-five minutes to tighten up a 700-word story on the body found off Monomoy, with liberal references to the other unidentified bodies found on the cape over the years.

She knew the story for the print edition would likely be chopped down to fit scarce space. But for the website, it would probably run in its entirety. She had an inkling that tying in the newly discovered body with the older cases would get some attention at the paper. The next best thing to *shahks* on the cape was potential *murder and mayhem* on the cape.

By the time she got to exit five in Plymouth while driving home, the night desk had called to ask a couple of questions. They said her story was probably running on page one in print and above the fold on the website's homepage.

This, of course, is every young reporter's dream.

◉

"No tips from the public?" Martin asked.

"Nada," Detective Clancy said. "Just whack jobs. Nothing credible."

"Sarah?" Martin said, turning to her.

Massachusetts State Police Trooper Sarah Langone was the youngest member of the detective team assigned to the Cape & Islands DA. She was adept at all things digital. At five feet ten inches tall, Langone was used to standing out in the crowd. Her short black hair, hazel eyes, and high cheekbones combined into a stunningly attractive woman. She was a devoted runner and tried to pound out 15-20 miles a week. The physical entrance exam for females to the state police academy required finishing a 1.5-mile run in less than fourteen minutes and fifty seconds; she beat the men's limit of twelve minutes and thirty-eight seconds.

But no amount of running could help her to be taken seriously in the DA's office. At twenty-nine years of age and with so little experience, she was acutely aware of her junior status. She had hoped to be mentored by Martin but found the opposite—Martin barely spoke to her.

"Nothing on the missing persons databases," Langone said. "But it might be too early for her to show up on those. It's only been two days since she was found, so we might get a hit soon."

"DNA?" Martin said.

"Nothing there either," Langone said.

"Fishing boats docking or in transit through the area?" Martin said, looking at Clancy.

"Mary, there's no complete list of commercial boats out there," he said. "Some of the boats are run by owner-operators, and some are part of company fleets. The fleets are easier to track, and we've got some stuff from New Bedford, Fall River, Provincetown, and Boston. Nothing from Gloucester."

"And?"

"There's not much fishing activity right now. Two scallopers out of New Bedford were working south of Nantucket. Neither had a female crew member, nor were they close enough to Monomoy to be relevant. Another scalloper out of Harwich was due back in later today. They're a veteran two-man crew and work the area east of Chatham. Wouldn't have been near Monomoy. I'll talk to them, though."

Martin took a long sip of her lukewarm coffee.

"What's your take on the charter boat captain?" she asked.

"Doesn't work for me," Clancy said. "Hard to believe he was involved in her death because he'd have to have accomplices. And his wife said he was asleep next to her in bed at one o'clock. I don't know. Not a great lead in my opinion."

"Is it worth subpoenaing his cell phone data?" she said, finishing her coffee.

"Why not?" he said. "Worth a poke."

"Now, what's the latest on that scumbag Gutierrez?"

"He's not talking," Clancy said.

"You find thirty-two ounces of fentanyl in his car, and the idiot's not talking? Come on, Clancy, for chrissakes, lean on the bastard."

"He's got a Boston lawyer," Clancy said. "We have to play nice."

"Oh, great, a Boston lawyer," Martin said. "Let me guess. Northeastern grad, then Suffolk Law at night. Grew up in Southie. He didn't want to walk the beat like his dad, an upstanding member of the Boston PD. Now he's making $300K a year defending drug lords and scumbags, and his poor old dad won't even talk to him. Why can't they just pretend to practice law in Boston and stay away from the cape?"

"It's a woman," Clancy said.

"Excuse me; why can't these *women* bastard defense attorneys just stay in Boston?"

CHAPTER 5

Stacie sipped coffee in her local Starbucks and read emails. It got her out of the apartment and into the working world. Breaking up with Neil had depressed her and getting momentum early in the day was important. If she had a bad habit nurtured over many years, it was to mire herself in endless ruminating on the wrong turns in her life.

"Holy shit," she muttered under her breath as she stumbled over an email addressed to her directly from Smitty, the *Globe*'s editor.

"Nice job on the cape story," he wrote. "Like the color you worked into it. Have asked Metro to keep you on the story. Happy hunting, Stacie. Keep it up—Charles."

Stacie had met Smitty only twice in her two years at the *Globe*: once at an orientation for new employees and another time in the elevator. Both times he seemed distracted and intense, which was understandable for an editor of a major metropolitan newspaper.

She forwarded his email immediately to two of her fellow reporters, Stephanie Norton and Fred Collins.

"Damn," Norton shot back. "Aren't you the hot shit reporter? Man, the last time he noticed me, he thought I was someone else. Good for you. Oh, and I'm officially jealous."

"Impressive," Collins jumped in. "It was a good story. You have a nice touch. Though, I had no idea the cape was creepy like that."

Stacie's phone rang; she could see it was Hanes, the Metro editor.

"Good job on the cape piece," he said.

"Thanks, appreciate it."

"I guess you know Smitty is all over the story."

"Yeah," she said. "He emailed me, which is a first."

"Well, we're sending you back there for a couple of days. It would be better if you stayed down there to keep working the story. Meet people, work in a little of the dark side. Stuff like that."

"I can do that," she said. "No problem."

"Looks like we have an artist's rendition and an official cause of death, but not much more from the DA. Keep on them, would you? People love mysteries in odd locations, and this one's got some legs."

"Got it. I'll pack up and be down there around noon."

"Great. Check in with the desk later."

◎

Carl picked up the young family off the public dock in Stage Harbor at seven thirty in the morning. The two children were barely awake, and the bedraggled parents looked like they were sorry for scheduling the charter in the first place.

But he launched his best charm offensive and had the foursome laughing within twenty minutes of shoving off. A light fog had drifted in overnight, but a northwesterly wind had already started nudging the misty blanket into Nantucket Sound. Carl initially kept the boat inside Stage Harbor, letting the children catch a couple of sea robins, an under-sized fluke, and plenty of seaweed. After an hour of this, he puttered out of the harbor and hit the throttle, turning west toward the artificial reef off Harwich.

To his relief, the two parents finally relaxed as the cool air and the speeding boat drummed away their suburban angst. They sipped their coffees, smiled at each other, and hugged the young ones as the boat roared over the waves.

They joined two other boats working the underwater structure, and before long, the girl landed a keeper black sea bass while her brother pouted and kept bouncing his jig aggressively off the bottom. Carl and the mother both took pictures of the girl holding the fish.

Carl moved the boat, searching his fish-finder for another school.

The father chatted with Carl at the console.

"Glad the fog lifted," the father said. "Wasn't sure we'd be able to get out. But this is great. Sun's out, the kids are catching fish, and they'll sleep like logs tonight."

Carl laughed.

"You got kids?" the father asked.

"Yes, one. A girl."

"Does she fish?"

"You bet she does," Carl said.

The father laughed.

"Hey," he said, suddenly turning to face Carl, "what's up with this body they found out here?"

His wife shushed him to avoid alarming the children.

He stepped closer to Carl.

"So, what happened?"

"Man, I don't know," Carl said. "Lots of chatter about it. Could be self-inflicted, if you know what I mean."

"Yeah, a waitress at the restaurant said as much last night. What do you think?"

"Paper reported today that she drowned, so I'm leaning toward the self-inflicted approach," Carl said.

"But didn't they say the body was pretty far from the mainland?"

"David!" his wife said, looking at the kids, who were staring at their father. "Really? Isn't there anything else that we can talk about?"

"Hey," Carl said, pointing to the multicolored display on the fish-finder, "I see fish. Let's get on them."

"Yeah," the boy said. "My turn to catch one."

◉

The room was clean but musty, and Stacie opened one of the windows to let in some air. Marie had teased her about whether she'd be staying at the luxurious Chatham Bars Inn.

"Only if you're paying," Stacie said. "I'm on the *Globe*'s per diem. That means a motel and Dunkin' Donuts."

Although he insisted that he had nothing to add to the investigation, Chatham Police Chief Norm Thompson agreed to meet her at eleven that morning.

She unpacked her clothes, set up her laptop, and used her phone as a hotspot. There was an email from one of the assistant Metro desk editors with a link to a *Cape Cod Times* story. The story reported that the medical examiner found no trace of drugs in the body found off Monomoy, and the cause of death was drowning. Any further questions should be directed to the DA's office.

Stacie called the number Assistant DA Martin had given her, and it went to voicemail. She left a message asking Martin to call her.

Twenty minutes later, she pulled up in front of the police station. The building was large, new, and not busy.

Chief Thompson, a small, thin man with a smooth, tanned face, listened politely as Stacie asked several questions.

"I'm sorry, Ms. Davis, but we're just not involved in the investigation. You'll need to ask the DA's office those questions."

Stacie tried a couple of additional questions, but he just smiled and shrugged by way of an answer.

"Did you see the body?" she asked, desperate to elicit a quote.

"Well, I saw the covered body, if that's what you mean."

"Who else was at the dock when the Coast Guard brought the body in?"

"Besides me and Sgt. Cooper, there was an ambulance, the harbormaster, and two men from the Coast Guard station. I think that was it. Oh, and a couple of workers from the commercial dock that's right next door. They were looking down on the scene."

"What was the demeanor of the crew on the Coast Guard boat?"

"Demeanor? I'm not sure what you mean."

"Were they upset? How did they seem to you?"

"They were pretty upset," Thompson said. "No fun pulling a body from the water."

"Have you ever had to do that?" she asked.

"Not me, no. The harbormaster's had to on occasion, but not us. We find bodies on land, if you don't mind a little dark humor."

She smiled.

"Do you have a theory on what happened to the woman? Your gut instinct?"

He smiled. "No comment."

"How about off the record?"

"No comment."

"Who in this town has an opinion on what happened to that woman?" Stacie asked, with a hint of frustration. "I mean, a young woman is found floating about eight miles from here, and no one knows who she is or where she came from. She's someone's daughter, or sister, or wife."

"Ms. Davis, you must understand that the police department's not going to speculate on things we know nothing about. We may be a small town here on Cape Cod, but we don't just make things up on the fly. If you want unbridled speculation, hang around one of the local bars. Talk to some of those folks. You'll get a hatful of speculation."

◎

Mrs. Debra Falcone had a full head of snow-white hair, facial wrinkles from too much sun, and ice-blue eyes that were still intense after eighty-two years of life.

"I was hoping to get some background on Chatham," Stacie said, sitting in the small office of the historical association. "I mean, I've read some things on Wikipedia, but thought I'd come to the source."

"Wikipedia," Falcone said. "Mmm."

"Like I said, I've come to the source."

"I'll try to help, but there is so much history here that it's hard to know where to start. I don't think any of us has the time to fill you in on several hundred years of history in a half hour."

"To be honest," Stacie said, "I had no idea the town was that old. I see that it was incorporated in 1712."

"For starters, you should visit our website and read the articles there. You'll find them highly informative. Afterward, feel free to send me an email with specific questions."

"That makes perfect sense," Stacie said. "But I was wondering if you could tell me anything about Monomoy Island."

"I gather you're interested in the body that they found down there recently."

"Yes, as a matter of fact, I am curious about the body. But right now, I'm trying to figure out what Monomoy Island is. I gather it wasn't always an island."

"You are correct," Falcone said. "For a long time, Monomoy Island was attached to the mainland, extending almost ten miles south towards Nantucket. Remember, before the Cape Cod Canal was opened in 1914, boat traffic between northern New England and parts south needed to pass around the cape. The sandy shoals off Monomoy are always shifting, and in storms, it can be quite dangerous for ships. If you remember your history lessons, the Pilgrims hit the sandbanks off Monomoy and turned back to Provincetown and later to Plymouth."

"Yes, I read that. And I gather you've had your share of shipwrecks over the years?"

"Heavens, yes," Falcone said. "A lot of lives lost. All along the outer cape beaches. They finally put a lighthouse down on Monomoy in 1823, and later a lightship offshore as well."

"So, no one lives down there now? Just the lighthouse keeper, I guess."

"The lighthouse was decommissioned in 1923, so no one lives there permanently. The island's owned by the National Wildlife Service now, and they use the lighthouse building as a research center. It's quite isolated. There are no docks and no overland roads to get there, just sandy beaches. But at one time there was a bustling little fishing town down there."

"On Monomoy?"

"Oh, yes. It was called Whitewash Village. Several hundred people lived there. They even had a small school. Quite a bustling operation."

"What were they doing there?"

"You know, fishing, cleaning, salting, drying, and shipping. Also, they repaired ships that stopped by, and sold provisions and bait—things like that. Nantucket Sound was chock-full of fish and lobster in those days, and there was a perfectly formed powder hole on the Nantucket Sound side, up from the tip of Monomoy. It made a perfect deep-water harbor for fishing boats."

"A powder hole?"

"Oh, that's the name given to a protected pool of water created by shifting sand. Some powder holes are tiny, but others are quite large, like the one at Whitewash Village."

"Is it there today? Whitewash Village?"

"Heavens no. It's long gone. A huge storm in the 1860s ruined the harbor, and the village slowly disappeared. Most of the buildings were either abandoned, dismantled, or floated back to town. Years later Monomoy broke off from the mainland and became an island. It broke again later and became two islands. The smaller northern island they call Minimoy, which is kind of cute."

"Have you ever been down there?"

"To the lighthouse?"

"No, to Whitewash Village."

"There's nothing there," Falcone said, "except a couple of cement pilings. And poison ivy. Lots of poison ivy and ticks."

"That's it?"

"Well, the lighthouse is nearby. And like I said, just some remaining cement pilings. And some bad luck. That's all."

"Bad luck?"

For the first time, Falcone's steely demeanor broke, and she smiled.

"Oh, the usual legends," she said. "It was a seagoing town for a long time. Lots of stories."

"What kind of stories?"

"Listen, why don't you visit the website and send me any questions you have? We'll be glad to help as much as possible. And there's always Mrs. Stanford, I suppose."

"Who is she?"

"Mrs. Stanford is ninety-six years old. She's a living repository of old Chatham. Pretty sharp lady. We've recorded her oral history. Quite a character. But I'd look at the website first. Most of your questions could be answered there."

"How would I get hold of Mrs. Stanford?"

"Well, you'd call her son, Hank Stanford; he looks after her. They live on Main Street."

"Thank you for your time, Mrs. Falcone," Stacie said, standing. "You've been very helpful."

CHAPTER 6

Stacie fumbled for her phone, which was stuck in the side pocket of her purse.

"This is Stacie Davis."

"Ms. Davis, this is First Assistant District Attorney Mary Martin."

"Oh, great. Thanks for calling back."

"We really don't have much to add that hasn't already been released," Martin said. "I didn't want you to think I was avoiding you. There's nothing new to report. The cause of death is drowning. There were no drugs in her system, nor any evidence of physical trauma."

"Are you investigating the circumstances of her death?" Stacie asked, the phone squeezed between her ear and shoulder, while she wrote in her notebook.

"The investigation is ongoing," Martin replied. "We still do not know who she is or how she got there. If she was on a small boat, it hasn't been found yet."

"Do you suspect foul play?" Stacie said.

"Until we have more information, nothing is being excluded."

"Do you think she fell from a fishing boat?"

"Again, Ms. Davis, we have no idea how she ended up in the water. It's an ongoing investigation."

"Could it have been suicide?"

"It's an ongoing investigation."

"Is there anything else you can disclose at this time?"

"We've released an artist's rendition of the deceased and have requested help from the public. You've already published the drawing."

"Yes, we did, but have you received any useful tips?"

"We cannot discuss that at this time."

Stacie sighed. "Would your department contact me if there are any new developments? We keep reading it first in the *Cape Cod Times.*"

"We have your number. We'll certainly contact you if there are new developments. That's why I called now."

"Thank you, I appreciate it."

Stacie sat in her car after hanging up and thought of the artist's rendering of the dead woman's face. When she got the image, she stared at it before sending it along. The woman had medium-length black hair, a high forehead, thin eyebrows, and pronounced cheekbones. Perhaps it was the artist's intention, or maybe it was Stacie's frame of mind, but the woman looked sad and lost.

She was jolted from her reverie by that nagging unease of a looming deadline. Smitty would be looking for her next story, and she couldn't let this opportunity slip away.

◉

neil, stop texting and leaving voice mail. it's annoying. please stop

Stacie had not blocked Neil. When she was busy doing interviews, or driving around Chatham, she barely thought of him. But during the downtimes, when she was sitting in her car, or in the motel staring at CNN with the sound muted, she would get lonely and look at her phone for his entreaties.

Was she reveling in his angst? Was she being cruel to him? Was she serious about not even talking to him? Maybe he did make a stupid mistake. Guys do stupid things all the time.

And yet, even with the doubt, she knew it was over. When he had texted those simple words: *this just isn't working,* it was the sad clarification that she needed. He was absolutely right—it wasn't work for either of them.

What was the point of *not* blocking him if she knew the relationship was over?

Slowly, with the deliberation of a nuclear scientist at a weapons console, she opened her phone settings and blocked Neil's messages and phone calls.

i just blocked neil. it's now officially over, she texted Marie.

So be it. on to the next neil. or bill. or jim, Marie responded. *get movin girl*

She put the phone down, checked her makeup one more time, then headed out to see if she could find some local gossip.

◎

It's always awkward for a woman to walk into a strange bar alone. But Stacie put on her best brash reporter's face and sauntered over to an open stool. She placed her reporter's notebook on the bar and nestled her purse on her lap.

The restaurant's bar was long, with standing room behind. When she walked in, several men and women were outside smoking cigarettes.

"What can I get you?" the bartender asked.

"I'll take a Sam Adams on tap."

Twenty seconds later she had a frosty Sam Adams sitting on a coaster in front of her. She took a sip and looked around. To her left was a man in his sixties, with long, scraggly gray hair protruding from the bottom of a faded Red Sox cap. He was chatting with a middle-aged woman to his left. She was drinking a glass of white wine.

Stacie turned to her right and found herself staring into the tanned and chubby face of a man in his thirties. He wore a mesh baseball cap with the logo of a fishing and tackle store on the front.

"Hey," he said. "You here on vacation?"

"No, actually I'm a reporter for the *Boston Globe*. I'm covering a story."

"No shit! Wow, a reporter. The *Globe*. Let me guess—you're writing about *shahks*."

She laughed. "No. I'm following up on the story of the body that was found off Monomoy recently."

"Oh, that," he said, taking a sip of beer. "Yeah, that sucked."

"Do you know anything about it?"

"Yeah. She was my sister. And she owed me money. So, she jumped off my boat. But she couldn't swim. End of story. And I'll never get my money back."

Stacie reached for her pad, pulling the pen off the spiral ring.

"It's OK to joke, but this is serious stuff. Do you mind if I ask your name and what you do for a living?"

"Sure. My name's Noog; that's N-O-O-G. It's my nickname. My real name is Nathan Hagopian. In the summer I run a charter boat; in the winter I work construction. Am I going to be in the *Boston Globe*?"

Stacie wrote down his name, then put down her pen and pad.

"No, I don't think so. Unless you have some insight into what happened to that woman found floating off Monomoy."

"Hey, Frankie. Frankie! Come here," he said, turning to his right.

Stacie watched as a young, reed-thin man with his own faded baseball cap walked over with a Bud Light in his hand.

"Hey, Frankie, this is a reporter from the *Boston Globe*. What's your name?"

"It's Stacie Davis."

"Say hello to Stacie."

"Hey, Stacie."

"Why don't you tell Stacie here what happened to the body that was found off Monomoy? She's writing a story about it. She doesn't believe me, so why don't you tell what happened to that woman?"

"She killed herself," Frankie said. "Jumped off a boat."

Stacie shot a smirk to Noog. "I thought you said she was your sister."

"That was a joke," he said, shrugging his shoulders. "I always wanted to be in the *Boston Globe*."

"And the suicide idea?" she said, looking up at Frankie.

"Well, it kinda makes sense. What the hell else is she doing out there?"

Stacie laughed, shook her head, and took a sip of beer.

"Seriously, what do you think really happened to that woman?"

"Who knows?" Noog said. "It's the ocean. It's always tossing things up."

"But aren't you a bit curious about the whole thing?" she said.

"Stuff happens all the time out here. You'd be surprised," he said.

"You'd be surprised," Frankie said. "Like *really* surprised."

"Give me some examples," she said.

"Mmm, like real ones or made-up ones?" Noog said.

"How about real ones."

"OK. Here's one," Noog said. "I'm out past Pollock Rip on a charter and I see this thing in the water. So, I pull up next to it, and it looks like a sail just floating there. I use my boat hook and pull it closer. And damn if it's not a windsurfing board and sail. And it's maybe fifteen miles from the mainland. I notice there's like a water shoe still attached to the board where the foot goes. And the customers I got on board are getting weirded out, you know? At any moment I'm thinking I'll see a body floating nearby. People get blown way off course on these windsurfing boards and kayaks all the time. I call into the Coast Guard and describe everything to them. And ten minutes later I get a callback, and they tell me the board was lost off Martha's Vineyard two weeks ago, and the person just swam back to shore. But the Coast Guard wants me to bring the board back, if possible, because, like, it's a navigational hazard to boats. And I'm like, well, I got paying customers on board, and I don't know how to store the damn board and sail, while I'm fishing with paying customers."

"What did you do with the board?" Stacie asked.

"I gave the Coast Guard the GPS location and left it in the water. Drag the damn thing back to shore with my boat? No way."

"Frankie, what about you? Find anything strange out there?" Stacie asked.

"I was on a dragger off Nantucket once, and the boat suddenly stops moving, and captain's yelling that the net got snagged, and everyone's all pissed off and throwing shit around. Then we start moving again. We pull in the net and what do we find inside with all the sea scallops?"

"What?" Stacie said.

"A refrigerator."

"A what?" she said.

"You know. A refrigerator. Maybe thirty miles from land. I think it was a Frigidaire."

"You guys," Stacie said. "You're making stuff up."

"I'm not shitting you, ma'am," Frankie said. "It was a goddamn Frigidaire."

"How about bodies? You ever come across a body in the water?"

"What kind of bodies?" Noog asked.

"Human bodies."

"Nope," Noog said. "No human bodies. I've seen seal bodies, whale bodies, turtle bodies. No human bodies."

"Me neither," Frankie said. "That would creep me out."

"So, tell me what you think *really* happened to the woman off Monomoy? No bullshit. Just your honest opinion."

"Honestly?" Noog said.

"Yeah."

He took a deep breath, looked at the bottles lined up behind the bar, and said, "I have no friggin' idea what happened to that woman."

"Come on," she said. "There must be some chatter on social media."

"Ha," Frankie said. "Social media. Don't get me started."

"Come on," Stacie pleaded.

"Everyone here's got an opinion," Noog said, raising his arm and swinging it in a circle.

"And the consensus?"

"Stacie—that's your name, right?"

"Yeah."

"Stacie, I'd say the consensus is that it was a drug overdose," he said.

"But the medical examiner said there were no drugs in her system," she said.

"Like I said, that *was* the consensus," Noog said. "But ask that guy. He knows everything. Hey, Carl, come here. Want you to meet Stacie."

Stacie swung around on her stool to see a fit, broad-shouldered man about six feet tall. He wore an engaging huge smile on his tanned face, highlighted by a pair of light blue eyes.

"Hey, Stacie," Carl said, reaching out his hand.

Stacie shook his hand and was struck by the firm grip and calloused palm.

"Nice to meet you, Carl. Noog here says you know everything."

She was not sure why she threw out that silly line, but they all laughed. And for a single woman, in a strange bar surrounded by three men, you couldn't beat the thrill of getting a spontaneous group laugh.

"So, what's your opinion of what happened to the woman whose body was found off Monomoy?" she asked.

"Careful," Noog said. "She's a reporter from the *Boston Globe*."

"Really?"

"Yes," she said. "But I don't bite. I'm just a normal reporter with a notebook." Perhaps it was the chug of beer, or the fatigue from running around interviewing all day, but she was vaguely aware that her bantering was a trifle flirtatious.

She stood up, grabbed her notebook, and said, "Hey, guys, nice to meet you. But I have a deadline and need to get going."

"But you didn't hear my opinion," Carl said.

"Um, OK. What do you think happened to her?"

"She drowned."

"See, I told you he knows everything," Noog said.

"Mmm," Stacie said. "I must be off now. Thanks again."

"Hey, you didn't finish your beer," Noog said.

"No, I'm sorry. I have a deadline." She reached into her purse and pulled out a bunch of business cards. She handed one to each of them.

"Email me if you learn anything important. I'd appreciate it."

◉

Back in her motel room, nursing a large Dunkin' coffee, Stacie pounded out a 700-word story on how the quaint town of Chatham was dealing with the unexplained and unidentified body of a woman found floating off its shores.

She was late with the piece and knew the assistant Metro editor was going to hold it for later print editions or simply run it on the website instead.

Stacie filed the story and turned on the TV to one of the local Boston stations for the early news. While she was brushing her teeth, she heard the announcer mention "Chatham," and she rushed out of the bathroom with toothpaste froth on her lips. A smartly dressed female TV reporter stood against the backdrop of the famous Chatham Lighthouse and reported that authorities were still investigating the mysterious death of a woman in the waters nearby.

"Shit," Stacie said.

Instinctively she looked at her phone and, sure enough, it rang just then.

"Good piece on the cape story," said Stanford, the assistant Metro editor. "Love the color. But what's the status of the investigation? WCVB's got the DA on camera talking about it. You've only got the first assistant DA."

"For God sake's, Frank, it's TV. I don't have a big truck with a satellite dish on top following me. And I can't promise the DA that his neighbors, his kids, and his mistress will see him on the nightly news."

"Can't you get a quote from him?" Stanford asked.

"To say what, exactly?"

"To beef up the story, Stacie."

"Look, I'm trying to build a relationship with the first assistant DA. She told me to go through her, and I think I can get more out of her than from that idiot Barone. You know he's just showboating."

"Well, Smitty will ask."

"I'll be glad to tell him the same thing."

Stanford's sigh came through loud and clear on the phone. "We're going to be able to get your piece in the print edition. Page one below the fold."

"Really?"

"Yeah, I think it holds up well. Nice flavor of a seaside town that's seen just about everything."

"Thanks."

"The copy desk may have some questions. And you're staying down there, right?"

"Just tonight. I don't think there's a lot more to get on the story except what comes out of the DA's office."

"Don't come back before checking in with the desk in the morning, OK?"

"Yeah, sure."

CHAPTER 7

The alarm went off early at five o'clock, and Carl stabbed at the phone trying to hit the stop button. He knocked it off the side table and cursed, grabbed it by the charge cord, and reeled it in slowly like a fin-snagged striper.

He quickly scanned the weather report, sighed, and fell back in bed.

"Crap," he said, staring at the ceiling. He could hear the patter of wind-whipped rain against the window.

He dialed the number and waited for it to go voicemail. "Hey, David, this is Carl. I'm afraid we've got a washout today for our charter. The wind is up, and it'll be raining all morning. Sorry we couldn't make this work. I have a couple of open slots in early July, if that works for you, so let me know. Just text me to confirm you got the call. Thanks."

Carl dropped the phone on the bed next to his shoulder and tried to get back to sleep. But the rain hammered away at the window, reminding him of another lost charter for a crappy start to the season.

Unable to sleep, he got up, showered, dressed, and drove his pickup to the local breakfast joint. He nodded to the usual suspects sparsely spread throughout the diner on a cold, wet spring day. The seasonal residents and vacationers would soon swamp the place, turning it into a madhouse of screaming children, exhausted parents, hungover college kids, and gooey-eyed young couples. Today, it was still a locals' diner.

"No work today?" one of the old-timers asked, not looking up from his *Boston Herald*.

"No, sir. Mother Nature wins this one," Carl said, sitting at a stool. He quickly started working on Instagram and Facebook, posting pictures from some of the previous year's charters, showing huge striped bass and gnarly bluefish being held up by happy clients on cloudless, calm days.

It wasn't enough these days to outfit his twenty-six-foot center-console powerboat with tackle, gear, ice, and drinks. Now every successful charter boat captain had to maintain a website and a social media campaign. Carl chased "likes" as much as he chased stripers and tuna.

He saw two inquiries about charters, and he pounded out answers while checking his schedule.

After breakfast, finishing his third cup of coffee, he bounced around some of the news sites, and saw a text come in from Noog:

check out the globe. maybe i'll be on 60 minutes now. fame is fleeting, dude

Carl clicked on the link to a *Globe* story headlined: "Chatham Shrugs Off Another Mystery."

The story, by reporter Stacie Davis, started:

"Living in a 300-year-old fishing town, Chatham locals aren't surprised at what the ocean throws on its shore. Four days after the body of an unidentified woman was found floating in the waters off Monomoy Island here, residents are curious but taking it in stride.

'It's the ocean,' shrugged charter boat captain Nathan Hagopian. 'It's always tossing things up.'

Hagopian and others in this tightly knit community are as perplexed as the authorities are about how the woman died and ended up floating facedown miles from the mainland. But for a town that had its first recorded murder in 1606, when a Frenchman named Samuel de Champlain lost two of his crew to an altercation with Native Americans, they've pretty much seen it all."

ur famous dude. bet bookings pop, u lucky bastard, Carl shot back.

already got 2 inbounds for charters, Noog texted, along with a smiling emoticon.

u suck, Carl responded and put his phone screen side-down. He looked out the diner's huge windows into the parking lot and watched the rain pummel his truck like metal BBs. Why in God's name did he ever choose to live and work down here? Four years of college and you pick a career that depends on the weather?

◉

"Another nice piece. Keep them coming, Stacie!—Charles Smith." Stacie forwarded the email from Smitty to several of her closer *Globe* colleagues. She was thrilled, of course, to be recognized by the paper's fickle editor. But that thrill was followed with the opposing, systolic dread: could she keep it up? Would Smitty still be sending encouraging missives next week when she was covering an MBTA mishap on the Orange Line?

She showered and threw on a pair of sweatpants and a sweatshirt to head to the nearest Dunkin'. Before she could leave, her phone rang.

"Hey," Stanford said. "Smitty wants you to stay down there. Can you do that?"

"I guess so. But I don't think there's much else to do here. I mean, it's in the DA's hands, and they ain't talkin', if you know what I mean. I could do that just as easily from Boston."

"No. Smitty likes the background you've got in your stories. He likes the color and the history of the cape woven in. And he likes your writing style."

"Thanks," Stacie said. "I can stay down here, though I don't have a ton of clothes with me. Thought I'd be here for only a day or two."

"Feel free to buy some items if you need to and expense them. Smitty is serious about this. He wants more of the same, and if it means you buying some clothes, then so be it."

"Well, OK then," Stacie said. "I'll keep filing from lovely Chatham. Though today the weather sucks."

"Try to file something today if you can, but if you've got nothing, we'll need something tomorrow for sure."

"Got it."

Stacie walked into the Dunkin', shook the water from her hair, and ordered a large coffee and a breakfast sandwich. Reporter's careers are made and broken on opportunities just like this, and she needed to step up.

"Hey, famous reporter," she heard someone say behind her.

"It's Carl. You met me last night, remember?"

"Of course I do, Carl."

"Nice story today. Noog is all over it. Good for his charter business."

"Well, I'm glad I could help," she laughed. "This your favorite breakfast stop?"

"Hell no. This will be my fourth cup of coffee this morning. I ate breakfast at another place and was just grabbing a final cup here. Had to cancel a charter today, so I'll just hang out. Weather should clear out tonight."

Stacie moved down to the far side of the counter to get her order.

"Good luck on the weather," she said.

"Good luck on your reporting," Carl said. "You going back to the same bar tonight?"

"Um, hadn't thought about it."

"We'll be there if you decide to hang with those 'tightly-knit' locals," he said.

"Ha," she laughed. "You're a careful reader."

Stacie collected her order and found a small table in the back. She pretended not to notice Carl leave, but after the door shut, she craned her neck to see him get into his huge black pickup truck and drive away.

She opened her computer, found the wireless signal, connected to the *Globe*'s VPN server, and started reading emails.

The *Globe* placed reporters' official email addresses into nearly every story. As a result, there was a constant flow of emails from readers, public relations professionals, and assorted riffraff opining, haranguing, or offering additional leads to a story. Stacie pored over a dozen emails from readers congratulating her on an interesting story about Chatham. There was one email that excoriated her for stereotyping the town and its residents using "timeworn tropes."

One of the last emails caught her attention, not for the message itself, but the signature.

"Nice piece of writing, Stacie. Like the reference to Champlain. It is indeed a nice town that has seen almost everything. Like your writing style, not the normal *Globe*-speak, if you don't mind me saying, filtered of all vitality by an overeager, undertrained copy desk—Winslow Prescott."

Stacie reread the email several times and could not believe that it was from *that* Winslow Prescott, the famous writer.

She quickly did an internet search and found that indeed, Prescott had a home in Chatham. Holy shit! Not only was she getting plaudits from Smitty but now from one of the country's most popular and respected mystery writers.

How strange, Stacie thought. One moment you're a lowly general assignment reporter finishing up a mundane piece on an MBTA accident, and the next you're getting noticed by the high and mighty.

Can this be true? Stacie took her forefinger and thumb of her right hand and pinched the skin on her left wrist.

Yes, I am alive, she thought. This is happening. Like, really happening.

She decided to answer Prescott's email, though she was smart enough to check his email address and noticed that it matched his author's website address. All reporters have been warned about sock puppet fakes, and she was not going fall for some pranking Maine fourteen-year-old boy.

"Dear Winslow, thank you so much for your kind remarks about the story. Chatham is indeed a charming town. Unfortunately, I guess unseemly things happen here too. Sincerely, Stacie."

Next, she called Martin's office and left a voice mail asking for updates on the investigation.

Then, nursing her large coffee, she explored the Chatham Historical Association website. She was soon lost in a maze of dry, historical pieces tracing the founding families and their interactions with the resident Monomoyic Native Americans, the same tribe that had the lethal disagreement with de Champlain.

Stacie tried to remain engaged poring through the endless pages of history but soon lost interest. There was simply too much information to swallow, most of it boring. She was covering a mysterious death, not a hardscrabble pioneering life of salting fish and surviving storms.

Before she shut down her computer, she noticed another three emails to her *Globe* account. The first one was a cranky complaint accusing her of sensationalizing a sad death. The second one was from Neil begging her to call him.

The third email stated: "Stacie, you are correct that unseemly events do happen in Chatham, but those are rare. It's a robust, diverse community of artists, shopkeepers, fishermen, young families, and wash-ashore old-timers like myself. If you'd like to chat sometime over a cup of coffee, feel free to reach out. Cheers, Winslow."

She quickly responded: "Dear Winslow, I would like to take you up on your offer to meet for coffee. There's so much about the town I don't know. Unfortunately, I'm on a tight deadline and have to return to Boston soon. Are you available for coffee today or tomorrow morning? Sincerely, Stacie."

The moment she got back into her motel room her phone rang.

"Stacie, this is First Assistant DA Martin."

"Hey, thanks for calling me back."

"I just wanted to let you let know that we are investigating the body found off Monomoy as a suspicious death. We have no suspects currently and are pleading for help from the public. We'd appreciate the *Globe* mentioning our request for the public's help again. If possible, we'd like the media to continue showing the artist's rendition of the deceased woman's face. It may jog someone's memory."

"We'd be glad to do that," Stacie said. "Have you received any leads from the public so far?"

"We've had some comments, but we need more. It's a difficult case. It would help a great deal if we could identify the woman."

Stacie continued to press Martin for more details on the investigation but to no avail. She let Martin go and returned to her emails on her phone.

"Dear Stacie, I'd be happy to meet you for coffee today. Would eleven this morning work for you at the Founder's Coffeeshop? It's on Main Street—Winslow."

"Absolutely," she wrote back. "See you there—Stacie."

◎

"It's not a precise science," Professor Phillip Noyce said. "There are three variables: the tide, the current, and the wind. That part of the cape is a little complicated because it's not far from the tip of Monomoy, which is a mixing bowl of water from the Atlantic Ocean on the east, and shallow Nantucket Sound from the west. But, since her body was found a mile and half north of the tip in the sound, well, the body might have been stuck in a small eddy. It's hard to say where the body entered the water."

"You're an oceanographer, correct?" Martin said into the speakerphone, staring out the window of her office at a hydrangea bush whipped by the rain. "You study currents and stuff like that?"

"Yes, of course," Noyce said. "I know you'd like better answers, but the fact is that I can only give you a best guess. You said the body was in the water for about six hours. If the body was found at seven a.m., then it likely entered the water at one a.m. The tide level at that time at Monomoy Point was dead low. It stayed slack until around one thirty when it started rising. It was high tide at four minutes past seven on Monomoy Point."

Martin locked eyes with Detective Clancy sitting in front of her.

"And your opinion is that the body didn't float from the mainland, either Chatham or Harwich, and certainly not Nantucket?"

"I don't see how the body—again, I'm using a six-hour timeframe—could have moved that far south from the mainland in that time. Nantucket is out of the question. And you stated the body was found only fifty yards from shore, correct?"

"Correct."

"Then I'm confident the body did not enter the water in Chatham or Harwich at one a.m. and show up off Monomoy at seven a.m. That's too far. The moon phase was a quarter moon, meaning we had a neap tide."

Martin rolled her eyes at Clancy, and he chuckled.

"A neap tide? What the hell is that?" she said.

"It just means the position of the sun and the moon counteracted each other, so the tidal differential was relatively low," he said.

"Meaning?"

"Meaning there was not as much tidal motion as there might be on a full moon or no moon. And combined with a drop in the wind that evening, there was no energy to push the body eight miles south of Harding's Beach in Chatham, the nearest public beach."

"Meaning?"

"Meaning that I don't think the body traveled far from where it first entered the water. Perhaps a half mile. Maybe. As I stated earlier, if you look at a current satellite picture of the tip of Monomoy, there is a curling sandbar to the west into Nantucket Sound. The sand would tend to protect that part of the island from turbulence on the rips. So, it's entirely possible that the body entered the water within a couple of hundred yards from where the body was found, and it traveled in an eddy, being kept near the shore as the tide rose."

"You'll summarize this in a report?" she said.

"Of course."

"And the bottom line, if I get this right, is that in your opinion, the body entered the water approximately where the body was found?"

"Within a half mile or so, at the farthest."

CHAPTER 8

Stacie drove through the spitting rain on Route 28 toward downtown Chatham. To the west, she could see the weather was starting to break up, and it couldn't be too soon for her. Nothing seemed to stay dry; her hair hung limp, her rain jacket dripped water on her khaki slacks, and her hands simply would not warm up. The smell of the ocean permeated everything.

Her phone rang, and she saw the caller on her car's display screen.

"Hey, Marie," she said into the car's microphone. "How goes it in the exciting world of human resources?"

"It's going swimmingly, and I mean swimmingly here in Boston. Some asshole drove through a puddle in the road and drenched me while I was walking to work this morning. You should have seen me, rubbing my hair between two paper towels in the ladies' room at work. I looked like an idiot."

"I'm still in Chatham and it's not much better here. I took a shower, then used the motel's hair dryer that appeared to have been manufactured in 1970. When I went to get coffee, it got wet all over again. My hair looks like a shag carpet."

"Are you hot on the trail of that body they found down there?" Marie said. "I read your piece today. Must be exciting doing that stuff."

"Some days are better than others," Stacie said. "Today sucks so far. But it's early. Maybe I'll find something to write about before deadline."

"You do well under pressure," Marie said. "I've always admired you for that."

"If you saw me today, you might reconsider."

"Well, go break a leg, or whatever they say in newspaperdom. But can you do me a favor?"

"Of course. Name it."

"Can you unblock Neil? He's driving me crazy. He calls and texts me several times a day. He's trying to reach you."

"I guessed as much. He even sent something to my public *Globe* email."

"So, do something."

"I've asked him to stop contacting me. What else can I do?"

"Maybe if you met him in person and just leveled with him, he'd get the message."

"God, Marie, I don't have the time for him. He was such a jerk and I've totally lost interest in him. I hope he's not going to turn into a stalker."

"Neil's not a stalker. Just unblock him and arrange to meet him when you get back."

"Maybe."

"Please? He really is driving me crazy. And I feel kinda bad for the guy. None of my former boyfriends ever acted like this."

"Then you date him."

"He's not my type and you know that. Unblock him. See him one more time. Move on."

"God, you're so sensible," Stacie sighed. "How did you get this way?"

"I'm in HR, remember?"

"Right. I'll unblock him. Mission accomplished."

"You'll thank me."

◉

She saw him sitting at a small, wobbly table in the corner of the coffee shop and waved. She had looked up photographs of him online, just to make sure. He was a very tall, trim man with a high forehead, gray hair thinning at the temples, and a pronounced dimple in his chin. He wore rimless glasses that magnified his intense hazel eyes. His Wikipedia page listed him as sixty-one years old, though he looked younger.

"Mr. Prescott?" she said.

"Please, it's Winslow," he said, standing to shake hands.

"If you don't mind, I'll just grab a cup of coffee and join you."

"Of course. I'm just reading. Take your time. Weather is frightful today and best to be inside with a warm cup of coffee."

Stacie ordered her coffee and rejoined him.

"For pretend writers like myself, there's always grudging respect for real writers like you journalists," he said. "We get to sit at our desks and make stuff up for hours; you folks must expend energy collecting information—sometimes at personal risk—then sit down and condense the information on the fly. That's real structured writing."

"If you say so! But coming from a man who's authored seventeen books, I would have to respectfully disagree. *That* seems like real writing to me."

"I suppose it's one's perspective, isn't it?" he said, smiling.

"What are you reading?" Stacie said, trying to make small talk.

"Oh, it's just an old book by Thoreau on Cape Cod. I try to read one book each month that is more than a hundred years old. Most of what is written these days is nonsense—including my novels—so going back is refreshing, if that makes any sense."

"It makes perfect sense," she said. "But I think you may be a little too harsh on your own writing."

"When you compare my writing to something like this," he said, tapping the book in front of him, "I feel like I'm writing a fourth grade book report. This man's writing is more like yours: personal experience condensed into a readable narrative structure."

"I'm sorry, what author are we talking about?" Stacie laughed, looking down at the book.

"Henry David Thoreau," he said.

"Thoreau wrote about Cape Cod?"

"He certainly did. He made three trips here in the mid-1800s and wrote about it in two magazines. Later, in 1865, the writings were turned into a book titled simply *Cape Cod*. He was a bit of an odd duck, but a good writer. Strong descriptive style. Some of it is quite amusing."

"Thoreau amusing?"

"Yes," he said, opening the book and pushing up his glasses with his forefinger. "Listen to this. He's describing an old man who walked the beach looking for bits of wood from shipwrecks: 'He looked as if he sometimes saw a doughnut, but never descended to comfort; too grave to laugh, too tough to cry; as indifferent as a clam,—like a sea-clam with hat on and legs, that was out walking the strand.'"

"That is quite good," Stacie said. "I'll have to grab a copy of that. How interesting."

"The cape is an interesting place, which I gather you are discovering."

"Well, I'm just trying to get my arms around Chatham."

"And you're trying to find out what happened to that poor, poor woman whose body was found nearby?"

"Yes," Stacie said, taking a sip of coffee. "But I'm not an investigator. I'm just trying to get a sense of the town and its reaction to the death. To be honest, it seems like people here have just shrugged it off to 'the ocean,' and left it at that. Seems odd to me. In Boston, there would be a lot of speculation and concern about the woman's identity and how she ended up in the water. The reaction seems a little muted here."

Prescott laughed. "I suppose it just seems that way. But since the body is unidentified, people here really have no personal stake in it. She wasn't from the cape or she'd be identified by now. And to your point, I suppose they are sort of shrugging it off. The ocean has been tossing bodies up on shore here for several hundred years. I mean, let me read you this," he said, leafing through the book.

"Ah, here we go. He's writing about bodies found after a shipwreck: 'Many days after this, something white was seen floating on the water by one who was sauntering on the beach. It was approached in a boat and found to be the body of a woman, which had risen in an upright position, whose white cap was blown back with the wind. I saw that the beauty of the shore itself was wrecked for many a lonely walker there, until he could perceive, at last, how its beauty was enhanced by wrecks like this, and it acquired thus a rarer and sublimer beauty still.'"

"Well, that was a long time ago," Stacie said. "Nowadays we don't find bodies of unidentified women floating in the water and just shrug. She got there somehow. She must have a name."

"No, of course, you're right. I don't mean to be callous. I think people here are concerned; they've just learned that we're helpless against the ocean. But it's not like there's a serial murderer on the loose. We read that she drowned. Many think it was a suicide."

"The DA is investigating it as a suspicious death," Stacie said.

"And so they should," Prescott said, closing the book.

"But you're not concerned that someone threw her off a boat and let her drown?" she said.

"Of course I am. We all know that it's a possibility. But what are we to do? We assume the Coast Guard and the police will be able to identify boats that were in the area."

"Well, they're not having much luck on that end," she said. "I guess there's no central repository for smaller commercial boat activity. And forget private boats; it's a free-for-all out there for those folks."

"Rest assured the authorities will get to the bottom of this. You'll see."

"Do you mind if I ask you a few questions? I was looking for quotes from some locals."

"Is this for attribution in the *Globe*?"

"Yes, unless you don't want to be identified."

He sighed and scanned the coffee shop. "I suppose I don't mind being identified. Sometimes people walk by my house and take pictures. Or leave letters in my mailbox. I had to get a post office box. Don't ask me why fans think they must contact writers. It can be a little creepy at times."

"In that case, I'll just quote you anonymously."

"That would be best. Fire away."

After fifteen minutes of questions and answers, Stacie thanked him again.

"The cape is an interesting place," she said. "It feels more isolated than I thought. I see a lot of boats in people's driveways and backyards. Has the feel of an old-fashioned fishing village."

"But with tourists," Winslow laughed. "Schools of them swarming over the town like menhaden in their annual migration."

"I gather there's a love-hate relationship with tourists?"

"I suppose so. It was simpler when there was just fishing and a little farming here, but times change. In truth, all that's left of the old days are antique homes, a lighthouse, and some legends."

"Legends?"

"Every town on the cape has its stories; some true, mostly not so much," he chuckled.

"Like Whitewash Village? On Monomoy?"

"That's not a legend. It was quite a little fishing village at one time."

"Have you been down there? Is there anything left?"

"No. Never been there. And I wouldn't like to, either."

"Really? Why not?"

"Oh, old stories," he laughed. "I know it's silly."

"What kind of stories?"

"All around Monomoy strange things happened. The lighthouse, Whitewash Village, mooncussers, the White Stallion, things like that. Too many bodies washed up down there over the years."

Stacie laughed. "What the heck is a mooncusser? And the White Stallion? Is that a legend?"

"Yes, a famous one. You can check with the historical association. I'm not superstitious, it's just there are so many places to visit on the cape other than Monomoy Island."

◉

The rain had stopped, though the wind continued to buffet Stacie's small Mini as she drove across the thin causeway toward Morris Island. To her right, she could see boats in the water pointing into the wind and struggling against their mooring lines.

At the end of the causeway, the road suddenly rose up a steep hill. She saw a sign for the National Wildlife Service and pulled in. The short road opened onto a group of small buildings and a radar dome.

The director agreed to meet Stacie to talk about Monomoy Island and its role as a critical breeding site for terns, piping plovers, and gray seals. Stacie had no interest in writing about wildlife, but she was desperate for information on the history of Monomoy, and she prayed that she could coax the director into commenting on the body found off the island. Her deadline was approaching, and she had nothing new to justify a story.

The small facility had two buildings and a public bathroom. She parked and walked to the larger building.

"Hello," said a young man coming out of a small office. "Are you Stacie Davis?"

"Yes, and you're Steve Scoccia?"

Stacie had no expectations about what a wildlife department director should look like, but she didn't expect a man who appeared to be twenty-five years old.

"Come in," he said, pointing to his office door. "Out here is our display area, showing the wildlife we see here on the cape. Typically, we have a volunteer docent at the desk, but he wasn't feeling well today."

Stacie sat in the office and struggled to convince herself that this young man oversaw a 7,604-acre national wildlife refuge, including several employees and researchers.

"It's great that you're interested in the refuge here," he said. "We get some local press, of course. But not much from the Boston media."

"Well, I was in town on another story and was just trying to learn a little about Chatham. Much more going on here than I knew, including places like this."

"Yes, I've been reading your stories," he said. "They're very good. Really interesting point of view on the town here. And of course, the body was found off Monomoy in the first place."

Stacie couldn't believe he brought up the subject on his own.

"Now that you mentioned it, I was interested in the area where the body was found. It was close to shore, I believe."

"Yeah, we heard it was about fifty or sixty yards from shore on the west side of Monomoy, down near the tip. A charter guy was out with a client and found the body. Terrible stuff. But you already know that."

"There's a deactivated lighthouse down there, correct?"

"Yes. We use it for a research station. It's pretty desolate down there. Part of the refuge is designated a wilderness area."

"Is the place they call Whitewash Village down there?"

"There's not much left of that, just some concrete pilings. But yes, that's where the fishing village used to be located. It's been gone for a long time. I gather it was a going concern back in the mid-nineteenth century for fishing and ship repairs."

"Do you maintain a staff out there at the lighthouse?"

"Yes, it's generally occupied year-round. We have a lot of researchers, especially graduate students who monitor the wildlife. Some stay at the lighthouse building, and others camp out farther north near the nesting birds. In the winter, the research is on the gray seal population."

"Is anyone allowed to visit the island?"

"Yes, of course they can. There are private tour boats that take folks out there."

"Can they stay overnight?"

"No, that's not allowed for visitors. But as I said, we do allow researchers to stay at the lighthouse."

"Were any researchers at the lighthouse the day the body was found?"

Scoccia laughed. "No. We've been asked several times by the state police, and the answer is no. Three graduate students were down there for two weeks, but they returned a day before the body was found. In case you're wondering, they were interviewed several times by the police."

"I'm assuming they didn't see or hear anything important when they were down there?"

"I have no comment on the investigation or what they told the police. To be honest, they were pretty upset when they found out about the body. Two of the researchers are women, and as I said, it's isolated down there. The lightkeeper's house is still being rehabbed, so it's not exactly the Hilton."

"It would be great to chat with the researchers who were down there, if you think that's OK. I'd like to report on the other things that go on in Chatham besides fishing and tourism."

"Um, I guess that would be all right. As long as you agree not to bring up the subject of the body. As I said, it creeped them out."

"Sure, are the researchers nearby?"

"All three of them are staying in the other building here, but they might be in town. I'll check if they're here."

As he texted, Stacie glanced around the sparse office. The walls were covered with maps and wildlife pictures; Scoccia's window faced the parking lot, and it rattled as the wind shook the building.

He put down the phone and said, "Meanwhile, do you have any other questions?"

Stacie rattled off several generic questions and barely took notes.

His phone pinged and he looked at it.

"Well, the two women are here. Jim is in town. I'll ask them to stop over."

"That would be great. Thanks so much."

◉

Colleen was short and petite, with freckles covering her ruddy face. Her hair was pulled back in a ponytail that poked through the back of her Washington Nationals baseball cap.

Natalie was a foot taller than her colleague, broad shouldered and rugged looking, with a fleece headband keeping her wiry brown hair barely tethered.

The four of them crammed into Scoccia's office while the wind rattled the windowpane.

"What's it like staying out there?" Stacie said. "Are the accommodations all right?"

They laughed. "It's a little rustic," Natalie said. "We sleep in sleeping bags on cots. I mean, if you're used to camping out, this is certainly better than that."

"Gets a little chilly in the evenings," Colleen said, "but we play cards. And Jim has a guitar, so we sing a bit. Feels like summer camp sometimes. But you get used to the solitude. And we're never alone. There's always Sandy."

All three laughed.

"Sandy's a dog or a cat?" Stacie said.

"I wish," Natalie said. "Pets aren't allowed out there." Both researchers looked at Scoccia with fake pouts.

"It's against the rules!" he said. "It's not my fault. You don't want a cat eating piping plovers for breakfast."

"So, who's Sandy?" Stacie said.

"They're getting acquainted with our resident ghost," Scoccia chuckled.

"Ghost?" Stacie said.

"Yeah," Colleen said. "We call him Sandy. He's harmless. An old guy in a black raincoat. It just takes some getting used to."

"We've had complaints over the years from researchers that there's a harmless ghost in the lightkeeper's house," Scoccia said. "I've never seen him. Could be that the old building creaks and sways a bit in the wind."

"Steve," Natalie said, "we told you that we've seen him. I heard him walking upstairs a couple of days ago. They were footsteps, not mouse steps or banging windows."

"I know, I know," he said. "You're not the only ones."

"What does the ghost look like?" Stacie asked.

"He's got, like, one of those old-fashioned long black raincoats," Colleen said.

"And a long gray beard," Natalie said.

"Does he say anything?" Stacie said, stifling a smile.

"No," Natalie said. "He just looks tired. And he's only there for a second or two. We think he's the spirit of an old lighthouse keeper that died here. Or something like that."

"And you're not frightened of him?"

"Naw," Natalie said. "He doesn't even notice us. Other researchers have said the same thing. We're not worried."

"Well, I kinda don't like it," Colleen said. "Wish he'd find another home to haunt."

Scoccia laughed.

"Besides," she said, "with that body washing up recently, it kind of spooked us."

"Ugh," Scoccia said. "We don't have to talk about that. Ms. Davis is not interested in that subject."

"Steve," Natalie said, "it *was* kind of creepy. Come on."

"But you didn't actually see the body," he said.

"Ms. Davis, the police are investigating it as a suspicious death, correct?" Natalie said.

"Yes. Have you seen any other unusual things out there besides Sandy? Have you been to Whitewash Village?"

"The old fishing village?" Colleen said.

"Yes."

"I wouldn't go there," Colleen said.

"Me either," Natalie chimed in.

"Why not?" Scoccia asked, sitting forward in his chair. "It's just a bunch of concrete blocks."

"Too weird," Colleen said.

"What's weird about it?" Stacie said.

"Everybody out on Monomoy avoids the place," Natalie said. "Lots of stories. Other researchers have talked about it. Even Jim won't go there."

"Are you serious?" Scoccia said. "It's less than a mile from the lighthouse. You say Jim won't go there?"

"Yup," Colleen said.

"You haven't said what you're frightened of," Stacie said.

"Things," Natalie said.

"I'm sorry, that's ridiculous," Scoccia said, standing up. "I think there's not much more to be gained from the interview. Thank you, Colleen and Natalie. Ms. Davis, I think you've got everything you need."

"I do. Thank you very much for setting up the interviews. If I have any follow-up questions, could I send you an email or text?"

"Sure," he said, handing her a business card. "Be glad to help. And why don't you two show our *Globe* reporter here the view before she leaves? It'll give her a sense of the two islands we administer to the south. And no more talk about ghosts and things like that."

The three women walked across the parking lot and chatted amiably. Natalie led the way past the public bathrooms, onto a path leading through a small copse of scrub pine and oak trees. After fifty feet they walked out onto a high bluff, protected by a wood railing that looked out onto a channel a hundred feet below. A quarter mile farther out rose a thin barrier island pounded by the surf.

Colleen pointed out Minimoy to the right, and beyond that, they could barely see the larger island of Monomoy.

"You can see how desolate it is," she said. "And when the wind blows, like today, you really can't hide. If there's going to be a big blow, like a nor'easter, they come and get us off the island."

Stacie tried to keep her hair out of her face as the wind whipped it fiercely. Now she knew why Colleen and Natalie held their hair in place. She could barely make out Monomoy in the distance; it looked more like a smear of sand than an island.

"You two must be hardcore researchers," Stacie said as they walked back to the parking lot. "Looks forbidding out there."

"You'd be surprised how beautiful it is on a nice day," Natalie said. "The outer cape is at the mercy of the wind and the ocean, and that's what makes it interesting and magical."

CHAPTER 9

Stacie finished writing her follow-up story by six thirty that evening and waited for feedback from the Metro desk. She felt the story was lame and would be spiked or moved to the inside of the print Metro section.

Her story led with the DA's request for help in identifying the body found off Chatham, and the suspicious nature of the death. The story then veered toward the larger, diverse community of Chatham trying to make sense of the death. She worked in an anonymous quote from Prescott showing restrained concern about the death. She included several on-the-record quotes from Scoccia about the wildlife on Monomoy, and one from Natalie commenting on the isolation. She included another anonymous quote from Prescott about the cape's history of strange objects being offered up by a restless sea. She finished with one of the quotes from Thoreau that Prescott had read to her.

Within twenty minutes of filing the story, she received a call from one of the assistant Metro editors saying they wanted her to move the Thoreau quote higher in the story, and to check on the spelling of Scoccia and the two researchers' names.

It was going to run on page one, below the fold for the first edition, and might slide to the front page of Metro in later editions.

Surprised and thrilled at the response to her story, she fixed it and resent it. After another twenty minutes, it went to the copy desk. Stacie relaxed, stretched her arms, and stood up at the small motel desk, and arched her back. If they liked this stuff in Boston, she knew she had to keep it going. Her phone showed it was almost eight o'clock, and Stacie put on some makeup, changed her shirt, tried to brush some life into her wind-assaulted hair, and headed out.

◉

All the seats at the bar were taken, so Stacie scanned the group of people standing behind the bar and found Carl's grinning face.

"Hey," he said, walking over. "If it's not the Pulitzer prize-winning journalist from the *Boston Globe*.

"Pleeease," she said. "That's embarrassing. I'm just a lowly single-celled organism in the vast news media ecosystem."

"Well, you just missed Felicia Sanchez from Channel Five," he said. "The guys here are still getting over meeting her. Couple of selfies taken. Already saw one from Noog on Instagram."

"What the heck was she doing here?"

"Same as you. 'Body off Monomoy. Town struggles for answers.'— stuff like that."

"Gee, you're good. Maybe you should have gone into journalism."

"How are things going?" he laughed. "Got any good leads for what happened to that woman?"

"No. Do you? What's the scuttlebutt?"

"Look at you," he said. "Using all these nautical terms."

"What nautical terms?"

"First, why don't I get you something to drink. Beer?"

"No, I'll pay. I can get my own."

"You get the next round," he said. "What'll it be?"

"Sure," she said. "Red wine. A cabernet?"

"You got it," he said, taking several steps toward the bar and barking the order to the bartender, who nodded. Carl returned thirty seconds later with the wine. They clinked glasses.

"Scuttlebutt," Carl said. "Do you know where the word came from?"

"No."

"In the eighteenth and nineteenth century, sailing ships had a scuttlebutt, which was a cask of water that was available to the crew to drink during the day. So, sailors would often congregate around the water and gossip. Scuttlebutt became a word meaning gossip. Like standing around the water cooler today."

"I did not know that," she said. "You fishing guys are a font of knowledge."

"Font of useless knowledge, you mean."

"So, what's the *scuttlebutt* on the body?" she said, drawing out the word.

"The scuttlebutt is that no one knows a damn thing, which by itself is a little weird."

"Why?"

"This is a small town, maybe six thousand year-round residents, exploding to thirty thousand visitors in the summer. But the year-rounders pretty much know what's going on, and people talk, if you know what I mean. It doesn't take long for the word to get out. A text here, forwarded, then a couple of emails, maybe a post on a private Facebook group page. Bingo. Mystery solved."

"What kind of mysteries do people solve?" she asked.

"Oh, you know. The pickup truck that split the telephone pole on Route 28 in North Chatham at one o'clock Tuesday morning was driven by Joe Blow. Or the drug overdose at the shopping mall parking lot was so-and-so, who just got out of rehab, and her old boyfriend is a dealer who OD'd with her in the car. And they have a kid who's being raised by the woman's parents."

"Sheesh, that's pretty intense. But I don't get the connection to the body off Monomoy."

"It means that there's no scuttlebutt on who she is, where she came from, who threw her off a boat, what the boat's name was, where it was heading. Stuff like that."

"What makes you think she was thrown off a boat?"

"I made that up as an example. People just can't figure it out."

"What do *you* think happened to her?"

"I have no friggin' idea. Noog thinks she was tossed off a rich guy's yacht. But someone said that the body was in the water for something like six hours and that it didn't float very far."

"Who told you that?"

"Someone whose brother works for the state police."

Stacie reached into her purse and pulled out her notepad.

"Whoa," he said. "You can't use that. That's just bullshit someone said."

"OK," she said, putting the pad away. "But I'll probably go back to the DA's office and look for confirmation. Don't worry. You won't have any connection to it. But it's worth asking the DA."

"Stacie, you've got to promise me that I'm not going to be tagged with this information. I'm not used to talking to reporters."

She saw the alarm in his face and reached out instinctively to put her hand on his tanned forearm to reassure him.

"Carl, you will not be involved in this. Reporters hear stuff all the time and ask officials to respond. And for the record, the state police and Boston PD are the worst leakers known to mankind. The DA won't be surprised that this stuff leaked, and they'll either deny it or confirm it, or just tell me to take a hike."

He took a swig of beer. "That makes perfect sense. I just don't want to get someone in trouble."

"It won't happen. I promise. Now, here's my treat for the next round," she said, downing the rest of her wine and pulling out a twenty-dollar bill.

Stacie and Carl were soon joined by Noog, a young woman named Naomi, and a middle-aged man named Gunny. The conversation roamed, though Stacie kept prodding them for ideas on the circumstances around the body.

"Be careful," Carl said. "She's a reporter."

"Carl, I told you this is just background information. Don't scare these folks."

"I ain't scared," Noog said. "I can tell you that the woman was one of the crew members on a private yacht that ran through Nantucket Sound around midnight heading west to Martha's Vineyard. The billionaire owner didn't like something she said or cooked, or whatever, and just tossed her."

Everyone laughed.

"I'm serious," Noog said.

"You're seriously full of shit," Gunny said. "If what we heard is correct—that the body didn't travel far—there's no way a big yacht was going around Monomoy that close at low tide at one o'clock in the morning."

The alcohol-fueled conversation meandered for some time until Stacie realized she was a little tipsy.

"Hey," she said to Carl, "I have to get going. Thanks for introducing me to your friends. It's been fun."

"You didn't finish your wine," he said.

"I had enough wine, thank you. Keep me posted on any *scuttlebutt*," she said, drawing out the word yet again.

"Aarh, matey," he said.

◉

"Nothing?" Martin said.

"Nada," Clancy said.

"No matches on the usual databases," Langone chimed in. "DNA was sent out but nothing there either. No semen or anything on the woman's clothes. And sand. Lots of sand. And a couple of fish scales that were found in her skirt pocket."

"Fish scales?" Martin said.

"Yes."

"Maybe she was a cook? Or worked in one of the processing plants in New Bedford. Clancy?"

"We've been down there twice; no one is missing. Most of the workers at the plants are immigrant men, not Caucasian women."

"The DA is on my case," Martin said, glancing out the window. "I gather he's taking a little bit of heat from the business community. It looks bad to have an unidentified woman found dead on the cape. Tough way to start the summer season."

"I talked to Manteo, Dr. Gupta's assistant," Langone said.

"You did?" Martin said. "I couldn't remember his name if you hadn't mentioned it. I've never even spoken to him. What did he say?"

"He said the woman's clothes were a little unusual," Langone said.

Martin and Clancy swiveled to look at the young investigator.

"And?" Martin said.

"He said Gupta thought the clothes were odd. Almost homemade.

Kind of old-fashioned, if that makes any sense."

"No, it doesn't," Martin said.

"You know, maybe she lived on a commune. Made their own clothes, grew their vegetables, stuff like that. Or a religious sect. Like the Amish or Mennonites. Or a cult."

"Anything like that on the cape?" Martin asked.

"We can check it out," Clancy said, writing in his notepad.

"Good work, Sarah. That would explain why she's not reported as missing. Some of these groups are pretty isolated and tight-lipped."

◉

There was nothing more jarring than waking up to a screaming phone with a mild hangover. Stacie squinted to see who was calling.

"Shit," she said, sitting up and coughing to clear her throat.

"Hello?" she said with as much buoyant enthusiasm she could muster at twelve minutes after seven a.m.

"Stacie, this is Charles Smith. I'm sorry if I'm getting you up early. I just read your piece from Chatham and I like it. Who would have thought of digging up Thoreau? Great stuff."

"Gee, thanks. I'm glad you liked it. But to be clear, someone else down here mentioned Thoreau. I just borrowed the idea."

"Doesn't matter. Gives a great sense of the nautical history of the cape, and the tragedies they've seen over the years. You have a nice narrative style. We'd like to see more of this. Can you stay down there a while longer? I know it's a hassle to be living out of a suitcase, but your pieces are getting extremely high readership on the web. The analytics reports show they're getting forwarded and cross-posted on Facebook, Twitter, and Instagram. We can't let this pass."

"I'm sure I can string this out a little longer down here," she said. "I'm just running low on ideas, to be honest."

"Whatever you need, we'll take care of it. Where are you staying?"

"Um, a motel here on Route 28. It's fine."

"Why don't you move over to Chatham Bars Inn? That would be more comfortable. I'll have my assistant Nora check you in there. I think we can get a good rate. That should make your stay a little more comfortable. Are you OK with that?"

"Yes, of course. Thanks so much, but it's not necessary. I'm fine here, if you don't mind."

"I insist. Just keep these pieces coming. Call me directly if you need anything."

"Sure, Mr. Smith."

"It's Smitty."

"Sure, Smitty," she said. "Thanks for your support."

After hanging up, she stared at her reflection in the dresser mirror across the room. Her hair was plastered flat on one side and puffed up on the other. Her eyes, even from that distance, were bloodshot. She had dark circles under her eyes.

Stacie felt a rush of anxiety flutter from her stomach into her chest. Writing stories with her own sense of pace, direction, and focus was fun. She enjoyed it. Writing stories that were being endlessly dissected and evaluated was pressure. Reporters advance their careers by performing under pressure, but pressure breaks young reporters as much as it focuses them. I'm *not* going to break, she told herself.

She took a deep breath and scanned her emails and texts.

The fourth email down was from Prescott, lauding her on another great story. He teased her for "borrowing" the Thoreau quote and invited her to dinner at his house that evening with several other cape authors he knew.

"Holy shit!" Stacie said out loud and looked up at the mirror again to see the wreck sitting in bed.

Get moving, girl, she told herself, bounding out of bed.

◉

Carl roared south along the eastern side of Monomoy, gliding over the gentle swells rolling in from the Atlantic. His clients were a young, adventuresome couple from Montreal in their early thirties. Noog and another charter captain had heard rumors of stripers feeding on schools of tinker mackerel a mile west of the southern tip of Monomoy.

The young couple clung to each other behind the console, smiling and enjoying the sunny, cool day. Carl had lost revenue in the two-day washout and was glad to have paying customers.

He slowed the boat halfway down Monomoy and ran closer to the sandy indentation informally known as Shark Cove. It was near high tide, and several hundred gray seals congregated in the water near shore.

The Canadian couple oohed and ahhed the seals as Carl nudged in to within thirty yards of a group of bobbing gray heads. The Marine Mammal Protection Act set fifty yards as the minimum distance that a boat should get to seals, but with thousands of gray seals now propagating on the cape, everyone got closer. The couple took pictures, and Carl used the man's phone to take several of the happy couple.

If Carl and most of the commercial fishermen had their way, they'd remove gray seals from the Marine Mammal Protection Act. There were too many seals, and they ate a prodigious amount of food that would normally be bait for striped bass and other game fish.

But the customers liked to see seals, so Carl often pulled in to give them a look. He was not only in the charter fishing business but the wildlife entertainment business as well.

"Where are the sharks?" the man asked. "Are they here now?"

"Yeah, there's probably some here now, but August and September are when they're really busy. These seals are staying pretty close to shore, so there might be a shark nearby."

"Will we see a shark?" the woman asked.

"I doubt it," Carl said. "Believe it or not, they're hard to see from a boat except when their fins break the surface."

"Oh look, a baby," the woman said, pointing to a young seal near the boat. "They're so cute."

Carl smiled. "Now, let's see what's down on the rips," he said as he slowly pushed the throttle forward.

◉

"I don't know where you got the information," Martin said to Stacie, "but I can't comment on that. It's an ongoing investigation."

"Can you at least confirm that the body was only in the water for six hours?" Stacie said.

"No, I can't."

"Do you have any new information on boats that were nearby when the body was found?"

"No, I don't."

"There's nothing new you can tell us?"

"No, I'm afraid not. It's an ongoing investigation."

Stacie hung up and looked around the Dunkin'. She was getting tired of the breakfast sandwiches and was intrigued by the idea of moving into a room at the luxurious Chatham Bars Inn. She decided not to share that information with her colleagues, knowing it would raise some eyebrows. The dark side of all hypercompetitive businesses was that for every thrilled overachiever, there were ten unhappy, envious, cutthroat, middling achievers.

Her phone rang, and she saw an unfamiliar number from the *Globe*.

"Stacie Davis," she answered.

"Stacie, this is Nora. We've checked you into Chatham Bars Inn for the next three nights. Smitty asked me to tell you that if you need to extend, feel free to do so. You don't need to use your credit card for the hotel room, just for incidentals, which you'll be responsible for."

"Gee, thanks, Nora. I've never stayed there before. It should be interesting."

"Oh, I think you'll be quite comfortable there. Have fun and keep up the good work."

Stacie hung up and felt another pulse of anxiety.

Crap, even Nora is pressuring me, she thought.

CHAPTER 10

Mrs. Stanford's thin, wrinkled face was highlighted by a pair of piercing eyes the color of weathered slate. Stacie looked around the small living room. On the walls were prints of sailing ships, hydrangeas, and ocean waves. Mrs. Stanford's elderly son Hank had left them alone while he worked in the yard.

"She's a little hard of hearing," Hank told her. "You gotta speak up."

"I'm not deaf, Hank," Mrs. Stanford said.

"Didn't say you were deaf, just hard of hearing," he said.

She waved him away.

"So, you're a newspaper reporter?"

"Yes, ma'am. I work for the *Boston Globe*. Thanks for agreeing to meet with me."

"What are you down here? Somebody got bit by a shark?"

Stacie laughed. "No. I'm just following up on a story about a woman's body found off Monomoy. There's a lot of Chatham's history that I'd like to learn about. Mrs. Falcone at the historical association suggested I talk to you."

"Who?"

"Mrs. Falcone," Stacie said, raising her voice.

"Oh. Mrs. Falcone at the historical association."

"Yes. I wondered if you knew about the history of Whitewash Village. Whitewash Village on Monomoy Island?" Stacie shouted.

"That place is long gone. Why are you asking about that?"

"There was a body found near there recently, and I was told you knew a little bit about the history of the abandoned fishing village."

"That poor woman," Mrs. Stanford said, pursing her lips and shaking her thin shock of white hair.

"No one knows who she is or how she got there," Stacie said.

"She got there in the water," the woman said. "That's how she got there."

"Yes, but they don't know if she fell off a boat or jumped into the water at a beach. Until they identify the woman, there is little for the DA to go on."

"Poor woman," Mrs. Stanford repeated, rocking gently in her chair.

"It appears that over the years there have been many shipwrecks off Monomoy. A lot of bodies have washed ashore. Is that your recollection?"

"That damn ocean is always tossing bodies up on the beach. Been like that forever."

"When was the last time you were on Monomoy?"

"Me?"

"Yes."

"I never set foot on Monomoy in my life. My husband was a fisherman and a clammer. He clammed those flats for years. That's when there was plenty of clams."

"On Monomoy?"

"Yeah. Used to be lots of clams there. Steamers and quahogs. Guys could make a living digging out there."

"Did you go with him out there when he clammed?"

"Heavens no. That's hard work. I had kids to raise."

"You never made it out there, even as a child yourself?"

"No. Who wanted to go out there? We got plenty of sand right here."

Stacie realized that Mrs. Stanford was not going to be a quotable source about Monomoy. She looked at the few notes on her pad.

"Did you ever hear stories about Whitewash Village on Monomoy?"

"Stories?"

"Yes," Stacie yelled. "Stories about strange things going on."

"Oh, there was always talk about Whitewash Village. My father—rest his soul—told a lot of stories about the lighthouse and Whitewash."

"Really? What did he say?"

"He said it was haunted down there. 'Too many bodies,' he used to say. 'Can't have that many bodies without leaving a few spirits behind.' He didn't like to use the word 'ghost,' he always called 'em 'spirits.' Used to drive my mother nuts. His talking about Monomoy and such."

"Do you remember any of the stories he told?"

"No, I can't remember. It was a long time ago. Well, maybe there was one or two. He swore that the Legend of the White Stallion was true. He said he saw that darn horse one night."

"The White Stallion?"

"Called the Legend of the White Stallion. Some call it the legend of the stone horse. Heck, I don't know. Been a long time. But he sure liked to tell us that story over and over."

"Can you recall the story?"

"Of course I can. In the old days, there was these mooncussers—that's what they called them people—that would lure ships to wreck them on a sandbar. Once a ship wrecked, why, folks would rush down and salvage everything they could get their hands on. Coal. Cotton. Wood. You name it."

"How would a mooncusser lure a boat to shore?"

"Well, especially during a blow, those ships rounding the cape from the north, they'd be looking for the lighthouse at night. But there was also a lightship off Monomoy, so the captain would see two lights and try to estimate how far he was from the shore, based on how bright the lights were. And how close they were to each other. The idea being that the crew would get confused looking at those two tiny lights and think the land was far off. Especially in a blow, you couldn't make out anything if it was snowing or raining real hard. So, this old mooncusser would take his white horse down to Monomoy and hang a lantern on the front of the horse, and he'd hold the other lantern. And one day, the story goes, the horse got spooked and just galloped right into the ocean, and the old feller drowned."

"And that's the legend?"

"Yup. According to my old man, the horse can still be seen on some nights when the wind is up and the moon is shining. He said you could see the horse swimming in the water with a lantern hanging from it."

"Did he have any more stories?"

"Well, just one about Whitewash Village. He said the reason the village got abandoned was not because of a storm. He told us that story so many times that my mother would just tell him to be quiet, that it was nonsense. But we liked his stories."

"What did he say was the real reason Whitewash Village was abandoned?"

"He said there was some killing going on down there. People couldn't take it anymore and they were scared."

"You mean murders?"

"That's what he said."

"Did he say who the murderer was?"

"He said it was either a crazy old fisherman, or it was one of those spirits, you know, that just hung around down there waiting to take someone to the dark side. To keep the spirit company."

"Did he say whether the spirit was a man or a woman?"

"I don't think he did, but I'm guessing it was a man because no woman would do something that stupid."

"Do you believe that part of Monomoy is still haunted?"

"Haunted, you say?"

"Yes, haunted. At Monomoy."

"It's probably just a story. I don't know. But I'll tell you one thing for sure—that ocean sure knows how to surprise you."

◉

Carl had finished washing down the boat after dropping off the Canadian couple at the dock. They had caught and released five undersized stripers, which was plenty of excitement for them, and they seemed happy and exhausted when he dropped them at the public dock in Stage Harbor.

Tied up at his mooring, he checked his messages and sipped a Diet Coke.

The early June weather was finally cooperating. He had most of the following two weeks booked solid, and the rest of the summer was filling in nicely.

He looked at his phone, toying with an idea that had been percolating all day.

Why the hell not?

hey, u interested in grabbing a bite to eat tonight? my treat

He put the phone down and finished stowing the rest of the fishing gear. Gathering his backpack, he pulled the tethered dinghy close to the boat. His phone pinged and he looked at his messages.

that's a nice offer mr. charterboat captain, Stacie answered. *but someone beat u to it. got invited to some fancy author's house for dinner. maybe tomorrow?*

tomorrow works. u like sushi?

i love sushi

great place nearby. should i pick u up or meet u there?

i'll meet u. 7?

great, c u there at 7

◉

Stacie was thrilled that Prescott had invited her to dinner but was uncertain how to dress. What should she wear to a dinner party on Cape Cod with other writers? A summer dress? She didn't have anything like that in her spartan travel wardrobe.

Worse yet, she was suffering a strong case of class consciousness after checking into Chatham Bars Inn. The view was spectacular from the main building's porch overlooking Aunt Lydia's Cove. The hotel maintained dozens of separate units closer to the water.

After checking into her unit near the fish pier, she opened the shades and found herself looking down on a seagrass-covered dune and the beach. It was beautiful. The bathroom in the suite was almost as large as the entire motel room she just left.

"Marie, you wouldn't believe this place," she said, sitting on the bed with the phone pressed against her ear as she took off her shoes. "This is how the other half lives, I guess."

"Well, have fun now, girlie," Marie said. "Because no place you stay in going forward will ever be the same. You're spoiled for life."

"How can people afford places like this?"

"Some people make a lot of money, darling. You know that, you lefty pinko Trotskyite."

"Well, I'm not so egalitarian that I can't enjoy the good life, if just for a day or two."

"You deserve it. I like your stories. They're always on the front page of the website. Isn't that supposed to be good?"

"Yeah, but I'm beginning to feel pressure to keep it going. There's only so much I can write about this charming old fishing village. With fancy hotels. And expensive clothing stores."

"And dead women floating in the surf," Marie said.

"Yeah, there's that. Still don't understand how a woman disappears and no one reports her missing."

"It happens all the time, or at least it happens on *CSI* all the time."

"Hey, and guess what?" Stacie said.

"Besides being invited to Winslow Prescott's home for a friggin' dinner party? You promised you'd get him to sign a book, right?"

"Yeah, I already bought the one you liked. They had it in a local bookstore."

"Hey, you said 'Guess what?' So, tell me."

"You won't believe it, but this charter boat guy—he's kind of hot, to be honest—asked me out to dinner tomorrow."

"That means you haven't talked to Neil yet."

"I sent him a text asking him to stop calling you and me. Is he still calling you?"

"Actually, no. Like I said, I just feel bad for the guy."

"And like I said, you go date him then."

After hanging up, Stacie held the phone in her hands for several minutes, and then finally texted:

hey winslow, what's the dress code for tonight? don't get invited to these cape cod dinner parties often. don't want to show up in jeans and flip-flops if everyone's wearing evening gowns. help!

He answered: *nice casual if that makes sense. pants are fine. it's the quality of the company, not the clothes! relax*

CHAPTER 11

Stacie bought a fashionable shirt at a store in Chatham and a pair of cute, black canvas slip-on shoes. She bought an expensive bottle of white wine as a gift to the host. She also decided she didn't have enough to file a new story and was surprised that she got no pushback from the Metro desk.

"Just give us something tomorrow," the assistant editor responded by email. "Smitty's in a tither about your stuff."

At a quarter to seven, she found herself driving into a section of Chatham off Route 28 that looked like it was near the tributary feeding Oyster Pond, yet she couldn't see anything but trees.

She finally pulled in front of the address and saw several other cars had parked on the street. Nervous about her attire and her ability to keep up a literary conversation with this crew of invitees, she nervously bounced on her toes after ringing the doorbell. Under her arm, she had one of Prescott's early mysteries that she had bought for Marie.

The door was answered by a short, extremely thin woman in her sixties wearing a string of huge pearls around a boney, weathered neck. She wore a fashionable summer dress sporting a nautical print.

"You must be the *Globe* reporter," she said.

"Um, yes. I'm Stacie Davis."

"Come," the woman said, turning and leaving Stacie at the door. She quickly stepped inside and closed the door behind her, hurrying to catch up to the woman.

Stacie followed her down a short hallway and entered a large living room with floor-to-ceiling windows and a spectacular view of a tidal river. Prescott left a small group and rushed over.

"Marci," he said to the woman, "did you introduce yourself to our guest?"

"Yes, of course, I did," the woman said, walking away.

Stacie was confused because she had not introduced herself, nor did she seem friendly.

"Stacie, my wife Marci can appear a little distracted at times, so I hope you don't take anything she says or does personally," he said. "Please come meet our other guests."

"First, here's a small gift for you," she said, offering the bottle of wine in a gift bag. "And before I leave tonight you *must* sign this book for a good friend of mine."

"Of course, I'd be glad to," he said. "Come along to the kitchen."

She followed him up several steps into a large, bright, modern kitchen with granite countertops and white cabinets. Two women wearing matching black slacks and white long-sleeve shirts busied themselves with the oven and what appeared to be hors d'oeuvres.

He put the wine down and grabbed a pen. "What is your friend's name?"

"Marie," she said. He wrote something quickly in the book, closed it, and set it aside.

"Let's not forget this before you go home," he said. "Now, let's do some introductions. But can I get you something to drink? Wine? Beer? Soft drink?"

"A white wine would be great."

"Chardonnay or Sauvignon Blanc?"

"Sauvignon Blanc, thank you."

He pulled an opened bottle out of an ice bucket and poured her a drink.

"Now, on to the festivities. We typically have a brief cocktail and then sit for dinner. Marci and I are getting so old that we have our dinner parties catered," he said, waving at the two women in the kitchen. "They're wonderful. And Marci can't cook anyway." He chuckled as one of the workers laughed with him.

Stacie was introduced to Wade Caldicott, a historian and college profes-sor who specialized in nonfiction books about the US Civil War. He was a slightly rotund, balding man in his early fifties, she guessed. He wore a kind of a men's Cape Cod wealth uniform: a blue, open-collared dress shirt, navy blue blazer with gold-colored buttons, khaki slacks, and a pair of boat shoes without socks.

Next was Barbara Silvestri, a striking woman perhaps in her mid-for-ties. She had long black hair, a beautiful gold necklace with a stylized gold oyster shell, and matching earrings. She wore a black V-neck long-sleeve top, white linen pants, and black canvas shoes that looked dis-tressingly identical to Stacie's. Silvestri was the author of eleven novels.

"I write whatever is hot," she laughed. "I did a vampire series, three romance novels under a pen name, and even dabbled in some steam-punk. If I could write convincing LGBTQ fiction, I would, because my agent says they're snapping those titles up left and right. But, alas, I'm 100 percent hetero."

"You are also 100 percent vampire, which brings authenticity to your writing," Caldicott said.

She threw her head back and laughed, her long hair flying all around her face.

"Wade, you are so damn funny," she said, taking a sip of her mar-garita. "Why don't you try fiction? A comedy on the Siege of Petersburg, or something like 'Ulysses S. Grant—the Man and His Favorite Cigars: The Untold Story.'"

Stacie laughed with the rest of the group.

The last guest was David Lean, an extraordinarily average-looking man in his forties, of average height, average length brown hair, and average weight. He did, though, have something unusual about his ap-pearance. It took her a few minutes to recognize that he had different colored irises; one was brown and the other black. Lean wrote science fiction and looked nothing like what Stacie *thought* a sci-fi writer should look like: Wild hair? Wire-rimmed glasses and a nerdy T-shirt with a likeness of Carl Sagan or Einstein or Nietzsche on the front?

After a while, the group retired to the dining room, and the caterers brought more wine, appetizers, and plenty of sparkling mineral water.

Curiously, Marci had not appeared since letting Stacie into the house. Prescott sat at one end of the table, and an empty seat for Marci was at the other end. Stacie sat beside Lean and across from Silvestri and Caldicott.

Stacie felt like an interloper sitting in on a family dinner. She guessed she was twenty years younger than the next youngest person, was not a published author, and did not think she could hold up her end in the repartee this group exchanged. It was exhilarating and intimidating at the same time, but everyone made her feel comfortable.

During the main course of caramelized sea scallops over linguine, Silvestri suddenly blurted: "Stacie, I just *love* your stories in the *Globe*. You have the most astounding way of describing people and places down here. You have such a gift."

Stacie embarrassed herself by blushing. She quickly grabbed her glass of wine and guzzled.

"Please, I'm a journalist! There's nothing special about what I do compared to the people at this table."

"Barbara," Prescott said, "Stacie here is much too modest. I told her that her writing is way above the norm, but she won't hear it. I think she has a career in fiction or nonfiction if she chose."

"Absolutely," Silvestri said. "God, and to dig up Thoreau. Who knew?"

"That was Winslow's idea," Stacie laughed. "He read me a couple of Thoreau's quotes when we met for coffee, and it was so perfect. So, I did what any self-respecting journalist would do in similar circumstances—I stole the idea."

Perhaps it was the giddy companionship, or the alcohol, or both, but the table erupted in laughter.

"See, I told you she was sharp," Prescott said, raising his glass. "Here's to all self-respecting kleptomaniac journalists and writers everywhere." They clinked glasses to another round of bonhomie and laughter.

"What am I missing?" Marci said, suddenly appearing from the hallway. She took her place at the end of the table and put down the martini glass that she brought with her. One of the caterers rushed over with a plate of the scallops.

"Our guest of honor was making us laugh," Prescott said.

"So," David Lean said, turning to face Stacie, "what the hell is the latest on the woman who was found off Chatham? Certainly, they must have identified her by now."

"According to the DA's office, she's not been identified," Stacie said. "It wouldn't be the first time someone's gone missing and wasn't identified or claimed."

"But what was she doing down there?" Caldicott said.

"No one knows," Stacie said, noticing that all eyes were on her as if she were an expert witness in a packed courtroom. "We don't have much more than what the DA has released. No one has stepped forward with information on who she is, and she doesn't match any missing person cases on file."

"It was a suicide," Marci said, nibbling a tiny wedge of scallop she had surgically removed from a caramelized disc.

"But, darling," Prescott said, "it would mean she walked into the water seven or eight miles from where she was found. There was no boat or kayak found nearby. And the woman would have had to traverse two islands to get down there. Without a boat."

"It was suicide," Marci said. "Don't know what all the fuss is about."

"I know what happened to her," Silvestri said.

"Really?" Lean said. "Tell us."

"It's a body from the past," she said. "There was a fishing village right near where her body was found. The village was abandoned over a hundred years ago. Bad things happened down there. She was one of the victims that were never found. She's back now."

"Do you mean Whitewash Village?" Stacie said.

"Yes! You know about it?"

"Well, I've heard about it," Stacie said. "I gather there's nothing left of the village."

"Barbara," Caldicott said, "I know you're into vampire legends, and science fiction, but you say that with such a straight face! There was a real body. Of a real woman found floating down there."

"She's not from our time," Silvestri said. "How else can you explain it? No boats have been identified that were in the area. No identification.

Right, Stacie?"

"That's true," Stacie said. "The medical examiner ruled drowning as the cause of death."

"You're saying she's a ghost?" Prescott said.

"No, not a ghost, silly. She's a real person. Who died over a hundred years ago and has resurfaced."

"Without decaying?" Lean chuckled.

"Science can't explain everything," Silvestri said. "Strange things have happened on the cape for centuries. I guarantee she'll never be identified and will be buried a Jane Doe. She was murdered and it happened a long time ago."

"It was a suicide," Marci said, standing abruptly. She grabbed her martini and exited down the hallway. No one appeared to pay attention to Marci.

"Barbara, you have a fertile imagination," Prescott said. "I love it. How about her theory, Stacie? Can you write a piece using that angle?"

Stacie laughed. "Might not get that one past the copy desk. But I did hear a rumor of a ghost lurking around the lighthouse."

"See, I told you," Silvestri said. "Strange things happen down there."

The rest of the evening was a haze for Stacie; they had dessert and after-dinner drinks. Later they stood on the deck overlooking the small tidal river that fed Oyster Pond. Stacie felt the breeze, breathed the pungent odors of the water, and watched the twinkling lights of homes surrounding the water. A dog barked nearby.

Lean asked Prescott about his boat that was tied up to a small dock at the bottom of a long flight of stairs from the deck. The men continued to talk about boats, while Silvestri pressed Stacie about the demands of writing for a daily newspaper.

"I could never do that," she said. "That's far too much pressure for me."

"But you must have deadlines for your books? You've written eleven of them."

"Oh, but that's different. The only pressure I have is from my agent, who wants to make money. But she can't push me too hard or I freeze, so she just sends texts and an occasional email. And sometimes a bottle of wine."

"A bottle of wine? Is that to nudge you along?"

"It's always the same wine she sends; an expensive cabernet I'm especially fond of. She sends me a bottle when she's getting really pissed off at me for dragging my heels. It's funny because it works. When I get one of those bottles delivered by FedEx, I know I have to get my butt in gear and finish the damn thing! Agents are funny people. Almost as funny and dark as writers." She laughed, her head thrown back and her hair whipping in the breeze.

◉

The following morning Stacie sat in her spacious, sunny hotel room and tried to pound out a follow-up story. The DA's office had no new information. She called the Coast Guard, but they referred all questions back to the DA. She even called Jack Wetzel, the charter boat captain who found the body. He said that his bookings were back to normal and that no one had asked him about the body. Wetzel asked not to be quoted, and Stacie agreed.

Next, she wrote a heartfelt thank-you email to Prescott for inviting her to dinner.

"You were quite a hit," he wrote back. "That's a rare feat with this group of renegades!"

Stacie tried to kick-start her article by staring at her laptop screen, watching the blinking cursor. Nothing happened.

She stood up, stretched, walked around the luxurious room again, and grabbed a photocopied article from the January 1864 issue of *Harper's New Monthly Magazine* that was given to her by the historical association. On page 305 was a story titled "Monomoy" that retold some of the folklore and history of Whitewash Village in the overwrought, flowery language of the nineteenth century.

The writer stated: "Whitewash Village takes its name from the tradition that, on its prominent edifices, there was, in some former era, bestowed a coating of that economical pigment, remains of which can even now be detected by a careful observation of the outer walls."

The *Harper's* article explained that village residents kept one eye on normal tasks, and another on the ocean, waiting for another wreck to be salvaged. "And when sounds the warning cry, 'Wreck, oh!' what a scampering there is among the Pointers! The longest legs and the longest winder then taxed to their utmost, and the runner stayeth not to look behind him…out comes cotton and flour, and topmasts and yards are sent down, and running rigging is straying on the breeze, and the stout ship is speedily stripped."

The article also describes a scene in which an old codger sat around a fireplace burning wood from wrecks and telling stories: "…the wreck fire meanwhile sputtering blue or yellow, or flaming up spitefully, as though infested with troublous ghosts of Malay, Portugee, or Beccaneer."

Stacie looked out the window of her room and saw a line of commercial fishing boats bobbing gently in the southwest breeze. Across Aunt Lydia's Cove, about a half mile away, she saw a low-slung sandy barrier island that was perhaps a hundred yards wide. Beyond that sat the Atlantic Ocean in all its majesty—and menace. She read that thousands of ships had wrecked along the outer cape over the centuries, and it was hard not to be impressed by the strange power and beauty of the ocean.

She started typing on her laptop: "Less than a week since a woman's body was found floating nearby, and more than 170 years since a popular magazine described windswept Monomoy Island, the town of Chatham does what it's always done: fishing, clamming, welcoming tourists, and getting on with life. The ocean, it seems, doesn't much care what's happening on land; it has waves to push and things to toss to shore."

An hour later she was finished and reread the piece, checking her notes.

She filed the story and decided to take a walk along the beach. Taking off her shoes, she walked slowly along the shoreline, peering down at the small shells and stones. Stacie guessed that the tide was out since she could see the damp high-water mark at least five feet farther up the beach.

A motorboat hummed nearby, and to her surprise, she saw two seals following her in the water. Stacie grabbed her phone and took a photo of one of the seals as it breached and stared at her.

God, I'm acting like a silly tourist, she thought. She put the phone back in her pocket and continued her walk, picking up a maroon-colored bay scallop shell.

Rounding a small bend on the beach she suddenly looked up the bluff and saw the top of the lighthouse at the Chatham Coast Guard station. Stacie had driven past the lighthouse several times during her visit and thought it was charming and quaint. A parking lot across from it was usually filled with tourists taking pictures or walking down the hill to the beach below.

Though it was a bright, sunny day, the rotating lighthouse beam was strong. Stacie stopped and stared at the light, which winked every ten seconds as if letting her in on a secret.

She smiled as an idea for another story flashed. Wouldn't that be interesting? she thought. Besides, I'm running out of ideas down here. I'll have to go back to covering the MBTA if I don't watch it.

Stacie retraced her footprints. Before leaving the beach, she tossed her shells into the lapping water.

"You can have them back," she said out loud, laughing. "I was just borrowing them."

CHAPTER 12

The meeting was nearly over when Martin turned to Langone.

"Nothing on a match for Jane Doe?" she said.

"Nope," Langone said.

"The only good news is that Barone seems to have lost his enthusiasm for the case. Still, we need to show some progress. Must be something we can release to the press."

"We've checked some of the small religious communities nearby," Clancy said. "Nothing there. Pennsylvania has most of the Amish and Mennonite groups, and that seems a little far from the cape. Should we be checking down there?"

"Of course we should," Martin said. "Check with state police there, then maybe locals."

"Mary, not to be a pain," Clancy said, "but I've got a boatload of open cases and it's hard to sit down and make all these calls. I know Sarah's full as well. There's only so much we can do on this Jane Doe. No fishing boats in New Bedford and Fall River report a missing deckhand, much less a female deckhand. Ditto for the small fleets on the cape. Nantucket harbormaster says no out-of-state yachts were docked there, and no pass-throughs either. He said the season hasn't got going yet."

"I have a crazy idea," Langone said. Martin and Clancy stared at her.

"OK," Martin said. "Go crazy on me."

◉

Stacie sat at the bar and sipped a glass of ice-cold sauvignon blanc while waiting for Carl. She was looking forward to chatting with someone besides the Metro desk editors. Her story, after a couple of rewrites, was accepted for the next day's paper. It was a soft piece, heavy on the seafaring history of Monomoy. She would need something meatier, or else her sojourn in Chatham was over.

But Stacie had hatched a plan on her beach walk and was ready to spring it.

"Hey, famous newspaper person," Carl said, sitting down next to her. "You finished for the day? I have no idea what the work cycle is for newspaper reporters. Do you write your stories at night? During the day? At two in the morning? I just paint houses, do some carpentry in the winter, and fish in the summer. That's the extent of my life."

"It's not that complicated," she laughed. "I've already filed my story. I can relax now. Speaking of work, when do you take people out on charters?"

Carl explained that he could schedule two half days or a long single-day trip. Either way, it could be exhausting, he admitted. "But it's not bad for a history major from Bates. I'm sure my classmates are teaching high school history or running tech start-ups in Boston."

"You majored in history at Bates?" she said, putting down her wine glass on the bar top with a bang. "Why didn't you say that earlier?"

"Why would I say that? What's that got to do with anything?"

"Bates is an expensive school with a great reputation," she said. "Hell, I couldn't get into Bates. I went into UMass Amherst and was lucky to get accepted there."

He shrugged. "I played lacrosse. Wasn't too bad at it. They don't have athletic scholarships in Division III sports, but it didn't hurt that some of the schools were after me. Union in New York was another one that liked me. And Roanoke College in Virginia."

"Wow, I'm impressed," Stacie said. "I feel kind of stupid for acting surprised. But how did you end up down here painting and fishing?"

"My parents summered here when I was a kid. I fell in love with the area and worked in some of the restaurants over the summers. One thing led to another, and I realized I felt comfortable here. I like working with my hands. I like being outside. And what the heck was I going to do with a history degree? No way I was going to graduate school."

"Your parents still have a place here?"

"No, they divorced when I was in high school. Me and my sister lived with my mom. My dad remarried. My mom didn't want to come here for summers, since he was coming here with his new wife. But I kept coming."

"So, he's here now? Your dad?"

"No, he died a couple of years ago. Cancer."

"Gee, I'm sorry, Carl."

"Not a problem."

"You just stayed then?"

"And got married," he said. "And had a kid. And got divorced."

"Holy shit," she said, grabbing her wine. "You don't sit still."

He laughed. "I was young."

"You're still young."

"OK. I was *really* young then. And impulsive. But I love my daughter. Her name's Shania. She's ten and lives with her mom Grace and her stepdad in Falmouth."

"Do you get to see her?"

"Of course. We spend as much time together as we like. She even joins me on some of my charters if I know young kids are coming. She's good with them. It helps with the tips too."

"I just broke up with a guy," Stacie said. "Actually, he broke up with me. Then he wanted to get back together, but I told him to get lost. He was a jerk. Men are jerks sometimes."

"Not all men are jerks," he said.

"I can't believe I said that," she said.

"You should withhold judgment until you know me better."

They both laughed.

After a few minutes into their meal, Stacie said, "I was wondering if you'd be interested in taking me somewhere in your boat?"

"A boat trip?"

"Yeah. I have this idea that I'd like to visit the lighthouse on Monomoy at night. It's near the ruins of Whitewash Village. I was going to ask the Wildlife Service if they'd let me in there for a couple of hours one night, just to hang around and see what it's like. And I need a ride out there and back. I'm sure the *Globe* would pay for the trip."

"I suppose we could arrange that, though I'm not crazy about night trips. And you know there's no dock down there on Monomoy. Depending on the weather and wind, it might be a little sloppy getting ashore."

"I was thinking of going down around dusk and staying a couple of hours. I'd like to get into the lighthouse if they'd let me. There's talk of a ghost in there. It would make a great story."

"You don't believe that stuff, do you?" he laughed, taking a sip of beer.

"About ghosts? No way. But people are fascinated with the subject. I met an author last night who said that the woman whose body was found off Monomoy is the body of a woman who was killed there over a hundred years ago."

"And the body is just showing up now? Was this woman drinking or experimenting with psilocybin mushrooms?"

"She did have a few drinks under her belt, but she was quite serious."

"All kinds of types down here, as you're finding out."

"So, would you be willing to ferry me down there?"

"Sure, I guess so, weather permitting. And no charge. Hell, I haven't seen a ghost in years."

Stacie found Carl easy to talk to. His smile was wide and engaging, and his eyes seemed to sparkle when he laughed. Yet, each time she tried to pry something out about his marriage and family life, he grew vague.

Perhaps it was the extra wine or the long day, but she finally blurted out, "So, why did you get divorced? You said things were going great with your young family. Your wife was a nurse. What gives?"

"I'd rather not talk about it."

"Carl, come on."

"Why are you so interested? That time in my life is over."

"I find you interesting, that's why." Stacie was intrigued with Carl and aware of her sudden attraction. Like a burrowing reporter plowing into a story, she could not hold back.

"I can still be interesting without you knowing everything about me," he said.

"So, why did you get divorced?" she said, her elbow planted firmly on the bar top.

He stared at his drink and swirled the beer in the glass.

"We argued sometimes. And I guess things got heated and some stuff happened. Simple as that. I thought things were going well between us, but I guess they weren't. And that incident led to a separation, a restraining order, and a divorce. There you have it."

"What kind of stuff happened? A restraining order? Seems harsh."

"Just stuff. I guess if you want to get out of a marriage and keep custody, you claim stuff happened. That's what my lawyer said. It was a while ago."

They both stared at their drinks over the clatter of the restaurant and piped-in music.

"Now you know pretty much everything about me," he said. "But I've done most of the talking. You were pretty sneaky not to talk about yourself."

"That's for another night," she said, finishing her drink and pulling out her credit card.

"Hey, it was my treat, remember?" he said.

"No, really, Carl. I prefer to pay my own way."

"I insist," he said, grabbing the check and putting his card on top of it. "But you have to promise we'll do this again so I can find out about you. My life was an open book tonight; yours is still open to only page one."

"I promise," she said. "Like I said, you're an interesting man." She placed her right hand briefly on his left forearm and smiled. It was a flirtatious gesture, she knew, but she was also genuinely curious about Carl and wanted to reassure him that his confession about an earlier rough patch was not an issue.

◎

"I can't let you stay at the lighthouse building overnight," Scoccia said. "That's just not allowed. Our researchers stay there. And some are camping out in tents farther north. We can't have people disrupting their work."

"Steve, I'm not asking to stay overnight, I'm just asking to be allowed into the building for a couple of hours after dark," Stacie said, sitting on her hotel bed. "I'd like to write about the great work your team is doing and the conditions they work under. It would add color and help promote the sanctuary."

"You just want to walk around in the keeper's house? At night?"

"Yeah. I've asked a charter boat guy I met to take me out there. He'll come with me. We'll get there at dusk and stay for a couple of hours. Then come right back. I won't bother your researchers, though it might help, if they were interested, to talk about their passion for the animals out there."

Stacie knew that if there was any chance of getting permission to make the trip, she'd need to tug at Scoccia's instincts for public relations. The refuge was not off-limits to visitors; in fact, visiting was encouraged. But she wanted to get into the lighthouse building, which was not open to visitors.

"When did you say you wanted to go?" he said.

"My friend—his name's Carl Lane—says tomorrow evening would be perfect, weather-wise."

"Tomorrow?"

"Yes."

"Well, that's a problem then. No one's at the lighthouse tomorrow night. They're moving to tents near the terns' and plovers' nesting areas. The house will be closed. Sorry."

"Steve, come on," she pleaded. "We'll just be there for an hour or two. Leave it unlocked. The story will be great, I promise. It'll give a good boost to the reserve."

Silence.

"You know there's no dock down there? It's a wet landing," he said.

"Carl's a charter boat captain. He knows what he's doing. He said tomorrow the weather and tides will be perfect for getting on and off the beach."

Silence.

"You won't even know we were there," she said.

"I need to think about it," he said.

"Steve, please." It was times like this that Stacie felt guilty for being so manipulative. Still, reporters are only as good as their access, and it sometimes took a little shove.

"All right, Ms. Davis. But for the record, you agree that you'll stay no longer than two hours and that you'll touch *nothing* inside the building. They have some personal belongings there. And I need an email from you agreeing to those terms."

"Three hours. Please? A maximum of three hours would be perfect."

"Fine. Send the email as soon as you can from your official *Globe* email address."

"You got it. Thanks so much, Steve. You won't be disappointed."

CHAPTER 13

"Another wonderful story," Prescott said, sitting across from Stacie in the coffee shop. "You should talk to my agent. He's got some nonfiction ideas for you."

"Really? Winslow, you're too much. I appreciate you helping me out. I'll be glad to chat with him after I get back to Boston. I can only squeeze out a day or two more here, then it's back to reality."

"But they haven't solved the case of that poor woman found in the water," he said. "Aren't you reporting on that?"

"There's nothing new there," she said. "Absolutely nothing. Perhaps one day they'll identify her, but right now the DA isn't talking. Which isn't surprising. Even if they knew something, they wouldn't disclose it since it could tip off the perpetrator. And that's even if there is a perpetrator. They still don't know whether it was a suicide."

"Didn't they say the body didn't travel far?" he said. "Perhaps I misunderstood."

"No, you're right. My guess is she was either pushed or jumped off a passing boat. But they haven't found the boat. And who knows if they ever will?"

"Ghastly and ghoulish," he said, shaking his head.

"That's a nice bit of alliteration."

"Well, aren't you the literary type?" he chuckled. "You reporters are quite impressive."

"Wish me luck tomorrow. I'm going to make a field trip to the

Monomoy Point Lighthouse. At night. I'm hoping to see Sandy."

"Sandy? Good lord, who's Sandy?"

"Some of the researchers at Monomoy say they've seen a harmless old ghost they call Sandy. I think it's kind of cute. I just need one more decent story about this part of the cape. I figured why not write about some of the stranger things that happened down here."

"A ghost story," he said. "Interesting idea. Reminds me of the Legend of the White Stallion. Have you heard of that one?"

"Yes. I researched it. The author Henry Beston seems to be associated with the story somehow, according to an old newspaper clipping. Another author named Elizabeth Reynard mentions it in an out-of-print book called *The Narrow Land*. A mooncusser and a white horse on Monomoy trying to lure ships to wreck on a shoal. Great stuff."

"Beston was another one of those ambulance drivers," Prescott said. "Life is full of oddities."

"Ambulance drivers?" Stacie said. "You've got me on that one."

"Oh, of course, you're too young. Wouldn't mean anything to you."

"Well, now I want to know what you're talking about. What ambulance drivers?"

"A slew of famous twentieth-century people were ambulance drivers in World War I. I suppose if it were two or three people, it wouldn't amount to much. But there were so many. Beston drove an ambulance in the war, as did Walt Disney and Ernest Hemingway. And there was the poet e.e. cummings, Maurice Ravel, Gertrude Stein, Somerset Maugham, John Dos Passos, and Ralph Vaughan Williams. Many more, actually. I believe even Ray Kroc—of McDonald's hamburger fame—trained to be one, but the war ended before he could get to Europe."

"Are you serious?" Stacie said.

"Yes, of course. Why?"

"That seems unusual. Wonder what it means? Ambulance drivers?"

"It's puzzled more than one researcher. Who knows? In Beston's case, I gather he was traumatized from the experience and needed some time to heal. So, after the war, he made his way out to the dunes in Orleans and wrote *The Outermost House*. He found it peaceful and life-affirming. Though he does manage to get around to talking about shipwrecks and death."

"Speaking of shipwrecks, were there really such people as mooncussers?"

"There are the legends, of course. Beyond that, who knows? Nefarious minds on shores everywhere have been luring ships to their doom for centuries. Alfred Hitchcock made a movie with that theme. *Jamaica Inn*, I think it's called."

"Really? I could look that up. Another great angle."

"It was a terrible movie! Even great directors make awful movies every now and then."

"I know this is going to sound silly, but do you believe in ghosts?" Stacie said, leaning toward him.

"You mean real ghosts?" he said. "Not in fiction, but in reality? That kind of ghost?"

"Precisely. Do you think they exist?"

"Mmm. That's a tough one," he said, swirling the coffee in his paper cup. "To be honest, I have no idea. I used to think that supernatural things were a hoax and believed by people who were uneducated and superstitious. But I'm not so sure anymore. Maybe it's my age; the world seems more nuanced and complicated as I get older. Why do you ask?"

"I don't believe in ghosts and probably never will," Stacie said. "Yet, there is something odd about the history of Whitewash Village. And the young wildlife researchers I spoke to were bright, intelligent people and they had no doubt there was a ghost in the keeper's house on Monomoy. And there's Barbara's idea about the woman they found off Monomoy."

"She said the body belonged to a woman from Whitewash Village who died a hundred years ago. Is that what you're referring to?"

"Yeah. If you believed in ghosts, you could almost believe that a body returned from the past too, couldn't you? Especially if she was murdered."

Winslow laughed. "I suppose so. But perhaps you've been reading too much about our legends. I want to remind you that's why they're called legends and not facts."

"My thinking was that for my last feature story from Chatham I could work in some color about the legends and mention my spooky night visit there. I keep getting feedback from the editors that readers are eating this stuff up."

"I'll have to tell Barbara that you're going down to the lighthouse at night. She'll love that. Watch out for vampires."

"And mice. All those old houses have mice."

"How about vampire mice? I can see Barbara's next tome right now—*Toothy Rodents: A Saga of Forbidden Mouse Bloodlust.*"

"You writers are bitingly funny."

"Touché, young lady!"

◎

"Are you really going down to that island with just the boat captain?" Marie said. "At night?"

"What's wrong with that? He's a really nice guy. And it's not like we're staying overnight, for God's sake. It's like a nature walk. But at night."

"Didn't you say he's divorced and had some problems with his wife?"

"Your point?"

"I could have sworn you mentioned something about a restraining order. Maybe he's a violent person."

"I didn't say that; I said his wife pulled out a restraining order to get custody. Besides, maybe *she* was the violent one. I believe him so I'm not worried."

"You hardly know him. And no one else is going?"

"Marie, you're starting to creep me out. Stop it. I've told a ton of people who I'm going with and what I'll be doing. Carl's a good guy. I like him a lot. Please don't worry. I'm a reporter. I know what I'm doing. I feel like it'll be a great way to finish off the series from Chatham. Then it's back to covering the MBTA. I can tell you one thing, though."

"And what's that?"

"I'm going to miss Chatham Bars Inn, that's for sure."

"I warned you; travel will never be the same."

◎

Langone walked down the hallway of the school and felt like she was in an art gallery. Framed photographs, paintings, and sculptures adorned the walls of the prestigious art school.

She found the door and walked into a suite of small offices. She saw a woman sitting at a computer in the nearest office and said, "Sorry to disturb you, but I'm looking for Professor Crimonini."

"You must be Sarah Langone," the woman said. "I'm Phyllis Crimonini. Please come in. It's not every day that I get a request from law enforcement."

Sarah looked around the small office and was stunned at the array of multicolored fabrics hung on the wall; some were held up with simple pushpins, others were in elaborate frames.

"I had no idea there was such a thing as a bachelor of arts in textiles," Sarah said. "What a wonderful subject. People like me study less uplifting subjects like criminal behavior."

Crimonini laughed. "That's an important area of study too. We focus on the arts, broadly speaking, including the fashion industry. Studying the weaving and dyeing of different fabrics is an important skill for designers."

"It looks fascinating, actually," Sarah said. They continued small talk for a while.

"So, tell me, how can I help you?" Crimonini said. "You wanted me to look at some clothing involved in an investigation?"

"Yes. Please remember that before we proceed, we request that you refrain from discussing the details of our exploratory discussion today. You should also know that our discussion today could potentially lead to other areas of investigation, which may involve subpoenas for expert opinions."

"Yes, you did mention that. But today is just for background, correct?"

"Correct."

"OK. So how can I help?"

Sarah reached into her large legal briefcase and pulled out a clear plastic bag with official notations, bar codes, and dates. The word "evidence" was emblazoned in large red letters across the bag.

"I wonder if I could ask you to examine the clothing that I have here," she said. "I'll give you some non-latex gloves to wear, if you don't mind. The clothing has already been tested, but it still would be prudent to keep contamination to a minimum."

"Where did the clothing come from?"

"This is one item of clothing that was removed from a woman who was found deceased floating off of Cape Cod recently."

"Oh, I read about that," Crimonini said. "But I'm confused. Why would you be seeking input from a professor of textiles? Seems a little odd to me."

Sarah pulled out a small sandwich bag stuffed with medical gloves. She removed four of them and put two on the desk for the professor, while she started to stretch on her pair.

"The item inside the bag is a shirt removed from the woman's body during the autopsy."

Crimonini grimaced. "Ugh. I'm not sure I'm the best person to be helping you."

"All I'm asking is that you look closely at the fabric and tell me anything that comes to mind about the construction, or color, or anything. The woman still has not been identified."

"Are you saying she was murdered?"

"No. Please don't misunderstand what I'm saying. The woman has not matched any reports of missing persons. Her DNA is still being run through public databases as well. The cause of death has been determined to be drowning, but we don't know how she got to the area where her body was found, and whether there was foul play involved. We don't have much to work with. If we could identify her, it might lead to who she knew and eventually how she ended up in the water off Cape Cod. It's a long shot, but we're getting a little desperate."

"I see. But that doesn't explain why you're here today. The woman's clothing could have come from a thousand different manufacturers and retail outlets."

"You are correct. But the coroner mentioned the clothing the woman wore was odd. He said he'd never seen anything quite like it. We wondered if there was anything an expert on clothing and fabrics could tell us that might help move the investigation forward."

"I see. I guess you're grabbing at straws at this point."

"You could say that. Please, would you mind taking a look?"

Crimonini pulled on the gloves, stood, and said, "Why don't we go into the lab?"

They walked out of the office suite and down the corridor to a closed door. Crimonini opened it, turned on the lights, and walked over to a table with an oversized magnifying glass attached to the moveable metal arm. The outside ring of the magnifying glass housed a bright light. She turned on the device's lamp and put a large white sheet of paper over the tabletop.

"Let's see what you've got."

Sarah opened the bag and pulled out a white shirt that had been loosely folded.

"The pull-on shirt has only three buttons at the top. At the autopsy, they cut the shirt off."

Crimonini spread the shirt out over the table and adjusted the illuminated magnifying glass down toward the fabric. She bent over and picked up the fabric and rubbed it between her gloved fingers. For several minutes she painstakingly went over the clothing and spent almost thirty seconds looking at the three buttons.

"I see what the coroner meant," she said finally, standing up. "This is not modern clothing. Not by a long shot."

"Um, can you explain?"

"Well, the fabric is cotton, but rustic cotton. If you look closely you can see modest imperfections in the cotton strands, which would suggest nineteenth-century cloth. The weave is broad and basic, and the stitching is heavy and industrial. This garment was mass-produced but by older machinery. To be honest, I'm a little stumped. This could be in a museum."

"Do you know of any religious sects that still use this kind of clothing? Amish? Mennonites? Hasidic Jews?"

"Sorry, no. I'm not saying that there's not some remote commune in deepest, darkest Vermont where they make their clothes the old-fashioned way, but I'm not familiar with it. Sorry, I can't help with that."

"Why did you keep looking at the buttons?"

"They're metal buttons that started to rust, presumably because the body was wet."

"Who wore metal buttons?" Sarah asked.

"Most any working-class person in the nineteenth century. They were mass-produced by stamping two metal discs together. Some of them were embellished with designs, but these buttons are quite plain."

"Can you suggest why a woman today would be wearing clothes from that era?"

"No idea," Crimonini said, arching her eyebrows. "I grant you, it's odd."

"Is there anything else you can tell me about the clothing? Anything?"

Crimonini sighed and shoved the magnifying glass down again. "I'll make one more pass."

While she fussed with the cloth, holding up parts of it to the lens, Sarah looked around the room, which she took for a fabric laboratory. There were several textiles on the wall with labels that she didn't understand.

"Mmm," Crimonini said.

"What did you say?"

"I didn't say anything," she said.

"You made a noise. Did you find anything?"

"Oh, maybe, or maybe not. Am I allowed to tease apart a seam?"

"I'm not sure what you mean."

Standing up, Crimonini arched her back to stretch it. "Is it appropriate for me to cut open a stitched seam? You know, two pieces of cloth are sewed together with thread to make a seam. I'd like to cut a tiny bit of the thread stitching to look under the seam."

Sarah could feel the professor's frustration growing, so she nodded. "Sure, go for it."

Crimonini reached for a box of small tools and removed an oddly shaped device with a curved metal piece at the tip. She bent over and started to tug gently at some threads. After a few moments, she put down the tool, picked up the fabric, and pulled it to within inches of the underside of the magnifying glass.

"What are you looking at?"

"It looked like there might have been a label sewn into the neckline, but the only piece of it remaining was underneath the seam. Can you see it?"

Sarah leaned over and looked. There was a white piece of cloth with the faintest outline of printed letters.

"Can I remove it?" Crimonini asked.

"Sure."

After several seconds of tugging, and with the use of a pair of twee-zers, she pulled out a square piece of white cloth that was one half inch square. They nearly bumped heads as they competed for position over the magnifying glass.

"Huh," Sarah said. "It does look like a label. Can you make out anything?"

"I don't think that's text, more like a design. Printed with red ink. It's badly faded."

Sarah looked at her watch. "Is there any chance you could look it up in your database for logos or designs like that?"

The professor stood up. "You're kidding. A database of clothing la-bels? From another century? I watch police shows all the time and that's a little too much even for them."

"Of course. Not sure what I was thinking."

"Look," Crimonini said, "I'll take a couple of pictures of this tag here and check around, if that helps at all."

"Yes, please. Anything will help. We're at a dead end here."

CHAPTER 14

"Murders?" Falcone said. "In Whitewash Village?"

"Yes," Stacie said. "Were there any recorded murders at the village? I didn't see anything in the online archives and just wondered if you knew of any that were mentioned at the time?"

"Ms. Davis, there is much that we don't know about Whitewash Village. As I explained to you before, a storm in the 1860s appears to have damaged the harbor and the village was not sustainable afterward. I don't know why you're asking about murders."

"But were there any reported murders?" Stacie said, standing in her room looking out over Aunt Lydia's Cove. She heard Falcone sigh histrionically into her phone.

"There were references in a woman's diary about some deaths that were suspicious," Falcone said.

"Really? When was the diary written?"

"I don't have it in front of me, but my recollection is it was written by the wife of a fisherman in the late 1850s, prior to the Civil War."

"Did she refer to them as murders?"

"She did."

"Did she say who the suspect was?"

"No."

"Did she say who died?"

"Two women several days apart, if my recollection serves me. Please remember that this was an isolated village and rumors were rampant about all kinds of things. This was a diary, not a police report. There is no police report of a single murder down there, only this brief mention in an old diary."

"Did the diary explain how the women died?"

"They drowned. Well, one did anyway. They never found the other woman's body."

"I appreciate you taking the time to summarize the diary," Stacie said. She sat down at her desk with the phone squeezed against her shoulder while she wrote in her notebook. "But how could they know that someone who drowned was actually murdered? How is that possible?"

"Are you going to write a story about this?" Falcone said.

"I don't think so, though I might make a brief reference to it."

"Hmm. There are so many other things to write about in the town's history than a single reference in an old diary. Ms. Davis, isn't that a bit sensational?"

"I appreciate your concern, but if it's part of the historical record in the town, it would be fair to at least mention it. Can I see the diary? Is it available to the public?"

"All our documents are available to be viewed by the public, though some of the older documents—like this diary—are too fragile in their original condition and have been copied."

"So, I can see a copy of this diary?"

"Of course, but we're undergoing a construction project in the archive area and there isn't access right now. I might be able to get you a copy, though."

"Yes, that would be great. But can you answer a quick question?"

"I'll try."

"How did the villagers know that the woman who drowned was murdered? Perhaps she fell off a boat and drowned."

"The diary said the woman disappeared from her home one night and was heard to scream out later. Her body was found tied to a mooring in the harbor. You'll have to read it yourself."

"And the other woman? You said there were two murders."

"She disappeared as well; a scream was heard late the night she vanished, but she was never found. Again, you'll have to read the diary."

"How could someone just disappear down there?"

"I have no idea. I wasn't there."

Stacie knew she had reached the limit of Falcone's patience, and thanked her profusely after getting her assurance that she could see a copy of the diary later. But first, she wanted to see some of the windswept scene herself.

◉

She stood at the end of the dock and marveled at how the salt air instantly stirred up memories of childhood. Stacie's parents took the young family to the Outer Banks in North Carolina every summer, and she loved it. She could remember rolling in the waves, getting sand everywhere, including in her ears. Her two younger, roughhousing brothers were almost tolerable. It was a perfect childhood.

Until she was twelve.

The divorce was like a bolt of lightning out of the blue, cloudless sky.

Her mother struggled to keep the family rituals normal afterward, including going to the beach each summer, but it was never the same. How could it be? Her father visited whenever he was in town, which was not often. And he had a new family.

Stacie looked around the harbor full of boats bobbing at their moorings. Carl told her to meet him at the public dock in Stage Harbor next to the harbormaster's office. The weather that day had been breezy, but sunny. Carl said the wind was going to drop and stay calm all night.

"Fog is a possibility, but we should get back before it rolls in," he told her on the phone. "You're only staying an hour or so after sunset, right?"

"Maybe a bit longer," she said.

"I have a full-day charter tomorrow, so the earlier we get back the better."

"It's so great you offered to take me out there," she said. "I'm looking forward to it."

"I've never been to the lighthouse," he said. "Most people I know have never been off the beach at Monomoy."

"What do you mean?"

"They're clammers. No need to go off the beach. Plus, as I warned you, Miss Famous Reporter, there are ticks and poison ivy all over that island. I'm told we can follow a path to the lighthouse, but we should cover ourselves with insect repellent and wear tall boots."

"I don't have any tall boots," she said.

"I've got some that will fit. I'll bring 'em."

"You don't know my size," she laughed.

"Wear thick socks. I'll pick you up at seven o'clock sharp. Sun sets at around eight twenty."

She waited at the dock. He told her to look for a "twenty-seven-foot, center console with T-top, and twin 200 Yamahas." Stacie pretended to know what that meant but had no idea what to look for except a boat with Carl on it.

She noticed a motorboat slowly coming toward the dock with its navigational lights on. The sun was already low enough in the west to coat the sky with a blush of pink.

Carl waved and gently pulled the boat into the dock.

"Permission to come aboard, Captain," Stacie said, saluting.

"Permission granted."

She wore a sweatshirt and light nylon jacket over it, as well as dark sweatpants and a baseball cap. She carried a small backpack with a camera, notepad, and her small purse.

Just as gently, Carl eased the boat away from the dock and started slowly toward the exit channel from Stage Harbor. "Beautiful night," he said. "Or dusk."

"You were right about the wind. It stopped. How do you know things like that?"

"The Weather Channel."

"Really?"

"Pretty much. I mean, some of the commercial guys listen to the National Weather Service reports, but most of the weather apps work just as well for inshore areas. And you get used to weather patterns."

"So, what's this weather pattern we're in right now?"

"Is this a test?"

"Yeah, sort of. I'm trying to figure out what's BS and what's not. You boat guys are prone, you could say, to a little BS."

He laughed. "I hope you're gonna score on the curve. OK, here goes:

this time of year, in early June, we get slow-moving high-pressure systems that always move from west to east."

"I suppose," she said slowly.

"Well, they do. And they get pushed offshore eventually. High-pressure systems in the northern hemisphere rotate in a big clockwise spin, so at the front end of the system, the wind is spinning down from the north, pulling cooler air with it. But as the high pressure moves out into the ocean, the circle of spinning winds now pulls warmer air from the south. Today the high pressure was moving out, so we had a southwest wind that was pretty brisk—too brisk for one of my clients, who barfed— but the weather report says a low-pressure system is moving up the coast and pushing the high pressure to Norway, or something. In between the two systems, we sometimes get a brief calm. Like tonight."

"I'm impressed," she said, standing next to him behind the plexiglass windshield. "Of course, I have no idea whether you made it up or not, but it sounds good."

He chuckled.

They puttered toward the harbor entrance and passed a handful of returning boats.

"When we get out of the harbor, we'll get moving pretty fast. I want to get down there before it gets dark. Luckily, it'll be a rising tide and we can anchor the boat close to shore."

Inside the harbor, the calm water reflected the surrounding landscape. Stacie turned and looked back at their wake, which was nothing more than a gentle ruffling of the surface. She noticed a V-shaped ripple radiating behind them.

She watched gangs of nearby cormorants disappear into the black water and return to the surface yards away from where they went under. A group of bickering terns swooped overhead, heading south to their nests on Monomoy.

"It's nice out here," Stacie said. "I can see what you like about it."

He looked around the harbor. "Yeah, it is nice. But to be honest, I rarely take the time to take it all in. I'm trying to make a living. But it is beautiful, I suppose."

Carl looked at his phone and quickly answered a text.

"Got a good charter tomorrow. All day. These guys are fun. Took them out last year."

"Is there pressure to find fish?" Stacie said. "What happens if you can't find fish?"

He grimaced. "That *is* a bummer, and it happens now and then. But some of us charter guys share where the fish are, so we don't go out completely blind."

"You must be good at it," she said.

"I like to think so, but then there are a lot of charter boats, and you have to market yourself. I think I spend more time on Facebook and Instagram than on fishing."

"Social media comes to fishing," Stacie laughed. "Who knew?"

They left Stage Harbor through a narrow channel. Two fishermen on the beach were casting into the channel from the west side. One of them waved and Stacie waved back.

Carl pointed to his left. "See that island there? That's the northern end of an island that some call Minimoy. Its big brother, Monomoy, is just south of that and runs for another seven miles or so. We're going to power up and head west for a while to get around a sandbar, then cut it back due south. We'll be flying, so hang on."

"Aye, aye, Captain."

The boat rocked a bit as it bumped into the current entering the harbor, and she held on as Carl pressed the throttle forward. It reminded her of the takeoff on a commercial jet; she felt the speed gather quickly and she leaned forward. At first, the bow was high, but as the boat sped up it leveled off and skimmed the water. The noise from the roaring motors and the rushing wind overwhelmed her at first and then became exhilarating as the boat flew over the calm, pinkish waters of Nantucket Sound.

It was too loud for conversation, so Stacie just hung on and enjoyed the ride. The air felt cooler, and she zipped up her jacket the last couple of inches. Carl looked at her and grinned; she grinned back.

It *was* fun.

They passed only one boat that was heading in the opposite direction. By the time Carl powered down near the shoreline at Monomoy

Island, she could see the distinctive red-painted lighthouse sticking up like a lollypop farther in the island. The glass top of the lighthouse caught the last of the sun's rays, giving it a strange radiance.

"Is this the right beach?" she said.

"Yeah. There's the mooring they use," he said, pointing to a white float the size of a beach ball. "I guess there's a path up there and it'll lead to lighthouse. Or that's what I'm told."

She looked up and down the beach and saw nothing for miles but sand and beach grass. Inland she saw assorted shrubs and bent scrub pine.

"Desolate down here," she said.

"Yup," he said, moving around to the front of the boat and pulling out a large anchor, chain, and rope. He tied the rope around a cleat, then stacked the anchor and rope in a pile on the bow. They were still about twenty yards from the beach.

He returned and pointed to a pair of tall, gray, rubber boots. "Time to get those on," he said. "I'm going to put the boat parallel and next to the beach and cut the engines. You jump off first. Try not to get water in the top of those boots or you're going to have a cold, sloppy walk. I'm going to toss the anchor up onto the beach, then follow you out. Tide is coming in, so the boat will be fine until we return."

The boots fit, and she wondered if they belonged to his daughter. When the time came, he ran the boat up to the beach and turned it sideways. He shut off the motors and the hydraulics groaned mightily as he raised the outboards out of the water. She jumped off and landed awkwardly on her knees; he tossed the anchor onto the sand and joined her on the beach.

He carried the anchor far up the beach and spent several minutes planting it into the dry sand, stamping on it, and adjusting the chain and rope so that everything seemed right. The boat drifted slowly out into the water, then stiffened as the rope tugged the anchor tight. Carl continued to stamp the anchor into the sand until he was satisfied.

Stacie checked her phone for messages but was surprised when the signal flickered from one bar to no bars.

Carl walked over, picked up his backpack from the sand, opened it, and pulled out insect repellent. He sprayed his pants, his shirt, and his neck, then held it out to her.

"Is that necessary?" she said.

"Not if you don't mind getting Lyme, or babesiosis, or West Nile."

"Fine," she said, spraying her clothing. Carl walked up the lip of the beach to the top of the dune.

"Here's the path," he yelled.

She followed up the beach and returned the repellent. The lighthouse was barely visible a half mile away in the gathering darkness. Carl led the way through the worn but narrow sandy path. Beach grass and spindly shrubs bordered the path as it meandered toward the lighthouse. In one area the path went around a large pond; it was wet and marshy underfoot.

Ahead she could see the lighthouse looming larger. The searchlight inside had been removed years before but the glass enclosure at the top reflected the reddish sunset, giving it an eerie shape against the cloudless sky.

They finally saw the attached, two-story wood house. It was dark and brooding. For the first time, Stacie felt a twinge of unease.

This place creeps me out, she thought. What the hell kind of story did you think you were going to get out of this lighthouse?

Carl stopped twenty yards from the house and said, "You sure they have lights?"

"Yes, Steve said they have solar panels out back and batteries. We need to turn on a master switch on the first floor. We have to remember to turn it off when we leave. It's too bad he wouldn't let us go up into the lighthouse. It's locked."

Carl reached into his backpack, pulled out a military-style metal flashlight, and started up a small rise to the structure. The lighthouse was attached to the left side of the keeper's house.

They walked onto a wood deck that surrounded the right side of the house and stood at the front door. Carl put his hand on the doorknob and turned. It was locked.

"You said it was going to be open," he said.

"That's what Steve said. He warned me that the researchers might have just locked it out of habit, but he said the back door should be un-locked." They walked around the deck to the back. It was nearly dark, and Carl pointed his flashlight at the door.

He turned the nob and it opened into a pitch-black room. The flash-light beam raked harshly across the small mudroom, reflecting garish black shadows. They entered and slowly walked down a hallway to the front of the house. They passed a stairwell on the right leading upstairs. Farther into the house they stumbled around until they found the room on the right with the electrical box. Next to it was a handwritten note explaining how to turn on the power. Carl studiously followed the di-rections then pushed the main switch forward and a single light flicked on in an adjacent room.

They found several light switches and turned them on. The room lights were dim and gave the house a gloomy, yellowish hue. The house smelled musty. The floorboards creaked underneath as they walked.

"Gotta love those terns to want to stay out here for a summer," Carl said. "I'd rather camp out on the beach."

Some of the walls were exposed to the beams, showing the ancient, skeletal two-by-fours. Steve told Stacie they were slowly replacing the walls with new sheetrock, but it was a long-term project since all the supplies needed to be boated out and dragged to the lighthouse.

"Well, here we are," Carl said, grabbing two white plastic chairs and dropping his backpack on the floor. "How long do you want to stay? Ten minutes?"

"At least until it's fully dark out here. I want to get a feel for what it's like on an isolated island. It's kind of cool, don't you think?" They sat down.

"No," he said, reaching into his backpack and pulling out a bottle of red wine, and holding it up. "But *this* is cool, not the house, or this stupid island." He took out two plastic wine glasses, a box of crackers, a small cheese board, and a block of cheese in a plastic bag. Reaching into his pocket, he pulled out an elaborate flip knife and put it next to the cheese.

Stacie felt a little shudder of unease looking at the large knife, but it passed quickly.

He saw her face and said quickly, "I just thought it would help kill the time. We don't have to have any of this. Sorry."

"No, it's a great idea. I'll take a glass. And one of those crackers with cheese on it. I'm starving."

They drank some wine and munched crackers and cheese. After a while, they got up and poked around the first floor. They unlocked the front door that they originally tried to enter, and walked out onto the deck. The air was much cooler outside, and they looked up at the empty lighthouse tower to their right. A small railing surrounded the glass lighthouse enclosure, and Stacie could barely see the outline of a decorative ball at the top with a weathervane on top of that.

"Shit," Carl said suddenly. "Holy shit! There's someone up there."

"What?" she said, startled. "I don't see anything. Are you sure?"

"Right there!" he said, pointing. "You can't see him?"

"No!" she yelled. "I can't see anyone."

He kept pointing. "There. Dammit, right there. What the hell is he doing up there?"

She felt her heart thump as if it were a huge bass drum. Her mouth fell open and her breathing grew shallow.

"Carl, I don't see anything—"

She realized he was howling with laughter.

"I'm sorry," he said, wiping tears from his eyes. "I couldn't resist. I'm sorry. That's not funny." He tried to control himself but had trouble muffling his laughter.

"Carl, I swear to God you are such a jerk," she said, her left hand on her hip and her right holding a wine glass.

He saw how distressed she was and stopped laughing. "Wow, I'm sorry, Stacie. I am a complete idiot. Totally uncool on my part. You have such a good sense of humor and I thought—."

She stared at him in the darkness, his silhouette outlined by light filtering from the house windows behind him. She took a sip of wine and made a face at him.

Then she chuckled. "You son of a bitch. You had me going."

"I'm sorry. I really am."

She started to laugh, partly out of embarrassment at her gullibility, and partly out of relief that he hadn't actually seen anyone. Her laughter grew until she spilled wine on the deck.

"Carl, I swear I will get you back one day."

"I have no doubt you will," he said. "And I deserve it. Really, I'm sorry."

"No, it's OK. It *was* funny."

They returned to the house and sat down in their chairs. Before he could speak, Stacie started laughing again and, finally relieved, Carl started laughing. After rehashing the episode several times, they regained their composure, had more cheese, crackers, and wine.

"So, have you had enough of this place or your jerk captain? Ready to head back?"

"Yeah, I'm ready," she chuckled. "Maybe it was Sandy you saw in the lighthouse."

"Oh, yeah. The ghost you said that was out here."

"Do you believe in ghosts?" she said.

"Ghosts? Mmm. I'd have to say that I'm agnostic on that subject. I've never seen one but sometimes when you're out on the water alone, well, it's not hard to imagine there might be a spirit lingering out here. And these waters around the cape and especially Monomoy have seen their share of deaths by shipwreck. Thousands I would think over the centuries."

"It sounds like you *do* believe in ghosts then."

He laughed. "I guess I do, sort of. How about you?"

She leaned back in her plastic chair and sighed. "I honestly don't know. I'm skeptical for all the normal reasons, like science as opposed to superstition. But you should have heard those two researchers I talked to. There was no doubt in their minds that they saw Sandy walking around here. How could that be?"

"Well, the isolation down here may play into it, wouldn't you think?" he said.

"Yeah, I guess. Seems strange that they were so certain."

"So, are you ready to head back now?"

"I'm ready. But let's at least go upstairs. Maybe we could see Nantucket."

"Tonight, I bet we'll see Nantucket Light for sure," he said.

They walked down the hallway, turned left onto a tiny landing area, and turned left yet again up the creaking stairs to the top floor. They entered a small bedroom on the right with windows facing east and south. Carl stooped and peered out the south-facing window.

"Yup, there you go," he said, pointing. "Just wait about twenty seconds or so. That's Great Point Lighthouse on Nantucket. Only about ten miles away from here."

Stacie leaned forward and waited at the window. It was warm upstairs, and the musty odor was strong in the closed-off space. After a few seconds, Stacie saw the flicker of light sweep briskly across the sky.

"Got it," she said. "I bet that lighthouse has been there for a while."

Carl said nothing, so she turned and realized he was staring out the other window facing east.

"See anything cool?" she said.

"Mmm," he said. "Maybe."

She joined him at the window. "What do you see?"

"Over there," he said, pointing at a glow of light a couple of hundred yards away on the island's opposite, east-facing beach. The light source was mostly hidden by dark, silhouetted dunes.

"Those must be researchers," she said. "They're camping out."

"No, the researchers are several miles north of here. That's the Atlantic Ocean side. Don't know what that light is. Funny."

"Oh, please, Carl. One trick is enough."

He chuckled. "You want to see the rough Atlantic before you head back? It's just over those dunes there."

"Is that where Whitewash Village was?"

"No, that's back on the Nantucket Sound side, just south of where we anchored the boat."

"I'm up for seeing the Atlantic if you are," she said. "Then we can go back."

"Let's do it," he said, leading the way down the stairs.

"The stairs are tricky," he said. "Be careful."

She heard a ping and looked at her phone. She had no signal.

Carl looked at his phone.

"You have a signal?" she said.

"Yeah, but only from up here. One day they'll have a cell tower down here."

"And a four-star resort," she said.

"Not sure about that."

Back downstairs they packed up the wine and food. They put their bags just inside the back door to collect on the way back to the boat on the other side of the island. Carl led the way with his flashlight. The farther they got from the lighthouse, the cooler it became as a small breeze filtered in from the north. The sky was clear and sparkled with stars. After the fuss about Carl's silly joke, Stacie was feeling happy again. She could assemble a good story about the quaint lighthouse and the devoted wildlife researchers, combined with a tongue-in-cheek reference to Sandy.

She liked Carl, even with his goofy sense of humor. She already dreaded leaving the cape and burrowing back into the itinerant life of a general assignment reporter.

They crested a tall dune and looked down on the frothy beach where the Atlantic Ocean exhausted itself. A thin crescent moon, partway up over the ocean, provided just enough light to see the water.

They walked down the sandy bluff to the beach and watched the waves break in the dark in front of them, leaving a white, sudsy foam at the waterline. They said nothing and took in the view and the smells of the ocean.

Stacie noticed that Carl kept staring to his right down the beach.

"What are you looking at?" she said, removing a wisp of hair from her mouth.

"That light," he said absently. "The same one we saw from the window upstairs. Funny."

"What's funny."

"There shouldn't be a light down there at the southern tip of the island."

"Maybe someone's camping out."

"Yeah, I suppose. They're not supposed to be here, though. Camping by tourists is not allowed. They'd have to swim to get here, or they have a boat beached somewhere."

"Oh, well," she said, walking down toward the water. "It's a nice night for them."

"Careful," he said, coming up behind her with his flashlight. "You'll stumble over something. Crap washes up here like you wouldn't believe. Lobster traps, plastic crates, everything the ocean can grab and toss."

He pointed the flashlight at the sand. They stood a few feet from the water's surge and felt the sand thump with each wave; the froth washed up and then retreated, accompanied by the twinkling chimes of thousands of shell fragments.

Carl walked a few yards to the right along the beach, flashlight pointed down.

She breathed in the salt air, again filtering a brief memory of a happy childhood on the beach. Turning, she saw Carl kneeling. She joined him and looked over his shoulder.

"See any more ghosts?" she said.

He didn't answer but pointed his flashlight toward the light glowing around the bend.

"Carl, what are you looking at?"

He didn't answer.

"Carl?"

"Oh, um. I've seen a lot of things over the years, but not this," he said, pointing the flashlight down at the sand.

"I don't see anything," she said.

"Look."

"Sorry, I don't see anything, Carl."

He stood up, walked a few paces farther along the beach, stopped, and kneeled again. She followed, kneeled, and looked down.

"Do you see it?" he said.

"Is it what I think it is?"

"I guess," he said. "They look like horse hoofprints to me."

"That's not possible, is it? Down here?"

Carl, still kneeling, looked up and down the beach, shooting his flashlight beam like a lance. He stood.

"Let's follow these for a while," he said.

"Is this another of your jokes?" she said, laughing. "You can't get me twice on the same night."

But he was already walking, looking down at the sand with the flashlight. She quickly joined him.

"Carl, do you think they're real?"

He didn't answer so she fell in next to him. Then he stopped suddenly and froze.

"Carl, talk to me. What's going on?"

He pointed the light ten feet in front of them. Stacie saw something dark in the sand. They walked slowly until they stood over it.

"You've got to be kidding me!" she said. "That's a pile of horse shit. A pile of *fresh* horse shit. What the hell is it doing here?"

But Carl was already off following the hoofprints. She raced after him and grabbed his arm.

"Hey, we can stop now," she said. "I get the joke. The White Stallion."

"I don't know what you mean," he said. "What stallion?"

"The legend. You know it."

"Nope, never heard of it. Come on. The light is right around the bend." He started walking again.

For yet another time that evening, Stacie felt a frisson of anxiety ripple across her chest. Carl was acting strangely. People act strangely all the time, but acting strangely on an isolated, forlorn beach was not her idea of a good time. Besides, she didn't know Carl well at all. And this horse gag was just a little bizarre. Why would he stage something so elaborate? Perhaps she had misjudged Carl after all.

"Carl!" she yelled. "Stop! I'm going back."

He turned. "Come on," he yelled, waving her forward.

"No, I want to go back," she yelled.

He returned and held out the flashlight for her to grab. "You stay here. I'm going to see what that stupid light is. Now and then tourists get blown off course on kayaks. Maybe someone's stuck out here. We can give them a ride back."

"Don't you think the Coast Guard would be looking for them? Leave them alone. Let's head back now."

"You can't leave people who are lost out here. There's a poor cell service here. Someone might be injured. You head back. I'll follow after talking to those folks."

"Fine, never mind," she said. "I'm going with you. You're not leaving me here alone on this damn beach."

They walked in silence. Stacie could see the glow of a light source around the bend, but it was farther than she imagined, and it was exhausting pushing through the deep sand.

"But what if they're kids having a party? They might be drunk."

"Then we'll just leave."

"What if they're researchers just having a toga party?" she said, trying to make him laugh.

"We'll join them."

"You are too much, Carl," she said, shaking her head.

They slowed as they rounded the bend and tried to focus on the light source. Near the waterline, a lone lantern sat tipped slightly in the sand. Before approaching it, Carl swung the flashlight beam around the beach, up to the dunes behind them, then down at their feet where the hoofprints were.

The sand also contained occasional footprints, dried seaweed, bits of plastic, driftwood, and a deflated balloon caught on a small plant. They walked to the lantern that sat cockeyed in the sand. Carl bent down and picked up the lantern. He looked at it closely, his face glowing harshly orange from the flickering flame.

"What are you doing?" she asked.

"Checking it out. Someone brought a horse down here and left a lantern."

"I don't see a lot of footprints on the sand," she said. "There's no one here, Carl. And no horse. Just you and me."

They stood and followed the flashlight's beam as Carl swung it in a circle.

"Carl, I want to go back now. I'm a little surprised you went through all this trouble to scare me. I'm sure your pals will be laughing about this for years. 'Gullible city slicker reporter scared shitless by sneaky prank.'"

She turned and started retracing her steps. Carl raced up behind her with the flashlight.

"Stacie," he said, grabbing her arm. "I had nothing to do with this. I don't even know what you mean about the white horse thing."

She pulled his fingers off her arm, trying to remain in control as her heart raced.

"Please don't touch me, Carl. I want to go back now."

Be firm, she told herself. Show him that you mean business. How could you not have seen that he might be dangerous? She remembered the restraining order. Keep walking, girl. You'll get through this. Just don't threaten and don't confront. It'll be OK.

CHAPTER 15

It took them twenty minutes to walk back to the lighthouse. Carl stopped trying to talk to her and instead led the way with the flashlight.

They went through the front door and locked it from the inside, turned off the power, collected their belongings, and exited through the back door.

"Stacie," he said as they walked around the front of the house, "I had nothing to do with the horse thing. Really. And I'm sorry for that stupid joke about seeing someone in the lighthouse."

"Carl, can we please just go back now?"

"Sure," he said, leading the way again with the flashlight.

The walk back to Nantucket Sound took longer than she anticipated. The dark shadows surrounding them were disconcerting and gloomy; she could only see Carl's back and the minimal illumination of the flashlight on the path.

To the north, she could see the periodic swing of the lighthouse in Chatham. It seemed far away.

They finally reached the beach, stopped at the top to catch their breath, and then started down to the boat.

Carl stopped and Stacie ran into him.

"What now?" she said, her frustration mounting.

He swung the flashlight's beam across the water.

"Shit!" he yelled.

"Carl. Please stop it. I don't like what you're doing. It's not funny behaving like this. Can we just *please* go back now?"

"Go back in what?" he said sharply. "Where's my goddamn boat?"

He raced down the beach, the flashlight beam slashing wildly.

Stacie scanned the water; it looked black and oily in the dark. In the distance to the west, she could see the twinkling lights from homes along the shore. Stacie felt a strange sense of detachment; she was not standing on an isolated beach on a pitch-black night with a man who insisted on scaring her—she was watching someone else act out a scene.

She sat down in the sand and reached for her phone. There was no service.

"Dammit!" she yelled into Nantucket Sound.

Carl's flashlight continued to flash wildly about the water.

She stood up and walked slowly to him.

Stay calm and strong, she thought. He wants you to be scared so that he's in control. Show him your composure and strength.

"Carl, what's wrong?" she said.

He turned and inadvertently flashed the light into her eyes, blinding her.

"What's wrong? I'll tell you what's wrong! Someone stole my goddamn boat. They cut the line, those bastards." He pointed the flashlight to his left hand that held the end of a piece of rope. He swung the beam from his hand to the rope that led to the chain and anchor in the sand five feet away.

"Someone stole your boat? You want me to believe that?"

"I swear to God I'll kill them."

"Do people steal boats here?"

"Not that I know of. But it just happened. Who the hell would do this?"

Stacie took a deep breath and spoke clearly and slowly. "Carl, can you please call someone? The Coast Guard can get us off this island. You can report it to them. We need to get out of here. I'm a little freaked out and would appreciate you making a call right now."

"Yes," he said. "Of course. I'm sorry. This is very strange. I'd like to get out of here too."

He handed her the flashlight and reached into his backpack. The bluish glow from the phone made his face look inanimate, and Stacie looked away.

"Goddammit," he yelled.

"What's wrong?" she said.

"I don't have a signal. You must have one."

"No, I don't," she said. "Let's go to the top of the dune. It'll be better up there." She turned and hiked the thirty feet to the top of the rise. They both used their phones, showering their faces in an eerie bluish glow.

"Nothing," he said. "You?"

"Nada."

They stood side by side, staring out into the black waters of Nantucket Sound.

"Carl, your phone worked on the second floor of the house, correct?"

"Yeah. I guess we'll go back, and I'll call from up there. This is a huge pain in the ass."

"No, I'm staying here on the beach, Carl. You go by yourself, go through the back door, up the stairs, and make the call. Then come back and wait with me."

"You want to stay here?"

"Yes. I'd prefer to stay here. Just please make the call soon. I'll keep checking my phone to see if I can get service."

"All right. I'll hurry. I'm sorry about this, Stacie."

"I know you are. Please hurry." She looked at her phone. "It's twenty-two minutes past nine. You should be back here in about a half hour or so. I'll keep the beach warm for you."

He sighed. "This is bullshit. I will kill those guys who took my friggin' boat. I've got a trip tomorrow, goddammit."

"Carl, go please."

"Yeah, sorry." He turned, pointed the flashlight at the path, and walked back to the lighthouse. She watched him disappear into the black silhouette of dunes and gnarled brush. After ten minutes she could only make out the occasional glow of the flashlight. The lighthouse was too far away to see in the dark.

Stacie walked down to the waterline. The tide had risen. Now and then she turned to look back at the top of the dune where the path started.

God, what a strange night, she thought. Pirates stealing boats? Horses running wild on Monomoy? A random lantern flickering on the beach? This is seriously weird shit. And Carl. What to make of this guy? Did someone really steal his boat, or is this part of his complicated prank with his buddies? Get me the hell out of here.

It was getting chilly, so she zipped up her jacket. She tried to let the gentle waves from Nantucket Sound calm her. She remembered the stronger waves on the Atlantic side of the island. Two different bodies of water; one violent and rough, the other shallow and gentle. Two sides of Monomoy; two sides of a person.

Stacie shuddered and tightened her arms across her chest.

⊙

There was no clanging alarm that went off, only a slowly dawning recognition that Carl had been gone a long time.

A little before ten o'clock, she stood up and walked up the rise to the path's entrance. She could not see a flashlight beam anywhere. She returned to where her backpack lay on the beach and sat down. She pulled her knees up and put her arms around them, rocking gently.

Ten minutes later, she returned to the path entrance and peered into the black shapes of the dunes and shrubs.

"Come on, Carl, for chrissakes," she muttered. After another five minutes, she retrieved her backpack and sat down at the path's entrance, facing into the island. She refused to worry about what Carl was doing, or where his boat was, or anything else except getting off the island. If she let her imagination wander, she became frightened; so, she focused on the sky.

She used her backpack as a pillow and lay back in the sand, staring up at the stars. She tried to identify constellations, but only managed to find the Big Dipper, or what looked like the Big Dipper. She closed her eyes briefly; she felt physical and emotional exhaustion.

At one point she thought she heard something from the path and sat up. But she saw nothing except those ill-defined black blobs of shrubs and sand. Finally, after more than an hour had elapsed since he left, Stacie stood up, brushed the sand off her clothes, and yelled, "Carl!"

She tried that several times and gave up. She knew what she had to do and dreaded it. She looked at her phone's battery indicator and saw that it was down to 40 percent. Sighing, she turned on the phone's flashlight app and started down the path toward the lighthouse.

At one point, she thought she was lost. There were side paths they noticed on the way in, but they could always see the lighthouse in the distance to help choose the correct path. Now, without the advantage of seeing the lighthouse, Stacie was forced to guess. Her loss of direction added to the tension.

"Dammit," she said out loud when she came to another fork. She decided to use her phone's compass app and took the fork heading east. After another ten minutes, she saw the silhouette of the lighthouse against the sky.

"Carl!" she yelled one more time.

Slowly, and with a growing sense of unease, she climbed the steps onto the deck, walked around the house to the back. The door was open.

"Carl!" she yelled into the black house.

Nothing.

She entered slowly. Her phone light was not as strong as Carl's flashlight; she could only see a few feet in front of her. She knew the steps to the second story were on the right, but she decided to turn on the power first. The lights would make her feel safe. Where the hell was Carl?

After rereading the directions, she pulled the main lever, and a single light came on in the front room. Stacie looked at her phone and there was still no cell service; her battery was down to 20 percent. She went down the hall and turned to walk up the stairs.

That's when she saw him.

She screamed louder than she had ever screamed in her life. It felt good to scream; she released all the tension built into her body that day.

◎

The stairwell to the second floor started with three steps up to a tiny landing, where they continued forty-five degrees to the left for the long run upstairs.

Carl lay facedown on the landing. His backpack was up around his neck, and his body was crumpled unnaturally.

"Carl," she yelled. "Carl!"

Nothing.

She kneeled on the tiny landing area and leaned over to see his face.

She gasped. His eyes were closed, his mouth was partially open, and a small pool of blood had started to coagulate underneath his cheek on the landing.

"Oh God, Carl! Can you hear me? What happened?"

She put the fingers of her left hand against his neck, feeling for a pulse. She kept pressing, desperately seeking any sign of life, but could not find the telltale cardiovascular thump.

Stacie put her face within inches of his mouth to see if she could see or hear breathing. The house creaked as the cool air from the open back door forced the ancient wood to contract.

Then she did something she had not done in a long time: she started to cry. Small rivulets of salty tears ran down her cheek and fell onto Carl's face.

"Carl, please wake up," she cried softly. "Please."

She grabbed his shoulders and shook him.

"Carl!" she screamed. "Wake up!"

He moaned; his eyelashes flickered but did not open.

"Oh my God, Carl, can you hear me?"

He remained inert, lying awkwardly on the small landing.

"Wait. Holy shit, Carl. Where's your phone?"

It felt good speaking to him as if he could hear. She searched the landing with her hands, zipped open his backpack still hooked to his shoulders, but could not find his phone. After looking in vain up and down the stairs, she guessed that it might be underneath his body.

She kneeled next to him again and pushed her left hand underneath his body, shoving him a little with her shoulder. He moaned again.

"I'm sorry, Carl," she said, wiping away the last of her tears. "I can't find your phone. Where the hell would it be?"

She reached over with both hands and gently lifted his head. The gooey blood got onto one of her hands and she winced.

But she saw the phone; it was hidden underneath his neck. She grabbed it and gently let his head down. It was covered in blood and she wiped it on her pants leg.

She furiously tapped the phone and tried to remember how to get past the passcode to dial for an emergency. She held the volume and the other side button down on his iPhone. The emergency phone option popped up.

She raced to the top of the stairs and saw the phone had a single bar. She pressed "emergency SOS."

◎

The small house was packed with people and bright lights. Radios crackled with the truncated garble of emergency communications.

After an interminable, searing wait of forty-three minutes, the Coast Guard arrived in force with two boats and at least ten blue-uniformed personnel. Carl was judged by the Coast Guard to be seriously injured, and after an extensive back-and-forth with the shore station and personnel at a cape hospital, it was decided that Carl would be carried on a stretcher to one of the boats and sped to Stage Harbor. He'd be taken by ambulance to the ER in Hyannis.

Stacie was given a blanket and a bottle of water while she watched the drama. A young female Coast Guard officer named Fatima sat with her.

Stacie watched Carl's body being strapped to a stretcher. He remained unconscious, and Stacie could tell by the muted discussions that there was concern about his condition.

"He'll be fine," Fatima said. "They just need to get him to shore. It would take too long to get a chopper here, so they're going to run him to shore. Please don't worry. It's not too bumpy out there tonight."

She stood on the deck in front of the house and watched a group of guardsmen move swiftly on the path to the beach. They carried Carl's stretcher on their shoulders like a funeral casket. Soon, all she could see was the faint, bouncing light as they raced to the beach.

Stacie returned to gather her pack and sat next to Fatima. She was joined by two additional guardsmen: an older, dark-haired man named Petty Officer Krojec, and a young, blond, childlike man named Seaman Aronson.

"We found his boat," Krojec said to Stacie.

"Where was it?"

"About a mile or so southwest of here, near Handkerchief Shoal."

"Was anyone on board?" she said.

"No, it was empty."

"Was it damaged or anything stolen from it?"

"It doesn't appear damaged, and nothing obvious has been stolen. Hopefully, Mr. Lane can take a look when he recovers."

The two men and one woman in their dark blue uniforms and orange floatation devices looked at Stacie.

"You found him when you returned from the beach?" Krojec said.

"Yes. When he didn't return, I got worried and went back to the house."

"But you didn't go with him when he returned to use his phone?"

"No. I already told you. I stayed on the beach."

"Why did you want to stay on the beach? Why wouldn't you go with him?"

"Because I was tired," Stacie said. "And it was a long walk. Carl didn't need me to go with him. Why do you ask?"

"It just seems that you two would have stayed together," Krojec said. "People don't usually split up when there's an emergency. I gather Mr. Lane was upset about his boat."

"Of course he was, wouldn't you be?"

"Yes. But, again, it's unusual to separate," Aronson now spoke up. "Did you have an argument with him?"

"No, who said that?"

"No one, we're just trying to understand what happened."

"But I told you what happened. And once Carl comes around, he'll confirm it. I'm tired. Do you mind if we go back now?"

"Certainly," Krojec said. "But can you remind us again of the horse tracks you said you saw? And the lantern? On the Atlantic side."

"I explained that to you an hour ago, and you said you sent some guys out there. They must have found the tracks and the lantern. And the horse crap. It's all there."

They stared at her.

"Well," Krojec said, "it's high tide out there right now."

"So what?" Stacie said.

"So, there's nothing there. They couldn't find any horse tracks. Or horse manure. Or lantern."

"That's ridiculous. We saw it. Carl will confirm it."

"Of course," Aronson said. "We should go now."

◎

She had turned off the lights in her room and stared out the window onto the dark cove below. Beyond sat the whitish outline of the barrier beach, and farther out was the unsettled Atlantic.

Stacie looked at the room's clock radio. It showed one 1:22 a.m. She had dipped into the room's small refrigerator and taken out a half-bottle of white wine. She stood and gently swirled the wine in the glass. Looking down into the wine, she marveled at how liquid reacted to whatever force was applied to it. The ocean was like that, she knew. Without a disturbance, it remained calm and gentle; but when struck by wind and rain, it could explode.

She drank the rest of the wine, put down the glass, and buried herself in the bed's thick comforter.

CHAPTER 16

There had never been an ocean this deep, or a darkness that was so enveloping. So, Carl waited for a return to the surface. There was nothing else to do. Sure, there were strange undersea noises, but he was very deep in a very black ocean. He knew the ocean always tried to mislead and trick. Stay calm and vigilant, he thought.

"He opened his eyes," someone said.

"No, he didn't."

"Yeah. He did it again, look."

"Hey, Carl, can you hear me? Peggy, get the attending. Hurry."

Carl knew he was underwater because he could both see, and not see. Saltwater was like that when you were immersed in it and opened your eyes. At first, you could see, but then the brine would sting, and your eyes would close reflexively.

"Carl, can you open your eyes again? Try it again. Good. Excellent. How are you feeling?"

He squinted. A man was leaning over him, his face a gauzy white shape.

"Can you see me, Carl?"

Of course I can see you, Carl thought. I'm not stupid. Stop yelling. You're hurting my ears. But who's Carl?

◎

"That is one hell of a story, Stacie," Hanes, the Metro editor, said. "Do you know whether this charter boat guy is OK?"

"They won't release any information to me since I'm not a family member. I'm tempted to call his former wife. I'm sure she'll fill me in."

"Do it. Our cape stringer is back from vacation, and I'm going to put him on it too. Do you know Frank Costello, the stringer?"

"No, never met him. Have him call me before he gets going."

"Sure. I hate to ask, but can you stay down there a little longer? Smitty will be all over this."

Stacie looked out the hotel window on the beach below.

"I can stay longer."

"Great. Check in later. I think we'll need a straight news piece from Costello to start. You can't write it since you're part of the story, but you can help point him in the right direction. Wait, I think there's something just popped on the *Cape Cod Times'* website down there."

Stacie hung up and sat in front of her laptop. The *Times* had a short piece on their website headlined: "Accident at Iconic Lighthouse Sends Chatham Man to Hospital."

The story was sparse, but it detailed the Coast Guard response and the rescue of two people stranded on Monomoy, one of whom was injured in a fall at the keeper's house. Stacie was not identified in the story, nor was Carl.

Her cell phone rang.

"Shit," she said, looking at the number.

"I should have never let you stay there," Scoccia said. "I can't believe this happened. You told me you'd be there a couple of hours."

"Steve, I'm sorry. This was an accident. Carl fell. Someone stole his boat, and we didn't have cell service, except from the second story of the house."

"No one stole his boat. Who told you that?"

"He did. He was pretty pissed off about it."

"The police don't think so. They say someone cut his anchor line. If they wanted to steal it, the boat would be on a trailer and in another state by now."

"Steve, what police?"

"The police who have been here all morning and the investigators at the lighthouse. Those police."

Stacie felt the anxiety explode in her chest again. She took a short breath.

"Steve, I'm sorry for what happened. I'll be glad to exonerate you in any way that I can."

"Too late for that, I'm afraid. I've already had a call from Washington. My boss accused me of running a theme park."

◉

On the surface, the voice was polite and respectful, yet Stacie felt an undercurrent of manipulation in the tone.

"We'd just like to ask you a few questions about last night," First Assistant DA Martin said. "It won't take long. Can you drive down here to our office?"

"That won't be possible," Stacie said. "I'm working today. Perhaps tomorrow."

"In that case, can we come to you? Are you in Chatham?"

"Yes."

"Can we meet you at your hotel or motel?"

"I guess so. How long will this take?"

"Oh, not long. Where are you staying? We can visit you around one o'clock. Would that work?"

"I guess."

◉

"What in God's name happened last night?" Prescott said.

She sighed into the phone.

"It was a walking nightmare. I'm still trying to figure it all out."

"Do you want to talk about it? Maybe grab a cup of coffee? Barbara called me this morning. She'd like to see you as well. We feel terrible."

"You know, I'd love to grab a coffee with the two of you."

"How about the coffee shop at eleven? We'll meet you there."

Stacie stood up from the bed and caught a glimpse of herself in the mirror; she looked haggard and beaten. Although she had taken a shower, blow-dried her hair, and applied a bit of makeup, the bags under her eyes made her look like a sagging bloodhound. Her eyes were bloodshot and her face pale.

◎

"Is that man Lane going to be OK?" Silvestri asked. "How dreadful."

"I can't get them to release any information to me beyond the fact that he's a patient," Stacie said.

"Do you know anyone in his family?" Prescott said.

"No. Just that his former wife and his daughter live in Hyannis. I don't know what her new married name is, or I'd just call her. I'm thinking of going to a bar that Carl and his friends go to a lot. Maybe they could help."

The three of them huddled around the small coffee shop table as Stacie detailed the events of that night at the lighthouse.

"You really saw horse manure?" Silvestri said. "And a lantern?"

"I kid you not. I'm still convinced Carl was trying to prank me."

"That's an elaborate prank," Prescott said. "And the boat?"

"Now *that*, I have no idea," she said, taking a sip of coffee. "I mean, if he wanted to create some reason for us to be stranded, he could have had the rope already cut and loosely tied so that it would separate eventually. But why do that?"

"Well, perhaps he was trying to create a situation where you two would have to stay at the keeper's house, and, well, you know, maybe have to snuggle," Silvestri said. "Which would lead to other things."

"Oh, Barbara, for God's sake," Prescott said.

"I'm just stating the obvious," Silvestri said. "He's a young man, she's an attractive young woman. Men do strange things to get what they want."

"Stacie," Prescott said. "What does your boyfriend say about all this?"

"I'm not dating anyone now," she said. "Neil—my ex-boyfriend—and I broke up recently."

"I'm sorry," he said. "I didn't mean to pry."

"No, it's OK," she said. "I don't really think of Neil these days. It's Carl I'm worried about. I'm so confused about the whole evening on Monomoy. There were a couple of times that I was uneasy around Carl that night, I'll admit. Then again, he seemed genuinely upset about his boat. And if he was choreographing this whole ruse, what happened to him at the house?"

"I told you there were bad spirits down there," Silvestri said. "I told you not to go."

"Barbara, do you think that's helpful now?" Prescott said. "Stacie here is trying to recover from a horrible experience. Let her be."

"I'm sorry, darling," Silvestri said, squeezing Stacie's hand briefly. "My imagination gets the better of me sometimes. You've been through a lot."

"What's this about the DA's office," Prescott said, "if you don't mind me asking?"

Stacie sighed. "They want to talk to me about what happened on Monomoy. I'm not worried. Carl will be able to confirm everything. It's just that I'm used to covering stories like this, not being part of the story."

"I'm sure everything will be OK, including Carl's health, poor guy," Silvestri said. "Still, the horse thing is a little strange. And the Coast Guard found nothing?"

"Barbara let's leave this poor woman alone," Prescott said, standing up. "She's been through a lot."

"I was just—" but he had pulled her up by the arm.

"Please don't hesitate to call if you need anything," Prescott said as they walked out.

Stacie felt a sense of foreboding. Something was very wrong. She took another sip of coffee and looked around the coffee shop. Groups of tourists, some with strollers, laughed and munched on scones and croissants. They seemed happy and carefree, like normal people. No missing boats, no horse manure, and no ghosts.

◉

Stacie was running late and whipped the Mini into the parking space in front of her unit that was across the street from the main hotel building. She saw two women standing on the sidewalk. They were not dressed like vacationers.

"Nice car," the older woman said.

"Are you Mary Martin?"

"Yes, and this is Sarah Langone, a state police investigator in our office. Thanks for seeing us today."

Stacie did not shake hands. "Follow me," she said, walking briskly.

"This is quite a nice room," Martin said, following Stacie into her suite. Martin looked out the large window onto Aunt Lydia's Cove and the barrier beach beyond. "I've never stayed here. Have you, Sarah?"

"Yes, once. My husband Bill brought me here for Valentine's Day," Langone said.

"How romantic," Martin said. "I'll have to guilt Kevin into bringing me here for Valentine's Day."

Stacie was uncertain why Martin insisted on talking to her today and was willing to drive the twenty miles to Chatham to do so.

"We can sit here, if you don't mind," Stacie said, pointing to a round table and three chairs.

"Perfect," Martin said. They sat down, and the two visitors took out yellow legal pads and pens. Martin smiled, though Stacie noticed that when she did so, her mouth twisted slightly, and the tip of her right canine tooth flashed.

"We appreciate you taking the time to meet with us," she said. "I know we've had other brief conversations about your reporting on another story. I just want to acknowledge that."

"That is correct," Stacie said.

"I want to make clear that you are voluntarily talking to us today."

"Yes, of course. What are you implying?"

"I'm not implying anything," Martin said, flashing the canine again.

"Have you talked to Carl Lane yet?"

"No, we haven't."

"Shouldn't you start there? I've already talked to the Coast Guard. You must have the information."

"Yes. But we're doing a routine follow-up investigation of the accident. The jurisdiction for an investigation falls to the Cape & Islands District Attorney's Office."

"What is there to investigate?" Stacie said.

"We're just trying to understand what happened to you and Mr. Lane on Monomoy. Is it possible that you could just answer a few questions? This won't take long." She smiled again.

"Fine. Proceed. I don't have much time. I'm a reporter, remember?"

"Of course, this won't take long."

After the introduction from Martin, it was Langone who asked most of the questions. At first, Stacie found the two women sympathetic and even friendly. But as the questions grew more detailed, she started to worry. Langone had constructed a timeline of their visit to Monomoy and was fastidious in getting Stacie to affirm various events. Langone asked questions: "Now, how long do you think that took? Would you say ten minutes?"

When Stacie mentioned the walk that Carl and she took to the Atlantic side of Monomoy, the questioning grew slightly accusatory.

"You saw horse hoofprints in the sand? Real horse prints?" Martin said.

"Yes, I told you. We followed them. Ask Carl. He'll tell you."

"And the manure?"

"Yes. Like I said, ask Carl."

"It wasn't seaweed or something else from the ocean?"

"It was horse manure."

"You've seen horse manure before? At night?"

"You could smell it, for God's sake," Stacie said.

"And you told the Coast Guard about a legend involving a white stallion. You thought that maybe Mr. Lane was trying to fool you?"

"Yes, I think he was trying to tease or scare me. There's no other explanation for it. Unless you believe in ghosts and legends, which I don't."

"Neither do we," Martin said, smiling.

"But you also know the Coast Guard found nothing when they looked that night?" Langone said. "No horse manure, no horse prints, and no lantern."

"They said it was high tide and probably all of it washed away."

"Mmm," Langone said.

"Listen, I have to get going now. Please send me any additional questions by email or call me tomorrow."

"Can we just clarify a few things about how you found Mr. Lane?" Martin said. "It won't be but a few minutes more."

Stacie sighed, looked at her watch, and said, "Wouldn't it be better to talk to Carl, then talk to me?"

"You said you stayed on the beach when Mr. Lane returned to the keeper's house, correct?" Langone said, pressing ahead.

"Yes."

"Why did you stay alone on the beach? Why not go back with Mr. Lane?"

"I was tired and cold."

"But the house would have been warmer, no?" Martin said.

It was at that moment that a tiny bell rang inside Stacie's addled brain.

"Why are you asking me these questions? I'm beginning to think you suspect me of something. Do you?"

The two women stared at Stacie and said nothing.

"We're just looking for clarification," Martin said finally.

Stacie stood. "I'd like to ask you to leave, please. I don't like the drift of this conversation. It feels like an inquisition. Perhaps I need to talk to a lawyer."

Martin and Langone looked at each other.

"Well, it's your choice to have a lawyer present when you talk to us," Martin said.

"Our conversation is over," Stacie said. "Please leave now."

They stashed their notepads away in their briefcases and smiled again while Stacie walked them to the door.

"Have a nice day," Martin said, showing the tip of her canine one last time.

Stacie closed the door before Martin finished speaking.

CHAPTER 17

He was a nice enough doctor; he spoke slowly, smiled at Carl sympathetically, and did several things, like pointing a light at his pupils, asking him to follow his forefinger that he moved right to left. He even asked Carl to close his eyes and use the forefinger on his right hand to touch his nose, and then to repeat it with his left hand.

Carl could not find his nose with either finger unless he moved it off his forehead.

He was agitated by all their tests, including being put in a large, white, tube-like machine that made strange noises.

Perhaps the oddest experience was when he was visited by strangers. There was a woman and a young girl who spoke to him as if they were friends, but he had never seen them before. The girl started to cry, and he was glad when they finally left.

And he had a terrible headache that was relentless and exhausting. They gave him medicine that made him groggy.

Other people visited too, but he didn't like them. They appeared to be policemen and asked questions that he could not answer. He felt that they were trying to trick him somehow. After several visits, he told the doctor that he didn't want to see those men again. The visits stopped.

Most distressing of all for Carl was his confusion about why he was in a hospital. They told him he hurt his head, but he didn't remember how it happened. They told him he was a charter boat captain, but he only vaguely remembered something about a boat.

And they called him "Carl."

He was sure that he was *not* Carl, though he could not remember what his real name was. It was all very confusing. It made him frustrated and angry.

◉

"I called Scoccia at the refuge and he won't comment," Costello, the *Globe* stringer said.

"That's not surprising. He was pretty pissed off when I talked to him," Stacie said. "Have you been able to find Carl's former wife's married name? If the hospital won't talk, maybe she will."

"No luck on that either. And I told you, the Coast Guard is throwing it back to the DA's office. No one is talking. Should we quote you in the story? You were there."

"I don't know. Let me talk to Hanes. Either he or I will call you back."

"OK. I was told to file by six p.m."

Stacie hung up and emailed Hanes about whether she should be officially interviewed for the story. The DA's office still had not identified Carl or her by name.

Hanes emailed back: "Costello should interview you. Explain why you were at the lighthouse. He doesn't have to describe the details except that there was an accident, Lane was hurt, and Coast Guard was called in."

She emailed back: "Am I no longer on the story down here? Body of Monomoy drowning victim is still not identified."

"I need Smitty to weigh in. Hold tight," he answered.

Stacie got up from the table and drank a glass of water from the tap. The fleeting thrill of being Smitty's favorite reporter was now gone. One stupid boat trip to Monomoy had thrown the meteoric rise of a young reporter into a tailspin. Worse, there was the nagging fear that the DA's office thought she was involved in Carl's accident.

And what about Carl? she thought. Why won't they let me talk to him? Surely, he'd confirm everything she told the authorities.

A half hour later she got a follow-up email from Hanes.

"Smitty undecided on whether you should recuse self from coverage. Hang on down there."

"I need to check out," she emailed back. "Am I staying or going?"

She waited for twenty minutes, presumably because Hanes was checking.

"Staying for now," he finally emailed back.

Stacie no longer had a story to file; that was coming from Costello, and she had nothing to report on, so she took a long drive north to Well-fleet and Truro. She chatted with Marie while driving.

"That's insane," Marie said. "I don't like the DA's visit. Something is up with them. You need a lawyer. Don't you dare talk to them again without a lawyer present, you hear me?"

"Where the hell do I find a lawyer?"

"The *Globe* must have a retainer with a big Boston practice. You were on company time when the accident happened. Get them to provide one."

"But can you imagine what it would look like if I asked for a *Globe* lawyer? I mean, this isn't like I'm being threatened for writing a story about pedophile priests. The DA is focusing on me for doing something. It would look terrible at the *Globe*. I can't do that. It's professional suicide."

"What I don't get," Marie said, "is why the DA is focusing on you. Carl must have confirmed everything you told them."

"Yes, that's what's strange. I can't see him *not* confirming everything. Then again, I barely know the guy. Dammit, this whole thing feels like a nightmare."

"Hey, hey there, Stacie. Be strong. You can't be waffling right now. You did nothing wrong. Do you hear me?"

"Yes, I hear you. It's hard though. And I'm all alone down here."

"I'm going to poke around to see if I can find you a lawyer," Marie said.

"I can't afford a lawyer."

"You can't afford not to have a lawyer."

◎

The waves started to show themselves a hundred yards from shore as long, horizontal bumps in the otherwise calm Atlantic Ocean. As the waves approached the sandbank near shore, they suddenly rose higher into per-fect tubes until they collapsed and crashed into foam on the beach.

Stacie watched the surfers from on top of a high, sandy bluff at White Crest Beach in Wellfleet. Twenty feet away from her in the parking lot was a huge sign showing the face of a great white shark and warning bathers to be "Shark Smart."

There were only a handful of surfers in the water, and she marveled at their courage—or stupidity. There had already been several shark attacks on the cape in recent years, including a fatality.

Watching the rhythmic undulations of the waves rolling in, Stacie tried to make sense of what happened that night on Monomoy. She replayed the entire trip to Monomoy and was stumped by three events: the horse and lantern episode, the missing boat, and, finally, Carl's injury. Did something frighten Carl and he fell? Was someone else on the island? Who went through the trouble to put out horse prints in the sand, drop a load of manure, and leave a lantern burning? Ghosts? Like *real* ghosts?

Carl, she thought. I need your help.

◉

The bar was half full when she arrived, and she grabbed a stool. Stacie glanced around but could not identify anyone she had met before. She played with her phone and carefully sipped her white wine. After thirty minutes the place got busier, and the sound level rose.

"Hey," a voice said from behind her.

"Noog," she said, turning. "How are you?"

"How the hell are you?" he said. "What the fuck happened out there?"

"My God, I don't know. It's a complete and utter mystery to me. Have you talked to Carl?"

"No one's talked to Carl," he said.

"Why not?"

"He's not there, that's why."

"I don't understand. Did they move him to a Boston hospital?"

"No, there's a guy there that we call Carl. But the guy we call Carl says he's not Carl."

"Noog, what are you talking about? Does everyone here tease outsiders?"

He took a long sip of his beer, scanned the bar, then peered down at her on the stool.

"What did you do to him out there?"

"I didn't do anything to him, Noog. I found him on the stairs. I think he fell."

"Mmm," he said, taking another sip.

"I didn't hurt him. I'm sure he'll confirm that."

"Not any time soon."

"Is he not talking? No one will tell me anything about his condition. Maybe his former wife will talk to me? Do you know how to get hold of her or even her last name?"

"Nope."

"You must know how to reach her."

"Nope."

"Noog, what's going on here? Why are you being this way?"

"Carl is a very popular guy. We love him. Now this. Very strange."

"Noog, Carl will explain. I promise you."

"That Carl isn't here anymore. The new Carl doesn't know anything."

"What is it with the riddles? Jesus, I'm trying to help and all I'm getting are riddles and teasing. Sheesh. What a town. You folks don't like outsiders, do you?"

"We don't like bad outsiders, that's all."

"You think I'm a bad outsider?"

"All we know is Carl takes you to the lighthouse at night, and the next thing he's in a hospital with a brain injury and amnesia. You tell me."

"Amnesia! Carl has amnesia?"

"They say you pushed him to get a good story." He finished his beer in one long, accusatory gulp and put the empty glass on the bar.

"I wasn't even in the house when he fell, Noog. How could I push him?"

"Says who?"

"Says me," Stacie shot back, anger now rising in her voice. "I was there."

"Who else pushed him then?"

"Who says *anyone* pushed him? Why couldn't he just have slipped?"

"Carl wouldn't 'slip' down a set of stairs," Noog said, using air quotes with his fingers.

"Who stole his boat then?" she said.

"You cut the line. Everyone knows that. Makes a good story in the paper. You're the 'fame fatale.' That's your name on our Facebook group. Get it? 'Fame fatale' instead of femme fatale."

She closed her eyes and took a deep breath. When she opened them Noog was gone. When she looked around the bar, she saw several faces staring back. She paid her bill and left.

Driving back to the hotel, she called Marie.

"Hey, what's up? I'm out at a restaurant. Can we talk later?"

"He has goddamn amnesia!"

"Who?"

"Carl!"

"Oh shit. Stacie, I'll call you later. Really."

Stacie parked and decided to visit the main hotel building. Inside was a cozy bar, and she ordered a glass of white wine and ruminated.

Amnesia? she thought. Fame fatale?

After a second glass of wine, Stacie walked back through the manicured grounds of the resort to her room. The night air was cool, and there was a thin veil of fog filtering in from the Atlantic. Back in her room, she undressed quickly and went to bed. Tomorrow would be a better day, she told herself.

◎

She woke because of a ping from her phone. The clock radio showed 7:40 a.m.

There was a message from Neil.

Leave me alone, she thought, tossing the phone back onto the table.

When the phone pinged a second time she grabbed it and read the text:

u need to call asap

Stacie texted back: *stop*

He answered: *r u in trouble with police?*

She called him right away.

"I'm on the T," he said. "I can barely hear you."

"What's this about the police?"

"I got a call last night from a Detective Clancy of the state police."

"What did he want?"

"He knew we had dated."

"How'd he know that?"

"He wouldn't tell me. Said he was investigating an incident and was talking to people who knew you."

"Don't talk to him, Neil. Don't say anything."

"I already talked to him."

"What did you talk to him about?"

"Not much, really. Just thought you'd want to know."

"I do want to know. Thanks. Sorry if I sound harried. It's been tough down here."

"Where are you?"

"On a story in Chatham."

"Oh. Well, I hope everything is going OK."

"Not really, but that's just how it is sometimes. Thanks for checking in. Appreciate it, Neil. Take care."

"Wait. I suppose I should tell you something."

"What?"

"This detective spent a lot of time asking me questions about our relationship."

"What's there to tell? We dated. So what?"

"He kept me on the phone for a long time."

"Fine. Is that all?"

"He asked a lot of questions about your personality. And behavior. Stuff like that."

"My personality?"

"Like if you had a temper," he said.

"Temper? He asked that? And you told him what, exactly?"

"That you don't have a temper or a temper out of the ordinary."

"Well, that's damning with faint praise. Thanks."

"He asked if you were ever violent with me."

"I'm sure you detailed our vicious pillow fights."

"Ha. No, I didn't. There was mostly nothing to tell him."

"Neil! Mostly?"

"He kept pressing and pressing about any recollections I had of you being violent or physically aggressive."

"And the answer was 'no.'"

"All I could come up with was that time at my parents' house on Lake Winnipesaukee."

"Oh my God," Stacie said slowly. "Neil. What did you tell him?"

"I told him exactly what happened, so don't worry. Just thought I'd mention it to you."

Stacie's mouth felt dry and she licked her lips absently. She was still in bed on her side but suddenly sat up.

"What did you tell him?"

"I told him what happened, you know. It wasn't a big deal. I didn't think so. But, well, now that I think back—and that's why I texted you— he kept asking questions about that time on the boat dock. If there were any other witnesses. Stuff like that."

"Neil, please explain what you told him."

"I told him last summer we were at my parents' house at Winnipe- saukee, and that one of my sisters was there with her boyfriend. And that we had a dock."

"And?"

"And well, we were horsing around. And my sister pushed her boy- friend off the dock into the lake, and I shoved my sister in return."

"Oh shit," she said. "You didn't tell him."

"I just said that you snuck up behind me and pushed me in."

"And that was all?"

"No. I told him about the other part too."

◎

Stacie lay in bed staring at the ceiling for twenty minutes. When she first moved into the hotel room, it had seemed large and almost palatial. Now, it was smaller. Even the ceiling had gotten closer to her.

The phone rang and she reached for it.

"Hey, Marie," she said.

"I'm sorry I didn't call last night. But what's the story on the boat guy and amnesia?"

"I don't know for sure because I can't get any information on his condition. But that's what one of his buddies said. And rumors are floating around that I had something to do with his injury."

"That's ridiculous."

"Of course. But that's how they are down here. I've even got a nickname on a Facebook group."

"God, what a fine mess you're dealing with. So why don't you come back to Boston? Are you still on the story?"

"I don't think so. I should be checking out today and back in my apartment this afternoon."

"Great, let's grab a drink. Call me when you get in."

"Wait. I just got a call from Neil."

"Oh. Are you going to start seeing him again?"

"Not on your life. Maybe I'll see him in court, but not romantically, that's for sure."

"What are you talking about?"

"He said a state police detective called him about our relationship."

"How did they know about that?"

"I have no idea. But Neil was asked if I was ever violent with him."

"Boy, are they grasping at straws."

"Unfortunately, Neil mentioned that time we were horsing around on his parents' dock at Winnipesaukee. Do you remember that?"

"Vaguely."

"I pushed him off the dock into the lake."

"Big deal, Stacie."

"But he hit his head on the edge of the dock."

"Oh, yeah. He needed stitches."

"Yeah. Five friggin' stitches. And he had a concussion."

"So? You were goofing around. Please."

"Think about it, Marie."

Stacie waited while the line was silent. Outside the window, she could hear the whine of a groundskeeper working a leaf blower.

"Oh shit," Marie said.

CHAPTER 18

"You don't believe that stuff about staying on the beach by herself, do you?" Martin said, tapping her desktop with a pencil.

"I don't know. If she was scared of the guy, she might have," Langone said.

"Why would she be scared of him?" Clancy said.

"Didn't she say he teased her about seeing someone inside the lighthouse? And the horse and lantern thing?"

"Sarah, I know you've only been on the team here for eight months, and it's good to have an open mind, but you also need to be skeptical," Martin said. "We need to follow the evidence. That's all we can do. There's not a single bit of evidence that the horse thing happened. No horse, no horse shit, and no lantern."

"Well, there might be some bullshit flying around," Clancy chuckled. Martin smiled.

"And the boat?" Langone said.

"She cut the line," Clancy said. "She panicked after pushing him down the stairs and needed a reason why they were separated after he 'fell.'" He used air quotes and a smirk to emphasize the word "fell."

"Sorry, I'm having trouble with this theory," Langone said.

"She's a young, ambitious, conniving reporter," he said. "Her quick thinking turns a disaster into a great story. Except in real life, there are no boat pirates and no ghosts. Just an ambitious woman with a history of violence around men. But you have to admit, it's a *really good* story."

"The old boyfriend hit his head on a dock," Langone said. "Happens a hundred times a summer on docks throughout New England. There's no other evidence that she's been involved in a violent incident."

"I'm just starting," Clancy said. "We'll find more stuff like this, I'm sure of it. Remember, this guy Carl Lane could have died."

"But that would make Davis a psychopath," Langone said to Martin. "I didn't feel like we were in the presence of a psychopath when we interviewed her. It doesn't work for me."

"Sarah, please. We're not forensic psychiatrists. But in my experience, Davis certainly fits the definition of a sociopath who made a terrible mistake and is furiously covering it up. This woman is good. Remember, she writes *stories* for a living."

Langone shook her head and looked down at her notepad.

"Let's keep looking," Martin said, tossing her pencil onto the desk.

"Can I just say something?" Langone said.

"Sure," Martin said, with a patronizing smile.

"A week or so ago, a woman's body was found floating about a mile from that isolated lighthouse. It's still officially a suspicious death. Now, a guy almost dies in that lighthouse, and his boat is found floating in Nantucket Sound. Am I missing something?"

They both looked at Langone.

"You think there's a ghost there?" Clancy said, trying to control a smile.

"No, but I think *someone* is down there. Or was."

"What makes you think the two things are connected?" Martin said, turning her head slightly to look directly at Langone.

"A feeling," Langone said quickly.

"We work off evidence, Sarah, not feelings."

"And we work for a DA who hates the *Globe*," Clancy said. "Like really hates the 'Glob,'" as he calls it."

"There is *that*," Martin said.

"Then is Stacie Davis now a person of interest?" Langone said.

"Yes," Martin said. "We have no choice. Unless Lane recovers his memory and backs up Davis's account, we need to move the investigation forward."

"What if she calls back as a reporter, looking for information on the Jane Doe case?" Langone said.

"That won't happen," Martin said, a thin smile crossing her face. "Barone is taking care of that."

◎

Stacie was shocked by its swiftness.

"You need to return," Frank Stanford, the Metro editor said. "And you're officially on a paid leave of absence until further notice."

"What happened?" Stacie said.

"Smitty said it's too complicated to have you involved in any more reporting down there. He got a call from the DA. I can't discuss it, Stacie. Please try to understand that we can't have someone who is considered material to a police investigation also writing news stories on that subject. And until the situation is clarified, it's best if you take some time off."

"What clarification do you need?"

"Stacie, please. Just do what we ask. Don't make it harder."

"I'm not trying to make it harder, Frank, I'm just trying to understand what's happening."

"What's happening is that you're taking time off."

After the call, Stacie sat hunched on her bed and felt a wave of doom wash over her. How could this have happened? she thought. What did she do wrong?

She finally stood and continued to pack in slow motion, mulling the absurdity of her situation. She looked out the large window facing Aunt Lydia's Cove one last time. She followed a speedboat as it raced north following the shoreline of the barrier island in the distance. Beyond the island lay the restless Atlantic, whitecaps faintly visible as an easterly breeze jostled the water. Below her on the beach, two young children walked in front of their parents and picked up shells.

Her phone rang and she looked at the incoming number.

"Hello?"

"Stacie, this is Debra Falcone from the historical association."

"Oh, yes. How are you?" Stacie strained to sound animated.

"I have the copy of the diary you were looking for."

"Which diary?" Stacie said.

"You know. You asked to see the diary of the woman in Whitewash Village."

"Yes, of course. Sorry."

"I just sent you a PDF of the pages you were interested in."

"All right. Thanks."

"Is there anything else we can do for you?"

"No, I'm all set. Thanks for your help."

"By the way, we're sorry about the incident at the lighthouse," Falcone said. "I'm sure it was a very trying time for you and Mr. Lane. He's very popular in the town."

"Yes, so I gathered. It was a nightmare, to be honest. But I'm sure everything will be fine in the end."

"Of course," Falcone said.

Stacie continued to pack away her clothes. Before shutting down her laptop she looked at her emails. Three of them were from colleagues at the *Globe* asking whether it was true that she had been placed on leave. She was too depressed to respond.

One email was from Neil that she didn't open.

She saw the email from Falcone and the attached PDF.

"Dear Ms. Davis, this is the only reference we have on file to murders at Whitewash Village. It is a single entry and is not verified by any other documentation. If you insist on mentioning this information in an article, please caution your readers that this by no means is evidence that murders took place out there. Please contact us if you have further questions. Debra."

She opened the file that contained images of several handwritten pages that were stained and blotched with ink.

Curious, she expanded the file and read the diary entry.

June 2, a cold day with a wind from the north that makes the eyes weep not just of wind but of sad mourning. there is no rest for the peoples of the village. the fishin is begun in the Sound & the men are busy loading their nets & floats to partake of the bounty the sea profers. It is a most strenuous busines & full of dangers to chase those cod still nearby after a dredful winter time. Now with murdur on the peoples mind, it makes for a weary friteful time on this forsaken hill of sand & beech grass. My husband William is of a mind to leave this place on account of the murdur of Jane Fenster who was a nice woman, but prone to fits & such. She being the second murdur on this forsaken spit of sand bar has put fear in the peoples heart. I nor William did hear the scream 2 nights ago that others hurd with their own ears of the Fenster woman as this devil took her into to the dark waters & drownned her. They says there was much splashin and such noise like that from a beached blackfish but the body of Jane Fenster was not found on the land and is disapeered into Neptunes waters. William is suspicous of mr. Fenster who is not kind and curses grandly on his boat to keep other boats distant from his catch & also he smells bad. But that is not the general feelin in the village nor is it the prouncment of Rev. Joseph Cummin, who arrived today from the mainland. It is the devil itself he says that got hold of the Fenster woman & also Kathleen the young wife of Silas Adams 4 days beforehand. The young Adams woman that was kilt & drowned was a good, kindly woman except for her left eye was crossed a bit & made her seem bewiched but I did not think so. The poor woman was found the next day tied to mr. coyles float in the harbor. Rev. Cummin he says he knows of this devil & his evil ways choosin the women who are week in spirit & killing them as a show of his diabolic strenth & to confirm the weekness of the female kind. William is not of the belief that it is the devil that is doing this dark work, but a man here of flesh & blood he says. William is not of the religious mind & i do not vex him with my thoughts on this subjec. But it is most shurly the devil himself who has desended on this village. the Parker family is the first to state there intension to float there house to the mainland & leeve this village to the murdurin devil. William is of the mind to do the same, but only after the fish are caught & salted & sold. I am sad for mr. fenster and mr. adams who have lost their wifes to this evil creatur. But i am not week of spirit & believe in the one true Lord who protecs his flock.

Stacie read the diary entry twice, then stood and went to the large window facing the water and watched the waves ripple toward shore.

Murders on Monomoy, she thought. And devils. And ghosts.

She sighed and finished packing.

◎

"Please turn off the machine," Carl said. "The noise is driving me crazy. I have a headache."

The nurse smiled.

"We have to keep the monitor on," she said. "I'm sorry, but it's necessary."

"Why can't I go home?" he said.

"You can when you're better. The doctor will release you when you've healed. You had a bad head injury."

"Yes, that's what everyone says, but I can't stand it here anymore. The noise. The confusion. It's too much. I'm getting tired of it."

"Let me see if I can get the doctor to stop by," she said.

"There's a new doctor all the time. They aren't helping me get better."

"Let me get the doctor," she said, hurrying out of the room.

He lay back in bed and closed his eyes. He tried to blot out the sound of the beeping monitors.

Why are things so confusing? he thought. They say I've lost my memory and that it will come back. But they don't say when, and even if, all of it will come back. What happened to me?

"How are you feeling, Mr. Lane?"

Carl opened his eyes and saw a woman with short, dark hair and a white coat smiling at him.

"Are you a doctor?"

"Yes, I am. I'm Dr. Kaminski. I hear that you'd like to go home."

"Yes, thank you! I'm getting tired of being here. I bet I could get better at home. There's too much noise here. And the food sucks."

She laughed.

"I'm sure going home would be a good idea at some point."

"I'm glad you agree. You have an accent. Where are you from?"

"Poland originally," she said.

"Is that far from here?"

"Yes, it is."

He stared at one of the monitors beeping next to his bed.

"Can you make that one stop?"

"Not at this time. I know the sound must be irritating, yes?"

"I hate it. I feel like turning the damn thing off, but I don't know how."

"Please don't touch the machines, Mr. Lane. We need them on all the time. Perhaps we could increase your medications to make you feel less irritated."

"I'm not irritated. I just want to go home."

"Yes, I understand that you want to go home."

"When can I go?"

"May I ask you a question?"

"Of course."

"Where is your home?"

"My home?"

"Yes, where is the home that you want to go to?"

"I'm not completely sure," he said slowly, angry now that they had tricked him again into admitting to problems with his memory. "I know it's nearby. Maybe someone could just take me there."

"But where is your home?"

"It's nearby."

"Do you remember the address or the town?"

"Someone must know where it is, for God's sake."

"Yes, but do you?"

"Why does everyone keep asking where my home is? Just take me there! I'll recognize it. I promise."

"Of course. Please don't be upset. I'm going to prescribe something to make you more relaxed."

"I *am* relaxed."

"Of course you are, Mr. Lane."

◎

The apartment smelled stale, so Stacie opened the studio's only window facing Clarendon Street in Boston's South End.

She liked the familiarity of the city, the sounds of people walking

160

by on the brick sidewalk in front, the cars, the sirens, the smell of diesel exhaust. The weather was warmer in Boston than on the cape, so she turned on the small oscillating fan.

There was almost nothing in her refrigerator except some plain Greek yogurt, a bag of carrots, wilted celery, and three eggs.

On the drive back to the city, Stacie talked to two of her colleagues at the *Globe* who had heard rumors that she was on a leave of absence.

Stacie explained to them, without too much detail, that an accident had occurred on a story assignment, and that the editors thought it was best if she took some time off. She left it vague, but like good reporters, they kept pressing her for details.

Marie called to tell her she had emailed the contact information for a lawyer.

"What kind of lawyer?" Stacie asked.

"What kind do you want?" Marie said.

"A good one?"

"You are too funny, girl. He's a defense attorney."

"Feels weird to have a defense lawyer."

"Please don't talk to those people in the DA's office until you talk to this guy first."

"Do you know him?"

"No, but someone else here knows him. He's good."

"Is he expensive?"

"Stacie, talk to him about it, OK? Just call him ASAP."

Once she felt settled into her small apartment, Stacie dialed the law-yer's number. It was answered by an older woman.

"Doherty and Robinson law offices," she said.

"I'm looking for Samuel Doherty," Stacie said.

"He's in court right now. Can I ask what this is about?"

"I was referred to him," she said.

"Referred by whom?"

"Is that important?"

"He likes to know, that's all. Can I have your name and a number where he can reach you?"

Stacie gave the number and hung up.

God, she thought. A friggin' defense lawyer. How far you've fallen. I should probably call my mom, but she'll freak out. Maybe I'll wait on that.

Stacie took a walk down Clarendon Street to Boylston Street, then took a right toward the Public Garden. It was a nice day, and the park was crowded. She sat on one of the benches overlooking the pond swarming with Swan Boats. She always thought the pond and the iconic Swan Boats were charming and quaint. Now, after spending time in Chatham, the pond looked muddy, the boats forlorn and a little ragged. Even the squirrels in the Public Garden seemed fatter and more aggressive.

Her phone rang. It was a Boston number she didn't recognize.

"Attorney Doherty here, returning your call."

"Oh, thanks for getting back to me. I was referred to you by someone I know."

"Who's that? Do I know them?"

"No. She heard of you though."

"Well, that's good. How can I help you, Ms. Davis?"

"I need a lawyer."

"That's a start."

"I'm a reporter for the *Globe*. You should know that."

"Is this for a story you're working on?"

"No. It's for me. I need representation."

"For what? DUI? Shoplifting? Stealing quotes from another reporter?"

"Ha. Funny."

"It's a grim business, Ms. Davis. We like to yuk it up every now and then."

"Can we talk in person?"

"Well, first I like to find out whether I can help. I specialize in criminal cases, with a little civil stuff when it shows up. What's the nature of your legal problem?"

"Are you familiar with the Cape & Islands DA's office?"

"Yes, of course. I've worked a few cases down there."

"I was involved in covering a story on the cape. In Chatham, actually. And there was an accident."

"A car accident?"

"No, a man fell and hurt himself."

"OK."

"And, well, the DA's office down there seems to think I was involved in the accident."

"How do you know they think you're involved? Did they tell you?"

"Not in so many words. But they interviewed me."

"When did they do that?"

"Yesterday. They came to my hotel room and asked me a lot of questions. Then I found out this morning that the police have already talked to my old boyfriend."

"Why'd they talk to him?"

"I don't know. They asked him about my behavior and whether I was ever violent with him."

"Hold on. This accident you talked about; what happened?"

"The man I was with fell down some steps at a lighthouse."

"A lighthouse? Where were you when it happened?"

"I was on the beach near the lighthouse. Someone stole a boat."

"Whoa. I think we should meet in person. Call my office again and speak to Phyllis. She'll book you in. We're in Dedham. Can you get there all right?"

"Yes, that won't be a problem. I'll call Phyllis. Thanks, Mr. Doherty."

"Quick question: Who did you talk to in the DA's office down there? Who interviewed you?"

"It was Mary Martin. I think she's the first assistant DA. And an investigator named Sarah Langone."

"Martin interviewed you in person?"

"Yes, why?"

"Do yourself a big favor, Ms. Davis. Are you listening?"

"Yes."

"I don't represent you yet. We still have to figure that out. But under no circumstances should you talk to anyone in the DA's office without representation. Do you understand that?"

"Yes."

"Good. Call Phyllis."

CHAPTER 19

Stacie felt some comfort after talking to Doherty. If nothing more, she was no longer alone in this nightmare. And it was a full-blown, blood-sucking nightmare that was derailing her career and her reputation, not to mention her mental health.

She walked across the Public Garden to the Boston Common, worked her way up to Tremont, and passed the gaggle of homeless people and addicts at the corner of Tremont and Beacon streets. She continued down Tremont Street and past Emerson College.

It was only three o'clock on a weekday afternoon, but the city was churning with the early exit of commuters. She crossed into Chinatown and onto Stuart Street, and finally made it to Columbus Street where it merged at Park Square. She stopped at the CVS at the corner of Columbus and Clarendon streets, and bought some bottled water, a small container of milk, and a box of crackers.

She had barely stepped foot inside her apartment when her phone rang. It was a cape exchange.

"Hello?"

"Is this Stacie Davis?"

"Yes, it is."

"This is Sarah Langone in the DA's office. We met yesterday."

"I remember."

"We'd like to set up a time when you could come into the office for some additional questions."

Stacie froze, pressing the phone against her ear.

"More questions? Is this an official request?" Stacie said.

"Yes."

"Do I have the option to decline?"

"Yes. But be advised that we may seek a subpoena requiring you to come in for questioning. Usually, it's easier just to answer the questions."

"I'll have to talk to my lawyer first."

"Sure. Have your lawyer call this office and ask for me."

"OK."

"Do you want the number?"

"No. That's not necessary."

Stacie put down the phone, opened the refrigerator, and put the milk in. She stood staring into the open refrigerator for several minutes. She felt scared and utterly alone as the cold air swirled about her.

She closed the door, sat down, and called Doherty's office. Stacie told Phyllis that she needed to schedule a meeting with the attorney as soon as possible.

Twenty minutes later Doherty called, and Stacie described Langone's request.

"For the immediate future, I will be representing you, Ms. Davis. Again, do not discuss this case with anyone. Is that clear?"

"Yes."

"I'm going to call down there and see what they're up to. I'll call you back if I hear anything. Meanwhile, I think we have an appointment tomorrow, correct?"

"At ten o'clock in Dedham."

"Good. Hang tight. Let me find out what's going on."

She hung up. Her mouth was dry, and she opened one of the bottles of water and took a sip. She opened the box of crackers and ate a handful of them to calm her queasy stomach.

Then she started to cry. At first, they were little sobs, but soon she was crying loudly. She got up and grabbed a paper towel to wipe her face.

can we grab dinner tonight? she texted Marie. *I need someone to talk to*

While she waited for Marie's response, she kept crying. Finally, she washed her mascara-smeared face. Looking at her bloodshot eyes in the mirror, Stacie could not recognize the cocky, intuitive reporter who had a knack for a nice twist of words and a fiery ambition to succeed.

The woman in the mirror was broken and lost.

She sat on the small stuffed chair, put in her earbuds, and played one of her favorite, up-tempo playlists: anything to get her away from the gloom that weighed her down.

shit, have a date tonight, Marie texted back finally. *maybe after date? will u b up?*

never mind, have fun, she answered.

hang on, Marie answered.

go on the date! Stacie texted.

After another ten minutes Marie texted back: *canceled date. 6 pm at chandler's*

◉

The law office was in the old downtown section of Dedham. Stacie had trouble finding a parking space. She was a little hungover from her dinner the night before with Marie. She tried to take Doherty's advice to not talk about her growing legal problems, but she couldn't resist with Marie. By the end of the dinner, she was depressed, a little tipsy, and scared. Marie walked her home.

Now, sitting in the law office's small waiting area, Stacie tried to read a two-year-old copy of *Sports Illustrated*, but only managed to turn the pages mechanically. Her stomach was acting up again and she felt nauseous.

A door opened down the hallway and she heard footsteps. She looked up to see a huge man standing in front of her. He had a full head of shockingly white hair, a bulbous nose, and huge ears. She guessed he was easily over six feet tall and weighed in the neighborhood of two hundred and twenty pounds.

"Ms. Davis?"

"Yes," she said, standing.

"Sam Doherty. Come on down." His huge hand enveloped hers whole, like a whale swallowing a mouthful of krill.

He led the way down the hallway and into his office. His desk was covered with loose papers and folders, as well as several coffee mugs, one of which held a dozen pens.

"Sit," he said, pointing to one of two chairs in front of his desk.

After settling, he smiled and leaned back in his heavy office chair.

"You seem to be in the crosshairs of the DA down there, Ms. Davis."

"Can you call me Stacie?"

"Sure. And you can call me Sam, if that works for you."

"OK."

"Before we get into the details of the case, I need to tell you that I spoke to Langone yesterday."

"Oh. Good, I guess."

"You're officially a person of interest, Ms. Davis—sorry, Stacie. Do you know what that means?"

"Not really."

"It means they believe you have important information about an investigation."

"Am I, like, a suspect? Are they charging me with anything?"

"No, you're not officially a suspect. There are no charges against you. But you are being asked to provide information. I can't say that one day they *won't* bring charges, but from the outline of the case so far, I doubt that."

"Do I have the right *not* to talk to them?"

"Yes, but I don't think that will help. I recommend you talk with them and that I sit in with you. But first, you need to agree to have me represent you, and you need to know my fee structure."

"I don't have much money," she said.

"That's OK, most folks don't have it right away. I require a $5,000 retainer to start."

"I don't have that much money in cash," she said.

"Don't worry about that right now. This is incredibly stressful for people suddenly caught up in the legal system. I'd like you to take a deep breath while I ask Phyllis to bring you some water, or do you prefer coffee or tea?"

"Coffee. With milk or cream. Either one."

"After that, I'm going to take out my legal pad, and you and I are going to sit at that little table over there, and you're going to start at the beginning. I've got ninety minutes allotted, so we better get going. We've got to get prepared for your interview."

◎

"I'm trying to be strong, Mom," she said. "It's just hard, that's all. And the leave of absence thing—that's embarrassing. All because of a stupid story about Cape Cod."

"Stacie, do you want to come home? Take a break from the city?"

"Not right now, unfortunately. I need to prepare for that meeting with the DA's office."

"Do you think this attorney is good enough?"

"I think he's going to be fine. I'm the one I'm worried about."

"Stacie, listen to me. You have *always* risen to the occasion. You're a strong woman, and you need to dig deep to find your resolve. You *will* get through this and be back to work."

"I knew you'd make me feel better," Stacie said.

"How much did you say the lawyer is charging?"

"He needs $5,000 to start. I've got $1,200 in savings."

"And the newspaper is not going to help you?"

"They haven't offered, and to be honest, I'd be just as happy if they didn't get involved. I need to keep my record there unblemished, if that's even possible now. My God, what a mess, Mom. It just happened completely out of the blue. One moment I'm on a charming little sand-covered island with an old lighthouse, and the next moment I'm in this huge mess."

"I'm sending you $5,000," she said.

"No, Mom. I'll put it on my credit card."

"I'm sending you the money. Cash the check or don't cash the check. I'm not leaving my daughter to the wolves."

"You don't have the money either, Mom."

"Stop worrying about me, Stacie. I'm a mother. This is what we do."

Stacie laughed. "Thanks, Mom. I love you."

"I love you too, darling. Stay strong, OK? And call me daily."

"Yes."

"And please consider coming home for some R & R?"

"I will. I promise."

◉

"This is Dr. Bentley, Carl. We've invited him to consult on your case," Dr. Kaminski said. "He's from Brigham and Women's Hospital in Boston, and he's an expert on amnesia. We don't see many cases down here."

Carl was tired of the hospital, the beeping machines, and the confusion. By now he understood something was wrong with his memory. He even had trouble remembering new information, like a nurse's name or what day of the week it was.

The most upsetting aspect of the disorder was his identity; the real Carl Lane was an accumulation of millions of pieces of stored memory, but this damaged Carl Lane could not access those memories. Therefore, he was no one.

"Hi, Carl," Dr. Bentley said. "I've looked at your chart and talked to your physicians here. Do you mind if I examine you?"

"No. Just don't make me touch my nose with my finger."

The two physicians laughed.

Dr. Bentley used a penlight and flashed it into Carl's eyes. He asked him to stand up and close his eyes. Carl had done this many times before, and he knew they watched to see if he swayed or lost his balance.

After the neurological exam, Dr. Bentley said, "You are doing well, Carl. Now, it's a matter of how much of your memory you're going to get back. We call this retrograde amnesia, and in some cases, your entire lost memory will return. Often though, some memories are lost. Do you understand that?"

"They already told me that."

"I see that you've been able to recover some memories, right?"

"I guess. I mean, I remembered I have a boat, but I don't know its name, or where it is."

"You also remembered that you were married once and have a daughter," Dr. Bentley said.

"Well, I sort of remember. I was told the woman who visited me was my former wife, and the girl was my daughter. I know the girl cried the last time she was here."

"I'm sure she's just trying to get used to your condition, Carl," Dr. Bentley said. "Hopefully, as you heal, you'll retrieve more memories."

"Why do the police keep asking to talk to me?"

"I guess they're hoping you can remember what happened. It appears you fell down some steps."

"That's what they say. I wish I could remember, but I don't. It's very frustrating, and I know I get a little angry at times."

"That's normal, Carl. It'll get better."

"When will it get better?"

"The brain is a very complex organ, and when it gets knocked around like yours did, we just have to wait to see how it heals."

"Why can't I go home?"

"You live alone, as I understand it, Carl, and you need around-the-clock care. Once you're at a certain point, you'll be going to a rehab facility to work on your coordination and stamina. We don't want you falling again."

"When can I go there?"

"Soon, Carl. Very soon."

After the doctors left, Carl got out of bed and wobbled to the window, and looked down on the hospital's parking lot. He wanted to leave the hospital so badly that he often fantasized about sneaking down the elevator and out into the parking lot to escape.

He was tired of talking to doctors. They never helped him.

Plus, he was keeping a secret from them.

Carl could remember some things that disturbed him about a lighthouse.

◎

Doherty drove Stacie down to the DA's office in his Mercedes sedan and rehearsed with her how she should respond to their questions.

"Remember, don't guess at an answer," he said as if he'd recited these directions a million times. "Just say you don't know, or you don't remember. You're not trying to please them, no matter how polite and friendly they appear. Don't let them suck up to you or compliment you to make you feel comfortable. They are *not* your friends. They're looking for discrepancies and anomalies in your story. Stacie, right now you are the only person able to describe what happened that night. The other person doesn't remember. Or that's what he says."

"What does that mean?"

"He could be lying."

"Why would he do that?"

"I have no idea. People are strange, Stacie. They have strange impulses and desires. They steal when they don't have to or lie when the truth is much easier. I don't write the rules, I just try to understand them. And rule number one is—people are just weird."

"Do you think Carl is lying?"

"He could be. Why do you act so surprised?"

"But he had a severe head injury."

"Meaning he can't lie? Since when is that a medical certainty?"

"Maybe you're being a bit too cynical."

"And maybe you're being a bit too naïve," he said. "I'm sorry if my view is a little harsh, but I live in the criminal justice ecosystem. It's a grim world."

"Mmm," she said. "I just want this whole thing to go away."

"It will if you're careful today. Remember—I know this is so stupid that you're going to laugh—but there will be a good cop and a bad cop today. The bad cop will bait you, and the good cop is going to be your friend. The reason they keep doing good cop, bad cop is because it works. And as I've already mentioned ten times, they can lie and will lie."

CHAPTER 20

The room was small and bright, with white walls and a simple rectangular white table. Sitting across from Stacie and Doherty were State Police Detective Clancy and Trooper Sarah Langone.

After introductions, Langone started by asking Stacie to describe the evening's events again. Doherty had warned Stacie that they were going to compare her current description to the details she already provided to Langone and Martin.

It took Stacie twenty minutes to describe all the elements of the incident on Monomoy.

Neither Clancy nor Langone interrupted, but both took notes and continued to consult notes in open manila folders each had in front of them.

When she finished, Stacie was sweating slightly, and her palms were wet with perspiration. It unnerved her that the two investigators barely commented.

Langone opened with a series of questions about timing—the exact time that she and Carl arrived at Monomoy, what time they started walking to the lighthouse, how long it took, and every other activity.

Stacie answered with vague estimates, just as Doherty had prepared her to do. As the questions continued, she wondered whether Clancy was simply observing, since he never spoke. But that changed.

"What was your interest in Carl Lane?" he said suddenly.

"I don't know what you mean," she said.

"Your interest. Did you find him attractive? He seemed like a good-looking guy."

"Attractive?"

"Yeah. Were you attracted to him?"

"Not particularly. He seemed like a nice guy."

"Is that why you went to dinner with him earlier in the week, because he was a nice guy?"

"Yeah, more or less."

"But you weren't attracted to him in any way?"

Stacie glanced at Doherty, who seemed to nod slightly.

Ah, she thought. The bad cop. Of course.

"If you're asking whether I was interested in having a romantic relationship with Carl Lane, the answer is no."

"But you weren't dating anyone at the time. You had just broken up with Neil, right? Your old boyfriend?" Clancy said, smirking.

"He broke up with me."

"That's not what he said," Clancy said, leaning forward.

"He's wrong or you misunderstood him."

"So, you knew Neil was seeing someone else then? He was cheating on you."

Stacie flushed; the blood rushed to her cheeks and her mouth grew taut at the corners.

"No," she said slowly.

"No, what?" he said.

"No, I didn't know he was seeing someone else. He never told me."

"He thinks you found out and were angry."

She shrugged, trying to control her composure. "I didn't know."

"You must have been furious," he said.

"I said I didn't know. How could I be furious if I didn't know?"

"He said you knew."

"He's an idiot and a fool," she said. She felt Doherty's eyes burning into the side of her face.

"It must be humiliating when a man doesn't return your affection," he said, smiling.

"No more humiliating than sitting here and listening to your garbage."

"My client would like to take a break now," Doherty said.

"No, I'm fine. Let's keep going."

Stacie *was* angry, and she could care less about hiding it.

"When you get angry, you sometimes get physical," Clancy said.

"I don't think so."

"You hurt Neil pretty bad that time you shoved him on the dock in New Hampshire."

"It was an accident and a while ago. It was a minor injury. We were all horsing around."

"You're kidding. Five stitches and a concussion. That's minor?"

"He was fine, believe me."

Clancy kept up the attack for several more minutes, raising his voice at times for emphasis. Stacie realized that she was following his emotional lead, getting upset as he upped the ante.

And before she knew it, he dropped the bomb.

"Carl didn't like you coming on to him that night in the lighthouse, did he?"

"What?"

"It must have made you furious. Another man rejecting you. Like Neil. So, you did to Carl what you did to Neil."

"What?"

"A shove was all it took. Gravity took over then."

"I wasn't even there!" she yelled. "I was on the beach."

"I don't think so. Our timeline shows you and Carl were never on the beach looking for his boat. You were still back in the house. You lured him upstairs."

"That's ridiculous!"

"And after he rejected your attempts to get intimate, you snapped and pushed him."

"No!"

"And then you raced back to cut the anchor line. You needed to come up with a crazy reason why you two hadn't left already. You needed pirates."

"You're out of your friggin' mind."

"My client would like to take a break," Doherty said.

◉

He took both her hands and enveloped them in his huge paws. Doherty drew his face close to hers.

"I thought you were smarter than that."

"I guess not."

"You're going to be in trouble if you continue to let them control you."

"Yes, I understand."

"Stacie, I'll repeat it one more time—they have no case. The only case they might have is one that you help them build. Stick by your original story and don't deviate. Don't get angry. Anger is a powerful emotion—emotion leads to outbursts, outbursts lead to mistakes, mistakes lead to charges. Make sense?"

"Yes."

The second session was run by Langone. She again focused exclusively on the timeline. Stacie could not read Clancy's demeanor since he simply stared at her. Langone appeared interested in two events: the visit to the Atlantic side of Monomoy, and the beach scene where they discovered Carl's boat was missing. It was clear that they did not believe Stacie and Carl walked to the beach, found the boat was missing, and then split up.

Langone had come up with a timeline that showed a discrepancy in how much time Stacie and Carl were apart.

Stacie repeated everything she had said before. When Langone insisted that Stacie's description of events did not make sense in terms of timing, Stacie simply shrugged.

"You're mistaken," she said.

Soon, Langone ran out of questions. Clancy never uttered another word, and they ended the session.

"You did good in part two," Doherty said on the drive back.

"Do you think they have a case?"

"A case for what?"

"A case that says I tried to come on to Carl and got angry when he didn't respond. That I pushed him down the steps. *That* case."

He laughed. "Let me repeat—there's nothing there! I'd be shocked if they got a judge to give them a subpoena for your phone records."

"My phone records? Like texts?"

"Yeah, why?"

"Doesn't that seem a little invasive?"

"Of course it is. It's what investigators do. Why are you concerned?"

"I never thought they'd check my texts."

"Is there a problem with your texts?"

"I don't think so," Stacie said, though she wondered if some of her texts to Carl were overly flirtatious.

"Listen, Stacie. Try to relax. I can't see them moving forward with this investigation. I get surprised now and then, but I can't see Barone giving this one the green light."

"I wonder if he was lying about Neil cheating on me?" she said, looking out the side window. "That caught me off guard, to be honest."

"He could have been lying. The only way to tell is to ask Neil, but I'd leave it alone for now."

"Still, it kind of hurts."

"Clancy was trying to shock you."

"It worked. I had no idea that Neil was capable of that. There are lots of things I don't seem to know."

His car phone rang. Phyllis was reporting in on a stream of other cases and inquiries. Stacie was shocked at how many cases he had going simultaneously. How did he keep it all organized?

He hung up and then used voice assist to dial a number. Stacie listened while Doherty jostled with a Suffolk County assistant DA about a plea bargain. It was a fascinating inside view of the hidden world of the criminal justice system. Perhaps she'd try to do a piece or a series on it one day.

Then her career predicament struck hard; she was a meteor that had risen and fallen to Earth in a flash. She'd be lucky to cover the MBTA after this ended. *If* it ended.

◉

"Sarah, I don't get what you were doing," Clancy said. "She was clearly hiding something and started to crack. Then at the break, you tell me that you're taking over. And all you do is ask about the stupid timeline."

"I felt your questioning wasn't productive," Langone said. "She didn't crack."

"She most certainly started to crack," he said, looking at Martin.

"If by cracking you mean crying, then yes, you 'cracked' her a little bit," Langone said. "But in my opinion, her tears are not going to get us anywhere."

"Since when are you an expert on when someone cracks?" Clancy said.

"Please," Martin said to Clancy.

"I feel it's my responsibility to raise questions about malfeasance," he said. "We had that woman. She pushed that poor guy down the steps."

"Says who?" Langone said.

"Says me, that's who."

"That's enough!" Martin said. "Jesus, Mary, and Joseph! To make this stick, we're going to need Lane to get his memory back. I'm not going to Judge Santini for a subpoena on her phone or geolocation data. He'd laugh me out of the courtroom with what we have so far. Sarah, keep checking with the hospital. We need Lane. Otherwise, this thing is closed. I know Barone won't like it, but he's happy enough that he got under the skin of the *Globe*. Small political victories are worth their weight in gold."

◉

The idea struck Stacie when she was shopping for groceries on Huntington Avenue. As she stood in the checkout line with her basket, a tall black man wearing blue hospital scrubs stood in front of her. He appeared fresh from work and hadn't changed clothes. Staring at his broad back and the baggy scrubs, she had an inspiration.

Why not? she thought. Why the hell not? No one else is helping me, except me. I'll do it myself.

CHAPTER 21

The physical therapy was not particularly helpful, but Carl went along with some of the simple exercises. He liked to walk the hallway, and they let him walk only if he held the arm of the therapist. He could not walk fast, nor let go of her, but otherwise he could shuffle down the ward, peeking into rooms with people in various forms of distress. It was depressing, and he wanted desperately to get out.

But complaining was not how to get out, he discovered. They wanted Carl to be calm, able to walk steadily, have no signs of balance issues, and to be able to see clearly. He no longer had excruciating headaches, and the medicine they gave him to ward off seizures seemed less troublesome. All in all, he knew they were going to release him soon.

Initially, he had a lot of visitors, but lately, they had tapered off. He knew it was because he didn't recognize them, and they would invariably lose interest in making small talk. What else could they talk about besides the weather and the hospital room? One guy, with the funny nickname of Noog, kept talking about huge schools of striped bass hitting the rips chasing squid.

Carl didn't know what to say to Noog; he could remember a little bit about the rips off Monomoy, but he had trouble talking at length. Noog had grown frustrated and finally left. That happened to most of the visitors: they lost interest once they had no common memories. The woman who was his former wife told a nurse that Carl might as well have Alzheimer's, whatever that meant.

The evenings were the worst. Many patients on the ward had visitors, and the sound of giggling children, the festive, metallic-looking vinyl balloons, the smell of flowers, and the laughter were depressing. He tried to watch TV detective shows or game shows, but he would invariably lose interest. Reading was impossible for him.

"Hey, Carl," someone said at the door.

He saw a young, attractive woman standing with some flowers in her hands.

"How are you doing?" she asked, moving closer.

"Same old, same old," he said. He had heard the patient in the next room use that saying, and he stole it. The nurses thought it was funny when he repeated it over and over.

"I brought you some flowers," Stacie said. "Kind of dorky, really, but I didn't know how to convince them that I'm your sister. Do you even have a sister?"

"I don't know, do I?"

"Tonight, you do."

"OK."

She put the flowers down on a chair and then walked over to his bedside.

"Your hair is growing back, I see," she said.

"I guess."

"It's darker now. It looked lighter before, but that must have been the sun." She smiled. "Do you know who I am?"

"Not sure."

"Do I look familiar?"

Carl stared. There was something about her face that he recognized. Or maybe it was her voice.

"My name's Stacie Davis. You don't recognize me, do you?"

"Your voice."

"My voice? You recognize my voice?"

"Maybe."

"Do you recognize anything else? I'm wearing the same clothes I wore that evening. Except for the boots. Those were your boots."

For the first time since he entered the hospital, Carl felt a rush of fear.

His emotions normally vacillated between confusion, frustration, and boredom. But now he was suddenly frightened.

"Go away," he said. "Don't hurt me."

"Why would I hurt you?"

He started to hyperventilate. His lungs felt like pricking needles. It was the secret he had been holding all this time. If he told them, they would think he was crazy, not just a person with amnesia, but a *crazy person* with amnesia. He could feel it next to him. The voice. The flash of pain. The darkness.

"Carl, I'm going to leave now. I'm sorry for what happened to you. I hope you get better soon."

After several minutes, a nurse came in.

"Carl, are you all right?" she said, looking at the beeping monitor. "Your blood pressure is pretty high right now. We need to get that down. You're scheduled to be released this week. They won't let you leave if your BP is too high."

She left and he stared at the wall; his eyes focused on a smudge.

◎

Stacie checked into the motel. It was already past ten at night, and she was reeling from the visit to the hospital. She thought her appearance would jog Carl's memory into some semblance of order, but the opposite occurred. He looked frightened, not to mention thin and agitated.

Why was he scared? she thought. What did I *do* that night on Monomoy?

There were times, usually late at night, when Stacie wondered what really happened on Monomoy. Did she remember events clearly? Did something terrible occur that she was blocking out? Did she come on to Carl and he rejected her? Did she get angry and shove him? Would Carl have gone through the trouble to recreate the Legend of the White Stallion just to scare her?

There were only two plausible scenarios for what happened on Monomoy that night: either everything happened *exactly* as Stacie remembered it, or something so horrible happened that she would not *allow* herself to remember.

Stacie crawled into bed, turned off the light, and tossed and turned for an hour. She had returned to Chatham to find out what happened. Her mother was right. She needed to dig deep inside herself to find strength and resolve. Either that or give up. Then she fell asleep.

◎

"My God, I thought you'd fallen off the face of the Earth," Prescott said. "Where have you been?"

"I went back to Boston," Stacie said. "I had to settle some things. And I took some time off from work."

"And you're here now?"

"Yes, and I have a favor to ask."

"For a mystery writer, those are interesting words."

"You have a boat, correct?"

"Yes," he said slowly.

"Would you take me to Monomoy and drop me off for a couple of hours?"

"Why would you want to go *there*?"

"I'd like to retrace the route that night. Maybe I'll remember something. It was a strange night."

Silence.

"Winslow?"

"Yes?"

"Is that something you can do?"

"I suppose. Are you sure you want to do that?"

"Yes."

"When did you want a lift out there? And don't say 'at night' because I won't do that. If I take you at all, it has to be in daylight."

"Today."

"Did you check with the Wildlife Service to see if it's OK?"

"I don't need their permission to visit Monomoy. It's open to the public."

"Well, I haven't checked the weather and tides," he said.

"I have," she said. "Five-miles-per-hour northeast breeze and high tide out there around one o'clock in the afternoon."

"Who are you taking out there with you?"

"No one; just me."

"I admire your enthusiasm," Prescott said, "but don't you think this is a bad idea?"

"Not at all. If you don't want to take me out there, I understand. There's a ferry service I can pay for, but I thought of you."

"How long are you going to be down there?"

"Two hours max."

He sighed. "I suppose I can take you down. Are you prepared to get your feet wet?"

"I'll be prepared."

"Very well. Can you be here at the house by ten this morning?"

"Absolutely."

"See you then."

"You're a peach," Stacie said.

◉

"Mom, I wish you wouldn't have sent the money," Stacie said, sitting in the motel. "You don't have the money for this. I've got it covered."

"Don't be silly. Your brothers chipped in. We're all worried sick. And why aren't you answering their calls?"

"Oh, Mom. I feel so ashamed of the entire thing. I can't even talk about it anymore. It's depressing. I did text them that everything was OK."

"But they wanted to talk to you, Stacie. Families do stuff like that. Your father called me too."

"He did? How did he find out?"

"He said a friend emailed him. He said you weren't answering his calls either."

"I haven't talked to Dad in a long time. And I would hate our conversation to be about my legal problems."

"He just wants to help, Stacie. You shouldn't cut him off like that."

"I'm too confused right now about everything. I'll be OK. I just need some time. I promise I'll check in with everyone soon."

"And you won't come home for a visit?"

"Not right now, Mom. Very soon though. Got some things to work out first."

◉

Prescott's boat was moored to a small dock at the base of his property. They walked down the steep wood steps that changed directions three times. He lived on the Oyster River near a popular beach. It was a tidal river that emptied into Stage Harbor near its entrance to Nantucket Sound.

His boat, a twenty-five-foot Grady White center console, was elaborate and new. It was powered by two 250-horsepower Yamaha outboard motors.

"I guess this is the good life," Stacie said, looking around the expensive homes with spectacular views.

"Well, it doesn't hurt to sell twenty million books," he said.

"But you're good at it," she said. "People enjoy your books."

"Then *you* can write my next one," he said. "It gets old and tiresome. The interminable book tours. Strangers gushing about my books as if they were literary masterpieces, for heaven's sakes. I write popular mysteries. In my books some people live, some get killed, and some get away."

"Maybe you're being a little too harsh about your talents," Stacie said.

"Perhaps. And perhaps I'm behind on my next book."

"I like your boat. Do you use it much?"

"No, of course not. I used to run down to Nantucket to see friends for lunch. It's only about forty minutes from here. But Marci now refuses to get on a boat. So, I pretend to go fishing now and then."

"Do you catch anything?"

"Heavens no. That's why they call it 'fishing,' and not 'catching.' I fish but do not catch. It would ruin the experience of endless frustration to actually catch something."

Stacie laughed.

Prescott suddenly looked at her, his face drawn and serious.

"Stacie, are you sure you want to do this? I told Barbara what you were doing and she almost fainted. We believe there's bad karma down there."

"It would be bad karma for me *not* to go down there. Please, let's go."

"I tried," he sighed. The engines roared to life. He asked her to untie the stern line and he undid the bow line. They navigated the small tidal river and were soon into Stage Harbor and out the narrow cut into Nantucket Sound.

"Hold on," he said, and pushed the throttles forward. The boat's nose reared up slightly, then flattened out onto a plane, and flew south past several boats returning from the rips off Monomoy.

Stacie remembered that this was the joy she had felt when she and Carl ventured to Monomoy that evening. The wind, the noise of the engines, and the fresh salt air were invigorating. She looked at Prescott and smiled.

He frowned and yelled above the roar: "I wish you weren't doing this."

She made a lame smile.

He shook his head.

It took only eighteen minutes from the moment they powered up leaving Stage Harbor to reach the beach on Monomoy. Stacie felt a swirl of anxiety when she saw the lighthouse jutting up like a single, forlorn red candle.

"I'm going to nose into the beach and turn broadside at the last moment," he said. "You'll have to jump off. I can hand you the backpack once you're on terra firma."

Stacie sat on the side of the boat, pulled off her hiking boots and socks, and stuffed them into her pack. She rolled up her pants legs. Prescott raised the engines slightly as he nudged the boat to shore, then turned them off and raised them completely out of the water. He swung the boat sideways and nearly onto the beach. She jumped and landed in two feet of water with a splash. He reached over and handed her the pack.

"I'll be back in exactly two hours, young lady. Your phone probably doesn't work down here, so be ready. *Please* be careful."

She gave him a thumbs-up. He drifted slowly away from the shore, then lowered the engines and started them up. He waved once, then roared north.

Stacie sat at the top of the beach, where the path into the island started. She had brought along a motel towel and dried her feet, brushing as much sand as she could off them, before putting on her socks and boots.

KEITH YOCUM

She brought a can of insect repellant and sprayed her shoes, pants, and arms liberally.

She scanned the beach area. It seemed different in the full light of a sunny day; that evening the colors had been impressionistic pastel splashes of pink and purple from the setting sun. The water that night had looked like squid ink gently rippling in the rising tide.

Now, the landscape was bleached out—brilliant white sand, dead black seagrass clumped at the waterline, and scraggly gray-green foliage in the island interior. The water was a clear blue-green color and lapped gently against the sandy beach. She stood and walked toward the lighthouse.

The path was narrow and winding, but she navigated the correct path when it forked. After twenty minutes of walking, with sweat now rising on her neck and face, she stopped a hundred yards from the lighthouse and looked up at the small promontory it rested upon.

The keeper's house was stark and out of place amidst the windswept sand and bent shrubs. The house's shingles were a weathered New England gray, offset by the blazing white window and door trim. The lighthouse was attached to the left of the house.

The lighthouse was the only object of unnatural color on the island. It was painted a dull red, with a black top section and black metal railing all around the glass windows. The railing supports were S-shaped, holding three evenly spaced thick metal wires to protect the keeper from falling. Above the lighthouse was a decorative round finial topped by a weather vane in the shape of a duck or goose with its wings flapped downward.

The lighthouse design looked overly decorative, almost Turkish. She stared at the vertical glass windowpanes surrounding the top, half expecting to see someone staring down at her. The lighthouse was empty.

To the right, about fifty yards from the building sat a small brick shed, painted a faded white. Stacie had not noticed the shed that night in the dark. She continued her walk to the lighthouse and up onto the porch surrounding the keeper's house. She peered into the single window facing north and saw a cot, some printed materials, and a rolled-up sleeping bag.

She knocked on the door and yelled, "Hello! Anyone home? Hello?"
After several attempts, she followed the deck around to the back
of the house. She knocked on the back door and yelled again. No one
answered, so Stacie reached for the knob and turned it. The door was
unlocked.

Her heart was beating wildly, so she released the door handle and
stood back to gather herself. Did she really want to go in there? Something was frightening and strange about this house. Finding Carl at the
base of the landing was the most disturbing event in her life. She walked
around in a small circle behind the house, challenging herself to enter.

What was she looking for? What did she hope to find? Was there a
ghost in there? Would it try to hurt her? What was *it* trying to protect?
More rationally, what was *Stacie* trying to protect? What did she do that
night that she was hiding from?

After several minutes, she took a deep breath, approached the door,
turned the knob, and stepped into the house.

◉

Carl's dreams were typically a kaleidoscope of nonsense. He sat on
the edge of his hospital bed, rubbing his chin, and thinking about the
strange dream the night before. Like other recent dreams, he fell a long
way into a deep black hole. But in this dream, his fall started differently.
He heard a high-pitched voice calling his name. And instead of effort-
lessly flying facedown into a void, he felt a sharp, painful jolt to his body
and landed in an unpleasant, viscous void that felt like drowning in oil.

He sat on his bed dressed in clothes his former wife Grace gathered
from his apartment.

"Hey, dude," someone said at the door.

Carl turned.

"You ready to get the hell out of here?" Noog said.

"Yep. Let's do it," Carl said.

"They said you got better fast. Like real fast."

Carl smiled. "Wicked pissah fast. They said it might happen that
way. But I just want out of here."

"Yeah, you're healed all right."

Noog came around the bed and offered to help him up.

Carl said, "I got it." He stood. "I'm ready."

They walked out of the ward, and several staff members wished him well.

Noog had his pickup truck idling out front, and he helped Carl into the passenger seat.

As they drove away, Carl said, "I haven't been in a car in a while. Feels strange."

"It's a truck. Wusses drive cars."

Carl laughed.

"You sure you can make it on your own?" Noog said. "You talked them out of sending a nurse to check on you. I'm going to stop in most days to see how you're doing. And I talked to Grace, and she's going to check in as well."

"Thanks, man, appreciate you helping out. I'm just trying to get my life back in order. Also need to make some money."

"Whoa. You're *not* taking customers out any time soon. I'll hide your damn boat if you try something like that. And you know Grace ran a GoFundMe for you. Something like twenty grand waiting for you. People from all over contributed. One anonymous person gave ten grand. I asked Grace if she'd run one for me, but, like, she told me to screw off."

Carl laughed.

"Yeah, Grace told me. It was great of her to do that."

"You gotta stop in at the bar. A lot of folks want to see you."

"One of these days."

"I don't mean to pry, but are you OK? Your memory is back?"

"Some of it," Carl said. "The doctors seem happy. They're letting me go home and chill. But the cops keep bugging me."

"Pretty weird shit that happened to you, Carl. Being pushed and all. You know that reporter chick stopped into the bar recently. I gave her a ration of shit."

"Mmm," Carl said.

"That's all you have to say about her? She almost killed you, dude."

He shrugged. "I don't know. It was a strange night. At least they found my boat."

"And she's still in town."

"Who is?"

"Stacie Davis. The reporter. Rumor is the DA is closing in on her for shoving you down those stairs."

Carl stared out the front of the truck, watching the landscape whiz by.

"I still get dizzy sometimes," Carl said.

"Did you hear me?" Noog said. "They're going to nail her for trying to kill you."

"Yeah. Well, that's good."

CHAPTER 22

Stacie stepped inside the keeper's house; it was hot and cloyingly musty. She walked several steps in and turned to the right to look at the small landing leading upstairs. The power was off, but there was enough natural light to see the dark stain from Carl's blood. She bent over and noticed that someone had tried to scrub away the stain, probably one of the researchers who was disturbed by the whole episode.

Stacie looked up the stairs and felt queasy. She remembered the room up there had two windows, one facing south and one east. The streaming sunlight upstairs gave the room deep shadows that sliced across the room.

She decided to walk around the first floor and poked into the disheveled rooms that held books, papers, wall posters of wildlife, and domestic items like backpacks, hairbrushes, a guitar, and noise-canceling headphones.

After a few minutes, she found herself back at the bottom of the stairs. Her heart raced as she started up. Each step creaked and she hung onto the handrail. Soon her head was through the opening and she scanned the room. It was smaller than she remembered. A cot was pushed against the south wall under the window. The room was empty except for the cot; maybe no one wanted to sleep there anymore.

Stacie looked out the south window and could see rolling dunes covered with shrubs and beach grass for half a mile or so. In the far distance, she could make out the tip of Monomoy and the agitated water that ran past it.

She moved to the east window and peered over plant-crusted dunes to the Atlantic. It was from this window that Carl saw the lantern light on the beach.

Stacie could barely control her anxiety, standing in the room, and revisiting that night. It was like returning to the scene of the crime, but *what crime*? What happened that night?

The floorboards suddenly creaked behind her and she shrieked.

There was no one there; the room was empty.

She felt a rivulet of perspiration run down her back; the heat in the room was suddenly overpowering and she took a deep breath and started for the stairs. She looked around the room one more time, then quickly hustled to the bottom, gingerly stepping over the stain on the landing.

Racing outside, she slammed the door behind her. She looked up at the south-facing window in the upstairs room.

What was up there? Who was up there? She could only see the washed-out reflection of the desiccated landscape on the glass.

Stacie walked around the front of the house, down the steps, and onto the path heading east that she and Carl had taken to the Atlantic that night. The sand was soft, and the walking was hard, but she managed to get to the high dunes overlooking the beach.

Looking up and down the beach, there was no sign of human existence. Out at sea, she could see a cluster of boats fishing atop the scattered rips.

She walked down to the beach, again looking up and down the lonely expanse of sand.

Horse hooves in the sand? she thought. A pile of horse shit? A burning lantern? Down here on an island? Really?

After thirty minutes of walking the beach, she returned to the lighthouse and was startled to see two people in folding chairs on the deck. As she got closer, she recognized Colleen and Natalie, the researchers she had met in Scoccia's office. She waved.

They looked confused and returned a muted wave.

Stacie approached the deck.

"Hey, you're the reporter," Colleen said.

"Yes," Stacie said. "We met in Steve's office."

Colleen leaned over and whispered something to Natalie.

"What are you doing here?" Natalie said.

"I was just taking a walk around the lighthouse and beach."

"How did you get here? We didn't see a boat when we got dropped off."

"A friend brought me down. I'm headed back to get picked up now."

The two women stared at Stacie, and she realized they were frightened.

Of course they'd be frightened, she thought. You're the maniac that threw a guy down the stairs.

"You really shouldn't be here," Colleen said carefully.

"It's a wildlife refuge," Stacie said. "People are allowed to visit."

They continued to stare, sitting forward on their chairs.

"Anyway, I'm heading back now. Have a good day," she said.

Stacie could feel their eyes drilling into her back as she made her way down the path toward the beach. After fifteen minutes she sat at the top of the beach. She removed her boots and socks, and walked slowly along the waterline, stepping over empty horseshoe crab shells and shattered, beaten clamshells bleached by the sun.

The water from Nantucket Sound felt cold and refreshing. In the distance, she could see an occasional boat traversing south to the rips. She vaguely remembered that Carl said there were optimal times to fish the rips, based on the flow of water that created the turbulence striped bass preferred.

She turned and looked back at the lighthouse; the only visible portion was the very top of the glass structure, like a giant eye staring at her. A frisson of fear ran through her and she turned away to look at the water.

Standing on the shore, she had the unnerving sense that someone was staring at her.

The sight of Prescott's boat buoyed her.

After her sloppy boarding of the boat, he said, "How was it?"

"Weird."

"I hope you're done visiting this place."

"I think so," she said. "I mean, there are parts that are breathtakingly beautiful and peaceful."

"Yes, but—"

"But I don't have great memories here."

He flashed a brief smile, then pushed the throttles forward and the craft took off.

◎

Langone's phone rang and she grabbed it without looking at the number. She was not in a good mood. There were too many cases, she was over-worked. She was grating under the condescending attitude of her older colleagues, including Martin herself.

"Sarah, this is Phyllis Crimonini. Remember me?"

"No, I'm sorry, I don't. How can I help you?'

"You came to the university with some cloth samples."

"Oh, yes. Sorry, Phyllis. The Jane Doe case."

"You asked me to look at the clothes and I confirmed they were in a very old style."

"I remember."

"And I took some pictures of a tiny fragment of cloth in the neckline. It looked like a label with a faded insignia."

"Yes."

"Well, out of curiosity, I sent the photo out to a network of people in the textile community."

"Oh. Well, thank you for doing that."

"And I got a response last night that you might find interesting."

"What kind of response?"

"It would be best if I could send you a picture. Or two pictures. Can you receive attachments there?"

"Sure."

"Then I'll send you two pictures; the first is the one I took of the label, and the second is another photo showing a similar label. I'll explain in the email."

"OK. I look forward to seeing the email. Thanks for following up. I'd nearly forgotten."

"By the way, have you been able to identify the woman?" Crimonini said.

"The one who drowned?"

"Yes, that one."

"No, we haven't. It's still an open case."

◎

Carl opened two windows. His apartment sat above a lawyer's office in a small, two-story retail zone on Route 28. He was lucky to get the place. Affordable rentals were hard to find in Chatham.

He looked at a calendar next to the refrigerator and counted the days that had passed since he was last in the apartment; he stopped at twenty-four.

Grace had been kind enough to gather some clothes for him to wear home. There were some flowers and a case of beer and some food that Noog and his friends had contributed.

He sat at the small round kitchen table and sorted through the stack of mail. He was late on several payments. He set those aside.

There was a handwritten letter postmarked from Boston. There was no name next to the return address on the envelope. He opened it.

Dear Carl,

There are no words that I can arrange on a piece of paper to explain how sorry I am for what happened to you. You were kind enough to help a young reporter in search of a story, and you ended up critically injured. When your memory returns, you'll know that I meant you no harm.

Hopefully, you'll read this when you can go home again and are fully recovered. You are a good man with a good heart. I wish you a speedy recovery and good health.

Sincerely,

Stacie

He stared at the letter. He noticed the cursive was strong, elegant, and purposeful. He sat back in the chair, put his hands behind his neck, and looked at the ceiling. He still suffered from dizziness and the deadening effects of his anti-seizure medicine.

But he was out of the hospital and rehab.

And his memory was returning in sudden spurts that startled him.

One moment he'd be watching TV mindlessly, the next moment he'd suddenly have a powerful memory of a charter trip for tuna that happened three years ago. It was both exhilarating and frightening to be assaulted with recovered memories.

But not all memories. He could not remember the boat trip out to Monomoy that night with Stacie. He could not remember much about Stacie at all. He thought she might have visited him in the hospital, but he wasn't sure.

Carl looked at his watch. He was expecting yet another interview by someone in the DA's office, though he warned them that he had nothing to add. A blank slate is a blank slate, zero is still zero. As far as he was concerned nothing happened on Monomoy that night because almost nothing remained of the memory.

One day in the hospital, with nothing else to think about, he ruminated on a classic dilemma from his only philosophy course in college. It went something like this: if a tree falls in the forest, and no one is around to hear it, does it make a sound?

It was more a mental exercise than a digression into the theory of knowledge. But the more he played with the idea, the more the philosophical dilemma became personal, not theoretical.

If he fell down a set of stairs and no one was around to see it, did it happen? Or more precisely, if he fell down a set of stairs and could not remember the fall, did he really fall?

He stood up and opened the refrigerator, bypassed the beer, and grabbed a bottle of water. He heard the knock on the door, looked again at his watch, and said, "Shit."

"Hello," the woman said when he opened the door. "I'm State Police Trooper Sarah Langone from the District Attorney's Office."

"Yes, I got your call," he said. "I'm hoping this is going to be last time. I have nothing more to add. Just got home and I'm tired."

"It'll only take a few minutes," she said, but he had already turned and left the door open. She closed the door and sat across from him at the small table. She pulled out a notepad and smiled.

"Where's the other guy?"

"Detective Clancy?"

"Yeah, that guy."

"We work together on cases. He was not able to make it today."

Carl shrugged.

"I feel a little woozy, so if you don't mind, could we get going?"

"Absolutely," she said. "First, I want to tell you how bad we feel about your injury and its aftermath. I'm sure this is a very trying time."

"That's an understatement."

"OK. So, let me dig right in. Has any part of your memory returned about the night in question when you visited Monomoy with Stacie Davis? Anything?"

Carl was cautious when talking to someone capable of making his life miserable, including medical staff and law enforcement personnel. He had learned too late that things he said or did could affect him dramatically. If he claimed—which happened his second night in the hospital—that he saw a large black dot in his vision, it created a cascade of new tests, questions, and examinations. If he told Detective Clancy that he *might* have some new memories of that night—which he had said only once—Clancy pestered him relentlessly until Carl pretended to fall asleep to get him to stop.

He did have a strange memory of that night, but he chose not to describe it to anyone.

"There's nothing new," he said.

"Do you mind if I ask you about your relationship with Stacie Davis?"

"Detective Clancy already did that. Many times."

"Do you mind if I ask?"

He sighed. "Fine."

"Were you fond of Stacie?"

"Fond?"

"Did you like her?"

"Yeah, I guess so. But as I said a million times, I have trouble even remembering what she looks like."

"Do you think she liked you?" Langone persisted.

He thought for a moment.

"I suppose so."

"Was she interested in you in a romantic way?"

He laughed. "That's the same question that Clancy asked over and over. The answer I gave him is the same: I don't know. You'll have to ask Stacie that question."

"Were *you* interested in her in a romantic way?"

"No. I barely knew her."

"But you offered to take her out to Monomoy. Just the two of you. At night. You must admit it sounds like the setting for a budding romance."

"She was doing a story and I offered to take her out there. I think you and Clancy have romance on the brain. Stacie's a reporter. At least that's what I remember she told me."

"I'm sorry these questions are repetitive. We're near the end of this investigation, and before we close it, we need to make sure we've exhausted everything. There are only two witnesses to what happened to you that night. Because you don't remember much, we only have a single witness. And when we consider the timelines, some things don't match up."

"That's what Clancy said. But I just don't remember that night. It hurts my head to even think about it."

"Would you be interested in revisiting the lighthouse to see if it jogs your memory?"

"No!" he said. "That's not going to happen. I'm not going back there. Are you crazy?"

"I didn't mean to alarm you, Carl. You will not be required to return there. I just asked."

"You know, I'm going to lie down for a while. Would you mind leaving? Go talk to Stacie. She was there. She's a reporter."

"Do you believe her story about what happened?"

"Why wouldn't I? Detective Clancy told me what she said, and I have nothing to remember, so I'd go with her story."

"Her story just doesn't sound right," Langone said.

"What part doesn't sound right?"

"The part about the horse hoofprints in the sand, the manure, and the lantern."

"I don't remember that. If she said it happened, then it happened."

"But horse prints? Horse manure? There were no horses on Monomoy hat night, Carl. You're familiar with the Legend of the White Stallion?"

"I am now. It's a stupid legend."

"But Stacie Davis has described elements of the legend as if they oc-curred that night. Don't you think that's strange?"

He rubbed his temple. "I don't know. I suppose it sounds odd. I'm confused, OK? I don't know anything. Just leave me alone."

"Has Stacie Davis tried to contact you since you've been in the hospital?"

"No. Wait—actually, she just wrote me a letter."

"She did? Can I see it?"

He reached over to the pile of envelopes and pulled her letter out. He pushed it across the table, but suddenly yanked it back before she could grab it.

"No, you can't read it," he said.

"Why not?"

"It was written to me."

"Yes, but it might be helpful if we could see what she told you."

"Nope."

"Are you sure, Carl? These little bits of information are important evidence."

"Evidence of what?"

"Evidence that something happened out there that only she knows."

"Leave her alone. And me. Please go now."

Langone slowly put away her notebook and pen, reached inside her purse and pulled out a business card.

"Carl, please call me any time if you come across something that would be relevant to the case. Who knows, perhaps your memory will return. That second number is my cell phone. Call me, OK?"

"Sure," he said.

CHAPTER 23

Stacie stared at her empty coffee cup and debated whether to leave the motel to buy another one. Caffeine was a drug she relied on. It helped her focus when she wrote articles. Today she was studying her notes from all her stories since coming to Chatham.

She pored over the first piece, reading it online and looking at her notes.

Her phone rang. She recognized the number.

"You wrote Lane a letter?" Doherty said.

"Yeah, why? I told him I was sorry for what happened."

"Stacie, didn't I ask you—beg you—not to contact him? At all? For any reason?"

"Yes, you did."

"Then why the hell did you send him a letter?"

"I guess I felt bad for what happened to him."

"Do you want me to represent you?"

"Yes, of course I do."

"Then you *have* to do what I ask. Otherwise, I can't help you. It sounds like they're going to subpoena that letter. At this point, they have nothing to go on, except your memory and the physical evidence. And even if this guy Lane does start remembering, I can easily make the case that his memories are not reliable, given his injury. But—are you listening?"

"Yes."

"But, if you singlehandedly offer up new evidence that something

·lse happened, or provide a new potential motive, then you will be in
.erious trouble. And even an old, overweight, asshole criminal attorney
ike me can't help you."

"I got it," she said quietly. "I'm sorry. Won't happen again."

She could hear him breathing, regaining his composure.

"Stacie, there are times when you have to break the rules because the
1ormal rules don't work. Your case is still normal in my eyes, so let's use
he normal rules. OK?"

"OK."

Stacie hung up and felt terrible. She had no idea why she wrote Carl
:he letter. It seemed like an honest thing to do. She genuinely felt bad for
1im. Still, Doherty was right. Follow normal until it's *not* normal.

She hadn't bothered to tell Doherty she was in a Chatham motel.
He probably would have been angry. Still, she knew there was a single
:hread of truth down here that she had failed to find. That little piece
3f figurative cotton thread would lead her to the truth. Or that was her
1ope. But Doherty's warning was sobering. *Her* instincts as a reporter
were in opposition to *his* instincts as a lawyer. She wanted to dig, pry,
and confront; he wanted her to shut up, lay low, and virtually disappear.

She stood up and decided to drive somewhere, park, and take a long
walk. She also needed a few food items to snack on and would stop at a
supermarket.

Fifteen minutes later she was walking the aisle in a busy supermarket looking for bottled water, yogurt, and some fresh fruit.

She stopped. In front of her, staring up at the shelf full of canned
goods was the diminutive, slightly shriveled figure of Marci Prescott.
Her casual but expensive summer dress hung loosely on her thin frame,
and her stylish, large round sunglasses made her look oddly like an insect examining a flower stalk.

"Marci, how are you?"

She turned to look at Stacie and then returned to stare at the shelf.

"It's Stacie Davis, Marci. The reporter."

"Yes, indeed. Tell me, where are the cannellini beans? He wants a
salad with those beans, and I can't find them."

Stacie was reminded of Marci's strange, distracted social behavior.

"Mmm, I think we're in the wrong aisle. They might be in the next one over. Do you want to follow me?"

"Yes, lead the way. This is so distressing. Shopping for food. Ridiculous. And why are there so many options? I feel like I'm in a huge mall. Ridiculous."

Stacie smiled and led the way to the next aisle.

"That was a nice luncheon at your house a while ago."

"Prescott loves those. I don't. They're tiresome. Writers are vain."

Stacie laughed. "I suppose they are."

"I *know* they are," Marci said.

"But Prescott is also a good writer, wouldn't you agree? Millions of people love his mysteries."

"Who cares?" she said, flicking her right hand up as if brushing a fly away.

Stacie reached for a can of cannellini beans.

"One or two?"

"Two."

Stacie put them in Marci's shopping cart.

"I hate cooking," Marci said. "It's too complicated."

"I'm sure you're an excellent cook. Please say hello to Prescott for me."

Stacie walked away, paid for her small stash, and drove back to the motel. The morning weather had been sunny, but cool. Now it felt warm and she changed into shorts and a long-sleeve t-shirt. A walk somewhere would be a good way to clear her mind.

◎

"Let's just name her a suspect and get on with it," Clancy said. "I'm tired of dancing around the facts. Once she's a suspect we can get her old boyfriend in, and some of her colleagues at the *Globe*. And we'll subpoena that damn letter she wrote to Lane."

Langone grimaced. "That seems premature. There's no physical evidence tying Davis to his injury. We don't have anything to go on, and I think we all know it."

"We need to put pressure on that woman. She'll crack, I promise you," Clancy said to Martin, who simply stared and listened. "The entire orse thing is ridiculous. There's not a single piece of corroboration for hat hallucination. She's the only person who saw the hoofprints, the norse shit, and the lantern. The Coast Guard found nothing. Let me re-peat—they found *nothing*. And of course, Lane can't confirm anything."

"But why would she make something like that up?" Langone said.

"Because she's crazy, that's why," he said. "She's a psychopath. She almost killed her boyfriend when she found out he was cheating on her."

"We don't know whether he was cheating on her back then," Langone said.

"Listen, I've worked on a lot of cases," Clancy said, looking at Martin. "This woman's a nut job. She's been violent in the past with men who reject her. She made up a ridiculous story about a ghost legend reoccur-ring. Let me repeat: a ghost legend happening now! And then Lane mys-teriously falls down the steps by himself while she's alone on the beach. What the hell are we waiting on? Make her a suspect and let's get this woman rattled. She'll crack."

"I don't buy it," Langone said.

"But, Sarah," Martin said. "The horse thing? You don't have an an-swer for that. Either it happened, or it didn't. And if it didn't happen—which is certain, for God's sake—then Davis's explanation for the other events that night is highly specious."

Langone sighed. "I guess so. The legend thing *is* pretty crazy."

"I'll talk to Barone and see what he wants to do," Martin said. "He's inclined to push her a little harder. OK, let's move on. Sarah, what have you got?"

"The Jane Doe. No DNA hits so far, and no one's sent in a credible tip on her identity. Still, there was a small item involving the clothes she was wearing. The textile expert I visited came back with an interesting twist."

"Well?" Martin said, tapping her pencil onto a legal pad. "Enlighten us."

"It looks like there was a faded label in the collar," she said.

Martin and Clancy looked at each other; Clancy rolled his eyes.

Langone blushed; they were mocking her.

"It's not a big deal," she said quickly. "I don't have anything else today."

CHAPTER 24

"Mom, I promise I'll be home soon," Stacie said. "This just isn't a good time. I'm trying to figure some things out."

"But you need to come home to relax."

"I thought you told me to dig deep and find some resolve," Stacie said. "That's what I'm doing."

"Being on Cape Cod, where this whole thing started, just doesn't seem sensible right now. Why not hang out at home for a while? We could cook together and have some mom-daughter fun."

Stacie laughed. "Mom, I love you dearly. You've always given me good advice. I *promise* I'll be visiting soon."

"I'm holding you to that. And I'm going to call you every day to bug you."

"You're not bugging me. You're being a good mom."

Stacie hung up and tried to cool down from a long walk through a conservation area. She felt coated in yellow pollen from the oak trees that powdered the walk. Stacie never noticed the massive annual release of pollen from oak trees in the city. Cape Cod was not exactly a wilderness, she realized, but nature seemed so much closer here.

Her phone rang again, and she stiffened as she recognized the number.

"Hello, Sam."

"A little bit of bad news today," he said.

"What kind of bad news?"

"Got a call from Martin today. She said they're considering making you a suspect in the Lane case. This is unusual. They either designate someone a suspect, or they don't. By calling me, they're playing games. They're trying to put pressure on you. Do you follow?"

"No, I don't."

"Martin says your story is full of holes. They seem hung up on the horse stuff. She mentioned the part about horse shit, and she laughed."

Stacie started to doodle on her notepad, drawing a big circle, making it smaller at each cycle until it ended in a small dot in the cluttered center.

"What exactly does this mean, Sam? I'm confused."

"It means that they *might* announce you're officially a suspect in the assault of Carl Lane."

"I didn't assault Carl," she said.

"Again, Stacie, that's their contention, not mine. I don't think they have a case unless they get something new from Lane. I gather he's regained some of his memory."

"Why do they keep focusing on the White Stallion stuff? It was a prank by Carl. Surely he'll confirm that."

"Lane is still fuzzy on that night."

"This is total crap, Sam."

"Believe me, if they had a solid case, Martin wouldn't have called. My guess is Barone isn't sold on pushing ahead with you as a suspect."

"Is that why Martin called you?"

"Probably. She knew I'd have to make this call to you, and they'd hope you'd start freaking out and make a mistake, like that letter you wrote."

"We're back to the letter again?"

"Well, you wrote it even though I made it clear you shouldn't communicate with him."

"Tell me, what kind of mistake do they think I'd make?"

"People under pressure make all kinds of mistakes, Stacie, even if they're not guilty."

"But I'm not guilty of anything, Sam."

"Why don't you come into the office and we'll talk? Sometimes it's better to sit face-to-face to hash these things out."

"I don't want to do that."

"Why not?"

"I've got nothing new to add. And I'm out of town."

"Where are you?"

Stacie delayed for a second, then took a big leap into the deep end. "In the Berkshires. I'm chilling."

"That's a smart idea. Just stay away from the cape."

"I'm far away from the cape, don't worry."

"So, call Phyllis and set up a time to come in."

"Sam, you told me a while ago that we should act normal until things become not normal."

"Correct."

"It doesn't feel like things are normal now."

"Things are certainly different. But I don't believe the DA has enough to push this case ahead. I'm still very much optimistic."

"I'm not. Something feels wrong."

"As I said, Stacie, they're trying to pressure you. Let's stay calm."

"I'm getting pissed off. I feel trapped in this giant spider's web that I can't get free from."

"Anger and frustration don't help right now. Calm helps. Call Phyllis." They hung up.

Stacie walked around the small motel room, trying to relax. All she could think about was the fear and humiliation of being a suspect in a criminal case.

She sat down and flipped her notebook back to the start of her reporting on the cape. The first story involved the body of an unidentified woman found floating off Monomoy. As news stories go, it was a straightforward piece involving the two men who discovered a body. Since that original story, Stacie realized she had heard nothing about the body.

She sat at her computer and searched the web for more information on the unidentified body, but there was no follow-up by any news organization.

If we're in the "not normal" zone, she thought, then it's time to act.

She looked up a phone number and called.

"Can I speak to Sarah Langone, please?" Stacie said.

"Who can I say is calling?" the receptionist said.

"Stacie Davis."

She waited for several minutes.

"This is Sarah Langone."

"Sarah, this is Stacie Davis."

"How can I help you, Stacie?"

"Have you been able to identify the body of the woman that was found off Monomoy a couple of weeks ago?"

"Are you calling as a reporter?"

"No. I'm calling as a citizen."

"We have no new information on the woman's identity. Why do you ask?"

"Don't you think that after all this time you'd know who the woman is?"

"These missing persons cases take time. Perhaps you're unaware of how many people go missing each year in the United States. That number's about six hundred thousand."

"You need to solve that Jane Doe case," Stacie said. "That case is related to my case."

"I beg your pardon?"

"You need to find out who that woman is and how she ended up in the water. It will lead to what happened the night Carl and I were at the lighthouse."

"Stacie, you understand that you're talking to a state trooper in the district attorney's office, don't you? Does your attorney know you're talking to me?"

"Find out what happened to that woman. It's critical. I didn't see it before, but now it's clear. Solve that case and you've solved what happened to Carl and me. The two events happened within a half mile of each other on a desolate island."

"Stacie, you can't just call the DA's office and—"

"I don't like the other guy there, Detective Clancy. I don't even know if I trust you, for that matter. But I'm taking a leap here, Sarah. Dig. Find out what happened to your Jane Doe. Then you'll find out what happened to me and Carl. Goodbye."

Stacie sat in the chair and took a sip of water.

That was either the stupidest thing I've ever done or the smartest, she thought. Which one?

◎

Langone reread the email from Crimonini. Then she opened the two images. The first image was of the faded label they teased out of the collar the second image was of a label that was not faded. This second image came from someone in the professor's textile group who recognized the label. It showed a red circle on a white cloth with the words "Simpson House" set inside the circle.

Crimonini said Simpson House was a specialty clothing company in England.

Langone was not going to bring up this tidbit with Martin until she was sure that she had something solid. It was clear that her junior status on the team was a liability. She found the website for Simpson House and sent off an email asking for information regarding a police matter.

She would have to cajole or sweet talk information from the company since they would be under no obligation to assist in a US police investigation without a subpoena. And a subpoena was impossible at this point.

Langone mulled how and when to tell Martin about Davis's phone call. It was extremely unusual—and unwise—for a person of interest to freely contact an investigator. It was clear that Davis was not acting in her best interest.

◎

"I saw her," Gunny said. "She was buying a coffee at Cumberland Farms."

Carl sat on a barstool, surrounded by friends.

"You're full of shit," Noog said. "Carl, pay no attention to him."

"I'm just telling you; it was her. Believe what you want," Gunny said.

"What's she doing here?" Carl said.

"See what you've done?" Noog said. "He's supposed to chill out, and you bring up that woman again."

"Fine," Gunny said, "I didn't see her. I saw her ghost buying a friggin' coffee."

"Well, if it *was* her, maybe I should talk to her," Carl said.

Noog gave Gunny a stern look.

"It could've been anyone," Gunny said. "Don't pay attention to me. I don't know anything. Relax, man. Have another club soda."

"When can you start drinking beer again?" Noog said.

"Not sure, exactly. They got me on some medications. To be honest, I'm not interested in drinking these days. Just trying to get my shit together."

"Been out to your boat yet?" Noog said.

"Yeah. Couple of times. I puttered around Mill Pond. Boat's in good order."

"You still drawing a blank on that night?" Gunny said. Noog shot him another fierce look.

"Yeah, mostly. Cops keep bugging me, but I don't have anything to tell them."

"How you getting by on money?" Noog said. "You still using the GoFundMe dollars?"

"What a lifesaver that was," Carl said. "Folks here were incredible. Can't thank you enough."

"Forget about it. You'd do the same for us," Noog said.

Carl drained his club soda.

"Do you think she's here?" Carl said to Gunny.

"Naw. I don't think it was her after all," he said.

"Guys, I'm outta here. Good to see you. Need my beauty sleep," Carl said.

Five minutes later he had started the truck and his phone rang.

"Hello?"

"Carl, this is Stacie."

"Oh."

"How are you?"

"Fine."

"You back home yet?"

"Yeah."

"Do you feel like grabbing a cup of coffee sometime?"

"I don't know," he said slowly.

"I thought we could talk things out a bit. I'm sorry about your injury But I'm still a little confused about what happened that night. Maybe we could go over it again, if you were up to it?"

Carl rubbed his temple with his free hand. "I keep telling everyone that I don't remember that night. Why do people keep bugging me about that?"

"Do you remember *anything* about that night?"

Carl didn't answer; the only sound was the rumble of the truck's engine.

"Carl?"

"Yeah?"

"Let's grab some coffee tomorrow morning. How about ten o'clock? That work for you?"

"I don't know."

"Tell you what. I'll meet you at the Chatham Lighthouse overlook at ten. You bring your coffee and I'll bring mine. We'll sit in your truck and chat."

"I don't know."

"I'll see you there tomorrow. Bye."

Carl sat in the running truck for ten minutes. His dull headache had returned, and he bit the inside of his cheek absently. He backed up slowly and drove home.

◎

Langone was surprised at the quick email turnaround.

"How can we be of assistance?" Katy from Simpson House wrote.

Langone explained that an unidentified deceased person in Massachusetts wore clothing with a tag from Simpson House. Was there any chance they could share a list of their customers in the United States? They were desperately trying to identify the deceased so the next of kin could be contacted.

"I'm afraid that would be an extensive list," Katy replied. "How far back did you want to go? Simpson House has been a clothing manufacturer for almost two hundred years. If the deceased was found in Massachusetts, perhaps I can look in our files for customers there for the last several years?"

"Yes," Langone wrote back. "Let's start with Massachusetts. Thank ˟ou very much."

The list of purchasers in Massachusetts came twenty minutes later. ˟This list includes clients from the past five years. To do a more thorough ˟earch I'd need to look through paper files. We do not have many cus-˟omers in your state. I hope this helps in some way."

Langone scanned the list of seven clients. She recognized two univer-˟ity theater departments and a film production company in Watertown. ˟f the four remaining names, two were nonprofits for theater groups ˟n Wellesley and Newburyport. The final two names were Carson Co. ˟nd Coleridge Enterprises. She did a quick web lookup for Carson Co. ˟nd found it listed in Great Barrington. There was no web listing for ˟oleridge Enterprises. She tried an online white pages lookup and found ˟othing.

"Please," she wrote back quickly, "can you provide the addresses ˟f these clients? I know this must be a chore, but it would be greatly ˟ppreciated."

"I will see if I can access that information," Katy responded. "I'm ˟fraid it will take a few days. We are quite shorthanded, I'm afraid."

"Thank you again for your help, Katy."

Langone sat back in her hinged metal chair and rocked gently. She stopped rocking after a minute and leaned over her desktop. She ˟earched for the Legend of the White Stallion on Monomoy Island.

Langone had originally listened while Clancy retold the legend, but ˟he paid little attention to it beyond the details of the horse and the lan-˟terns. Now she dug a little deeper and saw that the legend involved the ˟eath of a man trying to lure ships to sink on the sandbars off Mono-˟moy. The man's ploy was to use a white horse and two lanterns to trick ˟nwary ships into coming dangerously close to shore and wrecking on ˟he sandbars. Afterward, the ship would be salvaged for anything of val-˟ue. In the legend, the horse spooked and rushed into the surf, drowning ˟he man. The stallion could still be seen, the legend went, on moonlit ˟nights in the surf off the eastern side of Monomoy.

She leaned back in her chair again and rocked. Why would Lane ˟other to go through the trouble of teasing Davis about the legend? Did

Lane even *know* about the legend beforehand?

She leaned forward again and did a web search of Whitewash Village on Monomoy. She read about the bustling, but small, fishing village near the tip of Monomoy. The village was abandoned in the late nineteenth century after a storm wrecked the protected harbor.

Ghosts, legends, shipwrecks, and bodies washing ashore. Was Stacie Davis suggesting that ghosts were responsible for both Jane Doe's death and Carl Lane's near-fatal injury?

Langone stood up, stretched, and saw an email land in her folder. She bent over to see who had sent it.

It was from Katy at Simpson House.

The subject line was: "This was easier than I thought."

Langone opened the email and scanned the addresses of Simpson House's Massachusetts clients. She stopped at the address for Coleridge Enterprises.

She copied the address into Google maps and stared at the digital map for five long minutes. She erased the address and re-entered it. There was no mistake. Then she entered the address into an assessor's database of property owners.

CHAPTER 25

Stacie waved to Carl as she walked around the front of his truck. He didn't return the wave and peered at her intensely as she got into the truck with her coffee.

"Hey, Carl. Nice to see you again. You look great." Stacie did not think he looked great; he was gaunt and sallow-faced. His eyes were hidden behind sunglasses and his faded Red Sox baseball cap was pulled down tight over his forehead.

"Hey," he said.

"How're you feeling?"

"OK, I guess. I'm getting there."

"Nice of you to see me. Have you picked up your charter business again?"

"No. Friends have picked up my customers. Next year."

"Are you doing any kind of work to keep busy?"

"Some painting to help out a friend."

Stacie took a sip of coffee and looked out the windshield onto the beach below. A large channel of water ran in front, and a mile farther out she could see the thin barrier island they called South Beach, and beyond that the Atlantic Ocean. They sat in silence.

"Still get headaches?"

"A few. Not bad, though. I'm getting better."

"You feel like talking about that night?"

"Not really."

"I don't blame you. Not my favorite night either. But you're the only person that can help me, Carl. The police think I pushed you down the steps. They don't believe we saw the horse prints in the sand, the horse manure, or the lantern. They think I cut the anchor line to your boat after I pushed you to explain why you went back to the lighthouse alone to make a call."

Carl stared out the windshield. A young couple stood on the sidewalk in front of them to take a selfie.

"Carl?"

"Yeah."

"Did you hear what I said?"

"Yeah."

"I need your help. You were there. You saw the horse stuff. I know you were just teasing me, but if you owned up to it, it would help me a great deal. And you could confirm that we found your anchor line cut and you went back alone to the lighthouse."

He took a sip of coffee.

"Carl, please. Talk to me."

"I don't remember that night. I told everyone that. People keep bugging me. My memory isn't so good right now. I even forget where my boat is moored half the time."

"Do you remember *anything* about that night?"

Silence.

Stacie did not realize she was going to cry, because it came on so quickly. Two thick, salty tears rolled down her cheeks like twin waves. She turned away to the passenger window and coughed to provide cover for the quick wipe.

She had held out hope that Carl could help her, but he was a blank. And she was alone again, drifting in a vast, turbulent sea.

"Maybe," he said.

"Maybe *what*?" she said, whipping around.

"Maybe there is something."

"Carl, look at me, please—can you take off your sunglasses? I need to see your eyes."

He winced. "I need my glasses. The sun hurts."

"Fine. Leave them on. But can you look at me?"

He turned.

"What is it you remember about that night? I'm not the police, Carl. But you must understand that I'm in deep shit. Anything you can offer might help. I have *no one* to help me."

"There was a voice."

"A voice? What kind of voice?"

"Like a woman."

"What did the woman say?"

"She called my name."

"There was no woman on the island that night, Carl."

"You were there."

"Yes, I was there. But I was not in the house when you fell."

"The voice said, 'Carl.' So, I went to the voice."

"What did you see?"

"I don't remember. Maybe I saw you."

"Me? Carl, I wasn't there!" she yelled.

He drew back from her.

"Sorry. I'm just trying to process everything. So, you heard a woman call your name. And you went to her. Then what happened?"

"Something happened. I felt something. I saw a bright light, then darkness."

"Do you remember being pushed, or falling?"

"No. Just a bright light, then darkness. Like I said."

"Do you remember me calling your name, trying to wake you up?"

"No, I don't think so."

Stacie turned and looked out the windshield again. Her tears had stopped as fast as they started. She was exhausted, as if she'd run a marathon. Her shoulders drooped, and she let her head rest briefly on the passenger window.

"That's not going to help, Carl," she said softly. "I'm really sorry about your injury. Please take care of yourself." She got out of the truck, shut the door as softly as she could, and left him staring out at the beach and water beyond. She glanced up and saw the Chatham Lighthouse behind the overlook blink as it rotated.

Was it a blink?

Or was it a wink?

Stacie stared at the white lighthouse with its plain black top sec
tion. It was much less ornate than the decommissioned lighthouse or
Monomoy.

A blink or a wink?

Stacie stole a glance at Carl; he appeared frozen in place, staring ou
a thousand miles into the ocean.

CHAPTER 26

"There's something wrong with you, woman," Marie said. "What in God's name are you doing in Chatham?"

"Stop yelling," Stacie said. "I can't take any more drama."

"You want drama? I'll show you some drama. You have no friggin' business being in that town right now. Aren't you being investigated for hurting the charter boat guy? Hasn't the *Globe* put you on a leave of absence? Your career may be permanently stalled. Your old boyfriend is telling stupid stories to the cops that make you look like an ax murderer! Stacie! Are you out of your mind?"

"You said you'd stop yelling."

"I'm not going to stop yelling until you start listening."

"I'm going to hang up, Marie. I can't take it anymore."

"OK. Wait. I'm sorry. Is this tone better?"

"Yes."

"Good. Why don't you come back to Boston? We'll have dinner tonight. Better yet, stay at my place as long as you want. Get back here, please? I'm your closest friend. I love you and want you away from trouble."

"Maybe you're right," Stacie said, sitting on her motel bed.

"Hallelujah, there is a God," Marie said. "Why don't you check out and come back tonight?"

"Tomorrow. I'm tired."

"Great. Call me when you're on the road. Promise?"

"Yes. Thanks, Marie."

Stacie flopped back onto the bed. She was tired, although it was only two o'clock in the afternoon. She closed her eyes.

She woke up two hours later when her phone rang. She recognized the number.

"Hello, Winslow," she said.

"I assume you're in Boston getting away from all this madness," he said.

"No. Believe it or not I'm still in Chatham."

"Oh heavens, you are a moth drawn to the flame. Go home, young lady."

"Tomorrow," she said.

"I hate to tell you this, but a Detective Clancy just left my house."

"Oh God," she moaned.

"He asked about you and the dinner party we invited you to. How did he know about that?"

"I think I might have mentioned it to them. I can't remember. What did he want?"

"I couldn't figure it out, to be honest. He seemed very shifty. I had to tell him I took you back to visit the lighthouse recently. I mean, I couldn't lie."

"Shit."

"I'm sorry, Stacie. I had to. Don't be angry at me."

She sighed. "Don't worry. It doesn't matter."

"Listen, we're having another dinner party tonight. Why don't you join us? Pretty much the same cast of characters, with one or two additions."

"No. I'm not in the mood. But thanks anyway."

"I insist. You need to relax with friends who appreciate you."

After several minutes of pleading, Stacie realized she *did* need a distraction.

"Fine, what time should I be there?"

"Would seven o'clock work for you? Come a little early and let's chat to calm you down."

"Yes, see you then, Winslow. Thanks for thinking of me."

Stacie got up and took a shower to get ready for Prescott's dinner party.

Her phone rang. She saw it was Carl's number.

Oh what does that poor man want now? she thought.

She let it go to voicemail.

I promise to leave you alone, she thought. I won't bother you again.

◎

Stacie had the same summer outfit she wore to Prescott's previous dinner party, so she decided to accessorize with a new handbag. She shopped and found the perfect Lilly Pulitzer summer handbag and a floral print silk scarf. She also bought a half bottle of white wine and reached the Chatham overlook at six thirty. The sun was still strong and sent long shadows across the busy parking lot. Behind her grinned the lighthouse, flashing twice in succession every ten seconds.

She sipped her wine, which she had transferred to an empty water bottle. It was her private celebration for her last night in Chatham. She was done with this charming, old seafaring town. She'd attend a dinner party tonight and be back in Boston tomorrow.

Her phone rang, and she pulled it out of her new purse.

It was from Carl.

I can't help you, she thought. I should have left you alone. Don't worry about me anymore.

She let him go to voicemail again.

By the time she got to Prescott's house, she was a little tipsy.

Marci answered the door in another expensive size 1 dress that hung on her boney frame.

"Hello," Stacie said.

"Fine," Marci said, as if answering a question.

Stacie followed Marci into their large family room, where Prescott met them.

"Sit down, young lady," he said, beaming. "You look all gussied up."

"Well, you know," Stacie said, "a dinner party at Winslow Prescott's is never to be missed."

"Red or white?" he said.

"White, please." He pulled an opened bottle out of the ice bucket and poured her a generous glass.

He raised his whiskey and they clinked glasses.

"How do you stand having the perfect house with the perfect view?" she said.

He stared out the window onto the small tidal river below.

"It's not *that* perfect," he said.

"So how did it go with Detective Clancy?"

"Stacie, it's so interesting, to be honest. I mean, I've written many mysteries that involve policemen. But this is the first time I've talked to a real policeman on a real assignment. Fascinating."

"Don't remind me," she said.

"Oh heavens, I'm sorry," he said. "That was stupid of me."

"No. That's OK. This thing will sort itself out one way or another." Stacie took a big sip of wine. They continued to chat for a while. Prescott tried to reassure her that her legal problems would resolve themselves and she'd be back at her newspaper job before she knew it.

"You're very kind," she said as he topped up her glass. "I'm trying to be optimistic. It's just hard sometimes."

Marci appeared out of nowhere, sat down briefly on the couch with her martini, seemed to get bored, and then left again.

"So, where's everyone else?" Stacie said, looking at her watch.

"It's a late dinner party. We like having folks for cocktails later this time of year since the suns sets after eight o'clock in June."

"Do you mind if we wait on your deck?" Stacie said. "It's so lovely out there."

They walked outside, and Prescott brought along the wine bucket. Against her better judgment, she let him pour her a half glass.

"Is everyone who lives around here rich?" she said, sweeping her arm around the river.

"No, of course not. Many of the homes are passed down in families. The homes are worth a lot, of course, but unless there's a fight over an estate and some of the children want the money, the homes stay in the family."

Stacie took another sip of wine and realized she'd had enough alcohol. She put the glass down.

"You're very fortunate to live here, you know," she said. "And to have successful writing career. I envy you."

"It's Miss Serendipity raising her magic wand, that's all," he said. There are thousands of great writers out there who are never discovred. I showed up at the right time with an idiosyncratic private detecive. My agent liked it, and the publisher liked it, and *voilà*, here we are. Zou'd be surprised how arbitrary life is."

"You make it sound completely random, but you're talented," she aid. "Is this false modesty speaking?"

He laughed. "Perhaps. You know, I was just hoping in the beginning o sell one book, not twenty million."

"It's kind of chilly out here," she said. "I didn't bring a sweater. Do rou mind if we go back inside?"

"No, of course not. And the other guests will be showing up now."

They went back in. She sat on the couch and he planted himself in a tuffed leather chair.

He raised the wine bottle again.

"Oh no," she laughed. "I'm done with that stuff tonight. Just sparling water for me."

"So, what does it feel like?" he said, leaning forward in his chair and taring at her.

"Too much wine?" she chuckled. "Feels good in the beginning. But ask me later. Probably not so good."

"No. I mean about the effects of too much oxycodone?"

She laughed.

"I don't know," she said. "Why do you ask?"

"I'm nearly finished with my next mystery, and one of the key suspects is given an overdose of oxycodone in their wine. I was just wonderng what it felt like. You know, so I could be authentic."

Stacie laughed again but felt there was something peculiar about Prescott. Or was there something peculiar about her?

"What are you talking about?" she said.

He was giddy, smiling impishly.

"You know," he said.

"No, Winslow, I don't know. You're being funny tonight."

"You must have guessed."

"Hmm. I know this is going to sound odd, but I don't feel well right now, and I think I'll have to leave your dinner party early." She tried to stand but wobbled back onto the couch.

"*You* are our dinner party, Stacie. Relax. No one else is coming. Just you and me. And Marci, of course."

"I don't think this is funny," she said. "Please help me to my car. don't feel well. Better yet, can you please call me a cab or an Uber?"

"Relax. You shouldn't get worked up. But please try to describe what it feels like. Readers know when you're faking it. That's why it's important to be authentic in my mysteries."

Stacie tried to keep her eyes on Prescott but had trouble focusing.

"Did you put something in my drink?" she said, slurring slightly.

He acted disappointed.

"Stacie, we already went over that. You have overdosed on oxycodone, remember? You've been depressed since the terrible incident with Carl Lane. Your career is in tatters, remember? You managed to get your hands on some oxycodone and decided to end it all. Your suicide note will be a text, of course, to Mr. Lane. A very modern suicide note."

Stacie found herself blinking madly, as if she could wash the conversation away. She was both alarmed and sleepy at the same time.

How strange, she thought. I get it. It took me a while, but I get it How stupid.

"You killed the woman on Monomoy," she said.

"So, you *do* know!" he said. "Excellent."

"Who was she?" Stacie could barely speak. A huge wave of complacency suddenly overtook her, disrupting her thoughts. She bore down as hard as she could.

"Ana Vilovich. She was our maid. Our Bulgarian illegal immigrant maid."

"What happened?" Stacie's chin hit her chest and she fought to raise it to keep it steady.

"She drowned."

"How?"

"Well, I'd always been curious what it was like to kill someone. My mysteries involved so many murders, and they were all fabrications of my imagination. But how real is *that*? I needed to feel what it was like to kill someone. And, of course, to get away with it. I mean, what's the point if you can't get away with it?"

"She'll be ID'd," Stacie slurred.

"Impossible. Ana came here illegally through Canada. We found her through friends who introduced us to the smugglers. *They* don't even know who she is. I mean, I liked her. But Marci loathed her. Marci's game for anything, really, so I broached the idea to her. But I must admit, Marci hates doing the cooking now. She's never been comfortable in a kitchen."

Stacie tried to focus on his face, but finally settled on his sharp, dimpled chin; his eyes were too disturbing. While she was frightened by this bizarre confession, Stacie felt a strange dulling of emotions.

The bastard drugged me, she thought. I can barely think or talk. He really is crazy. Keep him talking.

"Why—drown—her?" she struggled to say.

"Good question. I had this idea of creating a mysterious death that no one could solve. I conjured up the perfect way to drown her and then dressed Ana in antique clothes so that it would be, well, a mystery. It was as if someone from the last century washed up on the shores of Monomoy. I put a bunch of fish scales I found at a dock in one of her pockets to add to the mystery."

Prescott chuckled, lost in thought for a moment.

"Her family. They'll come," Stacie garbled.

"How can they? She has no identity here, and her family in Bulgaria probably thinks she's a waitress in London. She's a ghost from 150 years ago, don't you see?"

"You didn't kill her," Stacie said, blinking wildly to keep her eyes open.

"I'll show you," he said, standing. "Marci!"

She sauntered down the hallway with a martini glass.

"Marci, darling. Get me the straitjacket, would you? The one we used with Ana. Please?"

Marci frowned and returned down the hallway.

"The only way I could think of drowning her without drugs or violence was to get her into a straitjacket, tie a rope to her, and drop her in the water. After she drowned, I just pulled her up, took her out of the jacket, and then put the old clothes on. I gently placed her in the water off the old Whitewash Village site around midnight. I mean, it took some tomfoolery to convince Ana to try on the straitjacket. First, I put it on, then Marci did, then she did it just for laughs. It was supposed to be fun."

Marci returned down the hallway with an old-fashioned, white canvas straitjacket. She flung it on the couch and left again.

"Thank you, darling," he said.

He held it up. "See? It will be easier to get you into it since you're so impaired."

And Stacie *was* impaired; her lips felt numb, her breathing was shallow, and she had trouble keeping her head from wobbling like a Raggedy Ann doll.

"Lighthouse," Stacie said with enormous effort.

"Ah, that. Well, I should have known that once you start doing things like this, it's hard to stop. Like smoking. Or drinking."

"Ahhh," Stacie said.

"Yes, yes, I know. It was mean of me. I had grown fond of you, to be perfectly honest, Stacie. And when you told me that Mr. Lane was going to take you down there for a night visit, well, I just couldn't resist. We tried to warn you not to do it, remember? Barbara begged you not to go. By the way, she's a little batty and knows nothing about my little games. But we did warn you."

"Horse," Stacie mumbled.

"Wasn't that brilliant!" he said. "My God, how creative! When I knew you were going down there at dusk, I got there about an hour earlier and left my boat a mile farther north. You wouldn't have seen it coming down. There's a couple of stables near Chatham, and I scooped up some horse manure, grabbed an antique lantern I had in the basement, and concocted the most ridiculous horseshoe contraption to leave hoofprints in the sand. It was kind of lame, but I suppose it worked."

Stacie shook her head.

"You don't believe me? Well, I knew the tide was coming up and
t would wash everything away soon enough. Hell, I wasn't even sure
vhether you and Mr. Lane would even *see* the lantern. But I saw you
voth going to that side of the island, so I knew it worked."

"Saw?"

"Of course. I was still there, silly. That little brick building near the
ighthouse was easy to get into. Do you know they originally stored oil
or the lighthouse lantern in that building? Now it's just for storage. I
vas in there when you arrived. It was hot and insufferable inside, I must
ell you. When you two left to find the lantern, I raced back to cut the
inchor line. I barely made it back to the lighthouse when you two went
orancing by on your way back to the boat."

"Why?" Stacie said, awkwardly twisting her lips that had stopped
working. "Why?"

"Why did I follow you to the lighthouse that night?"

She nodded.

"For fun. I thought it would be interesting to see how you and Mr.
.ane reacted to an old legend reappearing in the flesh. Especially you,
is a journalist. Would you believe it? And would you try to write about
t, even though no one would believe you? But I'm afraid I got a little
:arried away. It was thrilling to see you two stumbling around. Out of
he blue, I decided to cut the boat free. Don't ask me why, Stacie. I was
nspired; it was just too much fun.

"Now, you must understand, I never thought anyone would get hurt.
 sat upstairs reading something on my phone in the keeper's house for a
vhile, waiting for you two to call for help from the beach. After you were
rescued, I'd make my way back to my boat and just go home. I couldn't
vait to see whether you would write about it."

Prescott took a sip of whiskey.

"Alas," he sighed, "the next thing I hear is Mr. Lane walking up
he stairs in the dark looking at his phone. Boy, now *I* was frightened.
He looked ghastly. His face was lit by his phone, and the flashlight was
ointing at the floor. I had to get out of there, Stacie. What was I going
:o do? He stood at the top of the stairs trying to make a call. I raised my
voice in a high-pitched screech and said 'Carl!' He raised his flashlight

into my face, and I hit him with my flashlight. He fell on his back down those silly stairs. I thought he was dead, poor fellow. Then I ran to my boat. I raced back into the harbor just when the first Coast Guard boat was leaving Stage Harbor. Whew, that was close!"

By now Stacie was fighting an overpowering urge to sleep; her eyes kept closing and she fought bravely to keep them open. It seemed like there was a furious internal battle between feelings of fear and euphoria. She struggled to stay alert. Was this real? Was any of this happening?

"Me," she said, her head wobbling. "Me?"

"Oh, that," he said resignedly. "I feel terrible, Stacie, but I got scared that the police would eventually connect me to what happened at the lighthouse. That Detective Clancy bothered me for some reason. I decided right then and there that it would be best if the police had proof of their own theory that you pushed Mr. Lane. That meant you would have to confess. In a suicide note, of course. I feel horrible for doing this to you, Stacie. You must believe me.

"And, well, since I had perfected this method of drowning someone without signs of an assault, I thought I'd just repurpose it, so to speak. At first, I thought a simple overdose would suffice, but then the symmetry of dying in the ocean was just too much to pass up. You know, Stacie, we all start out living in water in our mother's amniotic fluid. We actually *breathe* that fluid. It's only natural that we should end the same way, don't you agree?"

Stacie's head had fallen to the right, and her eyes were slits.

"You poor thing," he said, shaking his head. "Marci!" he yelled. "Please come. It's time now."

CHAPTER 27

tacie watched a blurry, tilted Marci come down the hallway. Prescott tood and went into the kitchen. He returned into Stacie's field of vision wearing surgical gloves.

"Put the gloves on like we rehearsed," he said to Marci.

"Must we?" she said.

"Do as you're told," he said sharply.

"Hmmph," she said.

He opened Stacie's purse and removed her phone, motel room key, and car keys.

"Remember," he said, handing the items to Marci, "drive to the mo-el. Make sure no one is around, then enter her room, and stay there until nine thirty sharp. At that point take her phone and drive her car to that area on Bridge Street that I showed you. Park the car on the grass past the bridge. At exactly ten o'clock, you will take that piece of paper I gave you earlier. Use the password on the note to open her phone, then open her contacts like I showed you, and send a text to Mr. Lane. Text he exact wording of the suicide note that I wrote out for you. Then hit end. And remember, leave this bag and the phone on the front passen-er seat of her car."

He held up a plastic bag with several pills inside. "Gloves at all times, please. Walk back over the bridge and get into your car that is parked near the marina. Come home. Have a martini. We'll watch a movie later."

"This is all quite silly," she said, pouting.

"Go now, darling. And take a book to read in the motel. Stacie, w have your phone's passcode because you opened your phone severa times at our dinner party. We have video cameras everywhere. You ca see why we needed your phone. Technology is wonderful these days don't you agree?"

Stacie was vaguely aware of what was happening. She had slid far ther to her right on the couch so that she was nearly horizontal. Prescot stood over her and gently raised her to a sitting position.

"Mmm," he said. "This is the complicated part, Stacie. I hope I car do this without making it uncomfortable. You look very nice. I'll try no to wrinkle your scarf."

He reached for the straitjacket and began a cumbersome, arduou process of getting Stacie's limp arms into the jacket. He finished by hav ing her lie on her stomach while he buckled some items at her back.

"There you are," he said, pushing her into a sitting position. "You look like a trussed turkey."

Stacie was not quite unconscious; she could hear him speak. Yet much of what he said was confusing. He seemed interested in explaining what he was doing, as if he were running a seminar.

"As far as the police are concerned, you came here tonight for a drink," he said. "We'll report that you seemed *extremely* depressed and despondent. You confessed that you made advances to Mr. Lane tha evening at the lighthouse, and when he rejected you, you pushed him Marci and I will say that we tried to get you to stay over at our place fo the night, but you insisted on going back to your motel. The cell tow er data will show you went back to your room and stayed there unti around nine thirty, then you drove to the bridge and parked.

"Meanwhile, you and I will need to visit Stage Harbor on my boat Unfortunately, Stacie, you'll need to get wet, but I promise you won't fee a thing. Then I'll simply putter out to near the bridge and let you slir gently into the water. We're on an incoming tide now, and my guess is someone clamming at low tide tomorrow will find you."

◎

Mr. Lane, how can I help you? You called my cell phone three times, leaving very confusing messages. You realize it's eight o'clock at night?"

"She doesn't answer my calls or texts," Carl said. "It's important. You gave me your business card and told me to call you if anything came up. So, I called you."

"I'm not sure how I can help you contact Stacie Davis," Langone said. "Wait for the morning and try again. She has a lot on her mind these days. And I'm sure you do too. Please do not call my cell any more tonight. I gave you my card for official purposes."

"Are you a cop or not?" he said.

"Please try to get some rest," she said. "Call me in the morning. You've been through a lot."

"Don't you want to know?"

"Know what?" she said.

"About my memories."

◎

She was aware of being carried slowly, her stomach resting on his right shoulder. All the lights had been turned off in his house, except for a dimly lit bedroom window. He took a long time carrying her down the set of stairs and grunted several times.

Stacie could feel some sensation in her extremities and her face. He had placed her gently onto the floor of the boat. He took a long rope from a compartment and tied it around her ankles. He also tied something heavy onto the jacket that she could not see.

He kept muttering to himself, repeating phrases like, "Not too tight, don't leave marks."

The boat started and it slid slowly down the small river. Stacie was on her back and could see the clear night sky. The boat suddenly stopped; Prescott turned off the engines. They drifted for several minutes.

"Damn boat traffic," he muttered. "They come and go at all hours."

The boat rocked suddenly, then became calm as the wake rolled by. He started the boat again and it moved slowly.

Stacie wanted to speak to Prescott, but her lips were dry, and it was difficult to breathe. The straitjacket was tight against her chest.

"Winslow," she uttered, but it was barely a whisper and could not be heard over the engines and sloshing water against the hull.

After several minutes, the boat stopped, and he turned off the engines again.

"Winslow," she whispered again. "Don't. Please."

"What's that?" he said, leaning down to her. Stars sparkled behind his head in the black sky.

"Don't," she said.

"Oh heavens," he said, gently stroking her cheek, "it's too late to stop now. Breathe when you get in the water and it will be over quickly."

He grunted as he carried her to the back of the boat. She could see the lights of homes along the shore and the bridge nearby. The homes looked sad, forlorn, and isolated—like her.

"Don't," she said one more time, but he let her slip headfirst into the black water.

Her face felt the cold water, and then the rest of her body contracted from the sudden immersion. She found her body slowly descending, and though her arms were constricted, she found that she could use her legs to kick.

To her surprise, the kicking slowed her descent, and she was able to remain several feet below the surface. But the sudden exertion made her want to breathe, so she stopped kicking.

She continued to slide down. Looking up she could see a faint glow at the surface.

Perhaps this is how some people die, Stacie thought. There is no way out but down. She decided to give in. She relaxed and looked up, though her eyes stung. She thought of Prescott's comment on amniotic fluid and remembered her mother.

Stacie felt a powerful urge to breathe; she was dizzy and almost hallucinating. Looking up she could see a blue glow of light. Strange, the light seemed brighter the farther she fell into the deep.

She shuddered as her lungs screamed out for her to breathe.

And she did; in one final gulp of salty fluid her lungs flooded, and she shook violently. Then she stopped; the fighting was over. She floated like a graceful creature of the deep.

◎

four months later

There was a slight chill in the October air. The sparkling sunlight kept the memory of summer alive at this time of year. It was the golden period in New England between summer and fall, and Carl reveled in it.

On the cape, the air would be pungent with burning fireplaces and the briny odor of decaying eelgrass and the detritus along the shoreline.

But he was not on the cape today. He was in an outdoor restaurant overlooking the harbor in Boston's Seaport District. He sipped his soda water and lemon slice, watching the parade of powerboats and sailboats slice through the choppy Boston Harbor water in the distance.

It's the same water, the same ocean, the same fish even. But the city was different. He liked the vitality and energy, but only as long as he was here. The moment he drove away, Boston lost its luster. He wondered if some people felt that way about the cape.

Was it the weather, or just his injury that made him sad? Or was it the loss?

He sighed and looked at his watch. The Patriots game would be starting soon. He'd try to catch the last quarter in Chatham.

She sat down across from him without a word, slipping in like a wispy cloud.

"Hey," he said.

"Hey," she said.

"You look good," Carl said, "though all I can see are sunglasses the size of dinner plates."

Stacie laughed. "I'm shy."

"Right," he said.

They stared at each other. The waitress came over and Stacie ordered a cup of coffee.

"Late night?" he said.

"No. Little early in the day for drinking. You still not drinking?"

"Yeah. For now. Who needs that shit? I got better things to do."

She nodded.

"Been a while," he said. "About four months."

"Yeah. A lot of time has passed. How are you doing? Headaches still?"

"Gone. A little dizzy now and then, but otherwise doing good. You?"

"Hmm. Still some lung issues. And you seem to have given me you headaches. But I'm getting there."

"Back to work at the newspaper?"

"Yeah. I'm on a light schedule. They've been great. Couldn't ask for a better employer. And you? Back to painting houses?"

"Yup. I'm the Picasso of house painters, which as you know, isn't the ideal painting style for interior spaces. Picasso was a Cubist. I need to be more like Rembrandt."

She laughed, tossing her head back.

"You haven't forgotten how to be funny," she said.

"Some of the circuits still work, I'm happy to report."

Stacie noticed Carl's face had filled out since the last time she saw him. He looked relaxed, his face was tanned, and his hair had lightened a bit. He was the good-looking, mild-mannered man she remembered.

"Why haven't you wanted to see me?" he said.

"I don't know. Just didn't seem like I wanted to reopen that chapter of my life. Working on getting my sea legs back, if you'll pardon the pun."

He laughed.

"Well, you look great," he said. "Drowning did wonders for your sense of humor."

"Well, you try drowning, and let me know how it goes."

"I'm teasing you," he said.

They fell silent.

"Why wouldn't you see me? I texted a million times. I drove all the way up here two weeks ago and you stood me up. Half expected you to do it again today."

The waitress returned with Stacie's coffee. She took a sip and turned away to look at the harbor.

"I'm weird, what can I say?"

"But why wouldn't you see me?"

"Carl, you went through some terrible things. It took you a while to regroup. I just need some time too."

He looked over her shoulder into the harbor.

"I missed you," he said.

"Well, I missed you too."

"I wondered whether you were angry at me."

"Angry for what?"

"For not remembering things better."

"That's ridiculous. You were severely injured, Carl. Your call to Lan-one that night is why I'm sitting here today."

"It's strange how that worked out," he said. "It just came to me that night. The memory. Bang. Just like that. But you wouldn't take my calls."

"We've been through that, Carl. The police have hounded us with the details since then. Can we not talk about it today?"

"But we didn't talk about it," he said. "I talked to the cops, you talked to the cops, but we didn't talk to each other about it."

"That's true. But what else is there to say? We were lucky."

"I called Langone that night to say you weren't answering my calls. wanted to tell you that I remembered it was a man who hit me, and what he looked like when my flashlight lit up his face. When I described him, Langone went nuts. I had no idea what she was upset about. I didn't know anything about the clothing stuff. I guess Prescott had ordered some special clothes and had them sent to his home. Langone figured out who owned the home and had looked up stories and pictures of Prescott. When I described the guy who hit me, well, she knew it was him."

"It's funny," Stacie said, taking off her sunglasses. "Prescott was very cavalier about his writing success. He told me his success was random and arbitrary. He said it was because of a visit from Miss Serendipity that he was famous. I thought it was false modesty on his part, but, well, now I know that he thought everything was arbitrary. He took no responsibility for anything. His actions were just a series of arbitrary and capricious events, as he sees it."

"He's nuts," Carl said.

"It's an interesting view on life," she said, leaning back in her chair. Was it just happenstance that Langone took your call, connected your description to Prescott? Why did she feel pressure to drive to Prescott's house that evening to ask him about the clothing? And again, when she got to his house, she saw his wife Marci driving away in my Mini. I mean, how lucky is that? She followed Marci to the motel and watched her go inside and stay. Then she suddenly decides to rush back to Prescott' house and watched from his backyard as he loaded something tha looked like a body onto his boat in the dark."

They were silent.

"Maybe Prescott's view of life isn't too far-fetched," she said. "Do yo ever wonder about things like that?"

"No. I can't take life like that. I don't have a theory of existence. I'n not religious. I'm just a dopey charter boat captain and part-time hous painter who believes that most things have a cause and effect. I don believe in ghosts or spirits or legends. I do believe in some kind of lif force, but don't ask me to explain how it works."

"Mmm," she said. "I'm officially confused. I don't get anythin anymore."

"Stacie, you and I have something in common."

"We do?"

"Yeah, we got knocked around pretty damn hard. But we're botl survivors. How long were you underwater?" he said quietly, avoidin her gaze.

"I don't know, and I don't want to know. The Coast Guard pulled m up as fast as they could."

"Were you clinically dead? Someone said that."

"I have no idea what clinically dead means, Carl. I wasn't breathing But I am now. That's enough in my book."

They fell silent once again.

"So, Prescott's fighting the charges?" Carl said.

Stacie shrugged. "I gather his legal team is going for an insanity de fense. He has enough money for some heavy-hitting lawyers."

"He almost killed both of us."

"*Almost* is the key word," Stacie said.

"I guess we're both too strong," he said.

She laughed.

"I guess we are. Hey, are we going to have lunch?" she said.

"Yeah, I'd like to have lunch."

"Then let's eat, Mr. Charter Boat Captain. I'm hungry."

"You are an intriguing woman," he said. "I like that about you."

"Are you actively flirting right now?"

"Maybe," he said.

"It hurts my head, so go slow. I can only swim so fast these days."

POSTSCRIPT

As with many works of fiction, there are elements to this story that are factual.

Monomoy Island is part of the Monomoy National Wildlife Refuge totaling 7,604 acres, including 3,244 acres designated as wilderness. I is managed by the United States Fish and Wildlife Service. The island extends nearly ten miles south of Chatham toward Nantucket, and over the years it separated from the mainland due to the shifting sands and storm damage.

Monomoy Point Lighthouse was built in 1849 and decommissioned in 1923. The tower is forty feet tall and no longer contains a light source or lens. The keeper's house is used nearly year-round by wildlife researchers. Please note that the keeper's house is *not* open to the public and is *not* left unlocked, as described in the story.

Whitewash Village was a robust fishing and boat provisioning community that flourished for many years on the western tip of Monomoy about a mile south of the lighthouse. A natural sandy harbor provided deep water anchorage and protection for sailing vessels. The village served the fishing fleets that worked Nantucket Sound and surrounding waters. Nothing remains of Whitewash Village today, which at its height housed several hundred residents and a school.

Whitewash Village eventually disappeared due to the erosion of the "powder hole" harbor from a storm in the 1860s. There is no official record of murders occurring at Whitewash Village.

234

It is estimated that in the fifty miles between Provincetown and Chatham on the outer cape, there are a thousand shipwrecks. Many legends and ghost stories originate from Cape Cod, including the Legend of the White Stallion, sometimes also referred to as the Legend of the White Horse, or the Legend of Stonehorse. Stonehorse Shoal is a nautical hazard southeast of Monomoy today.

While there have been many references to "mooncussers"—men who used lanterns to trick sailing vessels into running aground in storms—on Cape Cod, there is no historical evidence that they existed on the cape.

There are no ghosts on Monomoy Island (that I know of).

MORE FROM KEITH YOCUM

Miraflores

MEMOIR OF A YOUNG SPY

At the height of the Cold War, young Nick Halliday joins the CIA to distance himself from a family tragedy and to do his part in the patriot fight against the communist menace. Rushed into his first undercover assignment in Panama in 1958, Nick finds himself mired in the humid, dripping world of deceit and lies. Pretending to be a left-leaning visiting professor at the University of Panama, Nick infiltrates an earnest, naïve group of students bent on Panama regaining ownership of the canal. But Nick's budding romance with Maria, a beautiful student activist, throws his mission sideways. The international clash of ideologies harshly intrudes on a young man's love for a woman. Both are expendable pawns in a vast worldwide deathmatch. Can they survive in a game that only values winning, whatever the cost? And what does winning mean, anyway?

Color of Blood

(BOOK 1 OF THE DENNIS CUNNINGHAM SERIES)

Dennis is glad to be back at work. His wife's death left him devastated but he'll do anything to lose himself into work at the Inspector General's office of the CIA. A brilliant, if prickly investigator, he's spent his career chasing down the Agency's thieves and liars. When his boss forces him to take a low-level assignment to investigate a missing employee in Australia, he soon finds that even in the red dust of the Outback, there is romance – and death – just a sweltering heartbeat away.

A Dark Place

(Book 2 of the Dennis Cunningham series)

An old case spills new blood. Dennis loves policing the CIA's network of spies for liars and thieves. But each time he plows into a case, it's harder for him to keep alive his relationship with Judy, an Aussie cop and the only woman who understands his passions and quirks. When Dennis and Judy meet in London to rekindle their relationship, they are sucked into the city's dark underworld. To save Judy's life Dennis must solve two cases simultaneously. If you like non-stop action, dark humor and complicated heroes, then you'll love *A Dark Place.*

Valley of Spies

(Book 3 of the Dennis Cunningham series)

When an American woman vanishes in New Zealand, it perplexes authorities. There is no body, no witness and no motive. But what looks like a sad, unfortunate case of foul play, slowly turns into something darker. The missing tourist is a female psychologist under contract from the CIA to see employees in strictest confidence. Was her disappearance a random act of violence, or an act of international espionage? Does someone want to know her patients' dark, dirty secrets? Dennis Cunningham, the gruff but uncanny CIA investigator, is tugged out of early retirement in Western Australia to rubber stamp a foregone conclusion by the agency about the real perpetrators. A brilliant but unusual sleuth, Cunningham can't help but pick at the agency's scab on this case until it bleeds red all over.

Daniel

Strange things happen in war – but Vietnam was always different

In January 1972, during the waning days of that sad war, a lone soldier crawled through the barbed wire and entered an isolated American fire base. He said his name was Daniel Carson, but a quick check found that a soldier with the same name and physical description was already buried at Arlington National Cemetery. Who was this new soldier named Daniel? Was he a crazy man, a common deserter or something else entirely? And why did he have such a profound effect on the unlucky company of grunts trying to survive the last days of the war? As a fierce regiment of North Vietnamese regulars prepares to destroy the forgotten hilltop firebase, the odd little soldier named Daniel seems to have all the answers to their survival. Several years after the war, three survivors of the firebase meet in Washington, D.C. and, almost by accident, discover the shocking truth about Daniel.

Titus

In the midst of carnage in the Civil War, is there a serial murderer at work?

A Union soldier is found dead on the outskirts of camp, his neck sliced open from ear to ear. But when more soldiers are found with their throats slit, an uneasy mood falls over the Union regiment. Who is killing these soldiers, and what does the strange mark on the dead men's foreheads mean? A young Union lieutenant and an eccentric field surgeon are ordered to get to the bottom of the killings. Can the two officers unmask the killer and motive before the fog of battle hides his identity forever?

KEITH YOCUM lives on Cape Cod. He is a former journalist and publishing executive that has worked for publications like *The Boston Globe* and *The New England Journal of Medicine*. He is the author of seven novels and welcomes feedback at www.keithyocum.com.

Made in the USA
Middletown, DE
03 July 2022